Praise for *ME THAT YOU SEE*

'Pacy, racy and so much fun! Anne Freeman's open, unreserved style is like catching up with friends. Pure escapism, with a side of humour, you'll fly though this.'
Ali Lowe, bestselling author of The Trivia Night and The Running Club

'A spicy delight of a story that hooked me from the first page. *Me That You See* gives a peek behind the cameras into a world of webcamming. With a diverse and well-defined cast of characters, there are powerful moments around friendship, trust, and love, with a creeping threat that will leave you shuddering. This book was satisfyingly unexpected, with plenty of surprises. As with Anne's first book, I was left with a yearning to stay with the characters and see what next unfolds for them. For me, that's a sign of a great book.'
Jo Dixon, bestselling author of The House of Now and Then

'The author's research about this fascinating profession is expertly and seamlessly woven into the narrative. It's no wonder she shortlisted in the Hawkeye Prize! Lexi and all of the characters are so well drawn, realistic and lovable; her dialogue is punchy, witty, and full of innuendo; and the suspense and tension she established kept me racing through the chapters. And those sex scenes! Quirky, original, and never a cliché. Loved the book, love the author!'
Camille Booker, award-winning author of What if You Fly?

'This book is a voyeuristic adrenaline rush, a glimpse into the world of women using their sexual power for money. It raises a thousand questions about masculinity, sex work, feminism, the power of female friendships and the importance of living your truth. From the titillating prologue, the novel had me turning the pages to the very end.'
Johanna Skinner, author

Praise for *ME THAT YOU SEE*

'I absolutely loved this book! The writing is so effortless and tasteful that the progression through some pretty exotic (and at times erotic) scenarios seems entirely natural and believable. The colourful descriptions are fun and often amusing, and the characters are fantastic and easy to empathise with. There's a really positive humanistic undercurrent running through the book as well... Highly recommended!' *David Bowley, St Kilda East, Victoria*

'The ultimate voyeuristic experience. Totally engaging and supremely readable, the characters are crafted with empathy and class. I loved this book!' *Marion Osmond, Eltham, Victoria*

'Freeman has done it again with another racy, riotous romance that will have you hooked from beginning to end. *Me That You See* introduces us to the lovely Lexi and a whole host of vibrant characters, and throws in some unexpected twists and turns to keep you on your toes. Just make sure you have a few good hours free, as once this book is picked up, it's impossible to put down.'
Victoria Hanlon, Brunswick East, Victoria

'Freeman brings a sexy, electric undercurrent to the familiar scenes of current-day Melbourne and an intensely modern perspective to women's fiction. As we are swept up in the tangle of Lexi's choices—conscious and subconscious, free and forced, benign and damaging—we are reminded that life is not linear, and that living authentically requires courage. Freeman's writing possesses an intense and empathetic curiosity about the interior lives of women, which so often conflict with their exterior lives. *Me That You See* is eye-opening, real, utterly absorbing, sexy and defiant, woven through with truths that resonate beyond the final page.'
Kasey Delben, Auchenflower, Queensland

ME THAT YOU SEE

Anne Freeman

HAWKEYE
PUBLISHING

First published in Australia in 2024 by Hawkeye Publishing.

Cover Design by Anne Freeman and Ellen Milligan

A catalogue record of this book is available from the National Library of Australia.

ISBN 9781923105089

Proudly printed in Australia.

www.hawkeyepublishing.com.au
www.hawkeyebooks.com.au

PROLOGUE

WAITING for her cue, Lexi Karas' heart pounded percussively against her ribs and she wondered if Jamie's virtual visitors could hear it. She stood off camera, in a corner of the curated bedroom, eyes flitting between Jamie's pantomime of preening and the door. *Is it too late to bail?*

Perched on the end of the bed wearing a silk robe, Jamie made a show of applying potions and powders to her already made-up face. Lexi watched as Jamie caressed her face and neck with a frothy white puff of luminescent powder. She traced the line of her craned neck, guiding it into the cleft of her cleavage, and let out a delighted giggle. Her false-lashed eyes flicked towards the webcam. Next came blusher which she loaded onto a pink brush before blowing off the excess powder through pouty lips.

'So, who's going to take me out tonight?' Jamie asked the webcam, alternately pinking her cheeks.

A *ding* chimed from the laptop on the table in front of Jamie.

She looked down and laughed. 'Thank you, Thommo88,' said Jamie, acknowledging the tip that came through.

She looked at the screen and laughed again. 'Dinner and dancing sounds wonderful,' she said, eyes downcast. Bashful.

She replaced the brush and made a start on her eyebrows.

Ding ding ding.

Jamie thanked three more usernames. Her demeanour was shy and a little sheepish. Like she couldn't understand what she had done to elicit such adoration.

Ding.

'Oh,' said Jamie, 'BigRob40 has tipped for a bra flash. Thank you, Rob, nice to see you again.'

Jamie ran a finger along the inside edge of her robe, teasing it out and loosening it to reveal the briefest whisper of lace. She wiggled her shoulders a little and laughed as more tips *dinged* to life on her screen. She thanked each user as she cupped her breasts and leaned forward, jiggling them in an alternating rhythm. Sitting up straight, she peeled back the silk from her bare shoulders and held the robe precariously over her strapless bra. *Ding ding ding.* Loosening her hold, the robe fell to her waist in one fluid motion. *Ding ding ding.*

Jamie gasped. 'BronteBoy has tipped to see my breasts,' she said, acting shocked. 'More like "Naughty Boy",' she added.

She cupped underneath her breasts and jiggled them softly. 'Do you think if I keep doing this they'll pop out on their own?'

She threw her head back and laughed, a singsong, pleasure-filled sound.

She bounced where she sat, her areolas rising like two suns over the horizon line of her bra. She continued until the bra slipped down, revealing the entirety of both breasts. She let them bounce a while, the *dinging* of incoming tips providing the soundtrack to her dance.

'I am never going to get ready for our date at this rate,' she said, re-dressing herself at a glacial pace and taking up her eyebrow brush once more.

Lexi realised she was holding her breath, astonished by her own arousal. The woman she watched wasn't Jamie, she was someone else. Someone new. Her lilting tone, her posture, her simmering sexuality all worked together to create a siren song. Lexi felt dizzy. Placing a steadying hand against the cool wall behind her, she tried to gather her thoughts and centre herself.

'I have a special treat for you tonight,' said Jamie, between lip gloss strokes.

She smacked her lips together audibly as *dings* punctuated the treacle-pour of her words.

I can't do this.

'I'd like to introduce you to a very good friend of mine. She'll be hosting her own chatroom here at Camnation, and I offered to show her the ropes because…' Jamie leaned in and whispered, 'it's her first time.' She sat back and resumed in her regular tone. 'We've known each other since… how long's it been, Jojo?' Jamie looked off camera and directly into Lexi's soul, using the stage name she had settled on the previous day.

Lexi felt possessed as she glided into view. She caught her image on the laptop and adjusted her posture as she sat on the bed next to Jamie.

'You need to stop changing the subject and get ready,' Lexi scolded. 'See, I'm ready to go out and you're not even dressed.' She ran her hands over the form-fitting bodice of her dress.

'But I don't know what to wear. I need help choosing,' said Jamie. She stood, allowing one leg to emerge from her robe, and walked off camera. Lexi picked up the hand mirror, fluffed up her hair and wiped a finger down one side of her bottom lip. She knew they were watching, could hear the incoming tips resounding like frenzied applause.

Jamie returned, clutching a cluster of hangers bearing a selection of dresses for consideration. She looked at the screen and read out the names of those who had tipped in her absence. 'I think you guys are hitting on my friend!' she teased.

'Come on, Jamie, it's not like that. We were just getting to know each other,' said Lexi, flashing a conspiratorial glance towards the webcam.

'Well, seeing as you like her so much,' said Jamie, head cocked. 'Maybe we should start a new countdown.'

Dings of agreement rang out.

'BronteBoy, you're so bad. Yes, I would like to know what it's like to kiss her,' said Jamie. 'But only if Jojo wants to.'

Jamie cast Lexi a sideways glance. Although they had discussed how this would play out, she made a show of considering the idea.

'I *have* always wondered what it would be like,' said Lexi, looking into Jamie's eyes. They stared at one another for a long moment and Lexi realised to her surprise that she wasn't faking. The idea that she wouldn't be able to do it until a certain number of tokens had been raised was giddying. Jamie dropped her gaze as if embarrassed by the declaration.

'Shall we say, 2,500?' Jamie asked the viewers.

'Let's make it 2,000, I don't want to have to wait too long,' said Lexi, using their prearranged dialogue.

Jamie laughed and leaned forward to set up the countdown. She positioned herself so that her admirers had a clear view into her robe as she typed. As soon as the countdown was live, tips to contribute poured in. Following Jamie's lead, Lexi thanked each user.

'But that still leaves the problem of you needing to finish getting ready,' said Lexi.

They passed the time with Jamie trying on clothes, stepping slightly off camera to undress and coming back into view as she was pulling a dress down over her lace underwear. Jamie turned this way and that, adjusting the garment by scooping her breasts into place or smoothing the fabric over her hips. Lexi rose onto her knees to do up zippers and straighten straps, letting her touch linger. The entire charade, designed to arouse the audience, was having the same effect on Lexi.

'Maccattack78 has tipped for me to get down to my lingerie,' said Jamie.

Adrenaline pulsed through Lexi's body, and she heard herself say, 'Maybe Maccattack would like it if we both did that?'

Jamie's eyes darted to Lexi in surprise.

'Well, it looks like Maccattack is in for a special treat,' said Jamie, recovering her composure. 'Who do you want first?' She read his reply and smiled. 'Well, I might have gotten jealous if you said Jojo.'

Lexi watched as Jamie peeled herself out of her dress, gingerly stepping out to avoid snagging her heels. It seemed to take an eternity.

'Are you sure you want me too?' Lexi asked the webcam.

Comments filled the screen and *dings* of confirmation rang out.

Lexi stood and checked the screen. 'We're halfway through our countdown already.' She turned this way and that before lamenting, 'I don't think I can undo this zipper.'

Jamie rose from her position on the bed and eased Lexi's dress open, helping to shuck it from her shoulders. Mirroring Jamie's earlier gesture, Lexi held the dress against her breasts, pushing them up in the process. Letting go, she peeled the fabric down and caught the band of her underwear to reveal her hip bones. 'Whoops,' she said, unhooking her thumbs from the lace and peeling down the dress only.

Tips continued to pour in, adding to their countdown as Lexi crawled onto the bed. She positioned herself lying flat on her stomach with her knees and elbows bent, chin resting in her hands. 'I don't think we're going out tonight,' she said.

'Oh no, we only have another ten minutes with you,' said Jamie, her bottom lip dropped. 'And we're still 500 tokens away from our countdown goal.'

Tips from new users *dinged* in while comments from those who'd already contributed encouraged generosity from others.

A *cha ching* sound rang out as the final 400 tokens was contributed by a single user.

'ZeroOneZero!' exclaimed Jamie. 'Does this mean you got the job?'

He commented in the affirmative, and Jamie clapped her hands. 'ZeroOneZero has landed his dream job and he's celebrating with us. Congratulations, it's so well deserved.'

Lexi moved to perch at the end of the bed, mirroring Jamie's posture with one leg bent, their knees touching. The sound of *dinging* tips melted away from Lexi's awareness as she looked into Jamie's slate-grey eyes. They exchanged sheepish smirks before Lexi whispered, 'Why am I so nervous?'

She took Jamie's hand and guided it between her breasts, holding it in place over her galloping heart. Jamie let out a breathy laugh and leaned in closer. Remembering their audience, Lexi raised her other hand to Jamie's mouth, parting her lips with her thumb before following with her mouth. Jamie's lips were full and soft. Although Lexi had kissed women before, the sensation always surprised her. She was so accustomed to Ethan's perpetual stubble, his modest lips and muscular jaw, that kissing Jamie felt like the first warm, foamy sip of an expertly made café latte. At first, their kisses were slow and measured, as if they were each tasting something delicate and delicious. Lexi moved her hand up to push Jamie's hair away and grasp her neck, their kisses growing deeper, tongues synchronising. They found themselves locked in a rhythmic push-pull dance. Breaking away, Jamie threw back her head, forcing Lexi's mouth to her neck as she laughed.

'Oh no,' exclaimed Jamie, rousing Lexi from her pleasure. 'Our time's up.'

Lexi felt disoriented. It was like losing yourself on the dance floor, only to have the house lights flicker to life. She blinked and tried to steady her breathing.

'Oh my,' said Jamie, scanning the comments. 'It sounds like a lot of you are going to need a moment to regroup anyway. NiceTwinTurbo said he came harder than he ever has before.' She laughed. 'I hope you guys will drop by and visit Jojo. I'll pop her links up. She'll be on at different times to me, so I guess you'll be able to date us both.'

Lexi, struggling to recover, tried to smile. 'Thanks for letting me crash your party,' she said, voice quavering.

Jamie kissed her hand and blew it towards the webcam before ending the transmission.

The screen snapped to black, reflecting Lexi's wide-eyed, breathless expression.

Two months earlier...

ONE

HEARING the bedroom door handle turn, Lexi slammed her laptop shut and turned to see Ethan framed in the doorway.

'I just got a call from the security company. The alarm has gone off again. I hate to ask, but do you think you could drop Lucas off at childcare while I run over there?' he asked, his face a grimace designed to pre-empt a slap.

Lexi exhaled, wishing she could decline. She looked up at Ethan's imploring face and smiled. His posture softened.

'Of course,' she said, rising from the desk.

Writing would have to wait. Again.

She followed Ethan downstairs and into the kitchen where Lucas sat, poking a chubby finger into the middle of his Vegemite toast before twirling it around exclaiming, 'Weeeeeeeee!'

'Mate, Lexi is going to drop you off today, okay?'

Lucas' solemn eyes landed on Lexi.

'You can show me the fish tank you were telling me about,' Lexi beamed.

Ethan ruffled his fingers through Lucas' thick mop of mousey hair and kissed the top of his head. He grabbed Lexi's car keys from the hook, and she had a vision of him folding his muscular frame into her dinged up Mini.

'Thank you, you've saved me,' he said, before kissing her and striding out of the room.

'Let's get you cleaned up,' said Lexi, taking in the fallout of Lucas' breakfast.

~

Lexi manoeuvred Ethan's army-tank of an SUV into the underground carpark's narrow driveway, unconsciously ducking her head to ensure the vehicle cleared the low-level ceiling.

Lucas' ceaseless chatter continued as Lexi unbuckled his seatbelt and scooped him out of his child safety seat. 'So that's what you have to do, just hide,' he concluded.

She led him into the elevator, the feeling of his clammy hand in hers sending nostalgia pulsing through her. In her mind, her two siblings were frozen in time and Lexi had to remind herself that they'd be teenagers by now. She shook the thought away as the elevator doors opened, depositing them at ground-level.

'Good morning, Lucas,' a saccharine, patronising voice cooed, filling the air around them with the scent of tobacco and breath mints.

'Hello, Cass,' Lucas mumbled.

'And you must be Mrs. Thomas.' The black-uniformed carer turned to Lexi. 'We haven't met yet, I came on board about a month ago…'

Lexi opened her mouth to correct the woman, but an almighty wail pierced the air as a reluctant child was pried from its father, allowing him to make a hasty departure to work.

'Excuse me,' said Cass, before hurrying off to assist her colleague.

Lucas tugged on Lexi's hand, and she looked down at him. He pointed with his free hand towards a large tank swarming with tropical fish. Lexi crouched and placed a hand on his arm.

'It's amazing, buddy. Thank you.'

Lucas grinned.

'Your dad will pick you up when he's done at the pharmacy, okay?'

'Kay,' said Lucas and shuffled off, his too-big backpack making him look even smaller than he was.

Back in the car, Lexi caught her reflection in the rear-view mirror. Her dark eyebrows, which framed green, thick-lashed eyes, were furrowed, giving her a perplexed and worried look. Her balayage-blonde hair did nothing to conceal her partial Greek heritage. As she put the car into reverse, the driver assistance squealed in response to a vehicle that had materialised out of the ether, making her jump. After reversing out of the parking space successfully, she gazed out the window at a harried woman in the process of extracting her children and their belongings from their car. Catching Lexi's gaze, the woman exclaimed, 'Mum life, am I right?'

Lexi forced a smile and accelerated.

Mum life. Lexi turned the phrase over in her mind. *Mum life.* Except that she wasn't a mum. Moving in with Ethan was meant to be a temporary solution. They'd only been dating for a few months when Lexi had been evicted from her apartment. How her landlord had found out about her subletting a room on Airbnb was beyond her. And with no affordable prospects close to her barista job, and with eviction imminent, Ethan had invited her to move in. To "crash" as he had put it, which sounded casual and temporary and not the kind of thing Lexi should run screaming from. And while Lexi was still looking for a place of her own, she now had Ethan's home as a benchmark. It was palatial compared to the fleabags that Lexi could afford, especially now that she had seen the error of her Airbnb-ing ways.

~

The Bean & Gone Café was already bustling when Lexi arrived early for her shift. It was no more than a hole-in-the-wall with a tight row of bar stools running down the left side. A place where morning commuters would dive in to grab a coffee and chia bowl or almond croissant, before rushing off to lives that Lexi could only wonder at. It was here, in a state of espresso-pulling hypnosis, that she watched the world go by. She used her observations as the basis for whatever short story or poem she was writing, or at the very least, for her journal, which seemed more like a friend than the Google Doc it was. She'd worked at a string of cafés since moving to Melbourne ten years prior, and her moments of introversion had often been interpreted as aloofness, especially by men. How could she explain her internal musings when she'd never had the courage to admit she was an aspiring writer, much less allow anyone to read her work? But it was different here, working alongside two other women. Paige, the café's owner, had spent a lifetime working in hospitality before scraping together the money for a place of her own. And Linh—a fellow barista who still lived at home with her mother despite being in her late twenties like Lexi—had become her first real friend since leaving Hamilton.

Lexi rounded the counter and threw her bag into the storage cupboard that doubled as Paige's office. She grabbed her apron from the hook and sidled up to where Linh was rhythmically pouring milk to produce fern fronds in a couple of café lattes.

'Hey, girl,' said Linh, without looking up.

'Where's Paige?' asked Lexi, putting the lids on and accepting payment from a guy with a man-bun.

'Roasters,' said Linh, wiping down the steam wand.

When the morning rush gave way to the usual lull preceding morning tea breaks and school mums, Linh turned to Lexi.

'I tried to call you on Saturday,' she said in an accusatory tone.

'Oh, yeah. Lucas spilled his juice, and my phone spent the afternoon in a bowl of rice,' said Lexi, banging a coffee puck out of the portafilter. 'What was up?'

'Xavier and his friends decided to have a bush-doof down at his parents' farm and I wanted you to come.'

'Oh, man!' exclaimed Lexi.

'It was so fun. One of the boys brought decks and everyone pitched tents. We were calling it "Woodend-stock",' said Linh, laughing.

'Oh, man!' Lexi said again.

'Someone brought mushrooms and that girl who's in the roller-skating troupe brought this big bag of costumes, so we all ended up frolicking around the paddocks wearing sequined unitards and stuff.'

Lexi laughed and gave her friend a playful shove. 'That sounds amazing.'

'Anyway, how was your weekend?' asked Linh.

'Okay, I guess. I got to meet Ethan's brothers and their families; they all came over for a barbecue on Saturday.'

'Oh, shit. How was it?' asked Linh, making a *yikes* face.

Lexi paused, replaying the one humiliating moment that had eclipsed the memory of the day.

'There were kids everywhere, it was madness,' Lexi began. 'One of them almost drowned. Ethan had to jump in and save him.'

'No shit, go Ethan.'

'Yeah,' said Lexi, forcing a weak smile before going on. 'In the chaos though… he, uh…'

Linh's face was questioning.

'He called me Justine.'

'Oooooohhhhhh,' said Linh, elongating the word so it seemed to wrap around them where they stood staring at one another. 'What the hell did you do?' Linh asked, breaking the reverie.

'Nothing really,' said Lexi. 'He realised immediately and was totally mortified, everyone was.'

Lexi paused.

'It confirms it though, don't you think?' she continued. 'There's no way he's over it. I'm living in her house, sharing her bed with the man who's clearly still in love with her.'

Linh's eyes widened and she nodded towards the door. Lexi turned to see Ethan, wearing his pharmacy whites, striding in.

'You don't know that,' hissed Linh quietly.

'Hey, Linh, new hair?' said Ethan.

'I'm glad somebody noticed,' she said, ruffling her undercut and darting her eyes towards Lexi.

'We've been busy!' Lexi protested.

Ethan looked around the empty café theatrically. He pulled Lexi's car keys out of his pocket and handed them to her.

'Thanks again, Lex,' he said.

'I'll grab yours,' she said, turning.

'Usual?' Linh asked Ethan.

'Only if you're not too busy,' he said.

'Shut up!' Lexi called from the storeroom.

TWO

THE airless stairwell smelled like the ghosts of dinners past as Lexi trudged up to the sixth floor. Catching her breath, she rapped on the door, which opened to reveal a smaller, more impish version of Linh.

'Hi Mrs. Pham,' Lexi said, leaning down to kiss the tiny woman's cheek.

'Lexi, how many times I tell you to call me Vien? Come in,' she said, ushering Lexi into the apartment. 'You look so pretty. Linh has been in the bathroom for one hour painting that black stuff on her eyes. She look like a *hát tuồng* performer! But you, so nice and natural,' she said.

Lexi walked in and the scent of turmeric and fried onions greeted her.

'Almost ready!' Linh yelled from the bathroom.

'Sit sit sit,' said Vien, motioning to the plastic-covered sofa.

The sofa groaned as Lexi sat, and Vien disappeared into the kitchen. She returned with a glass of iced water just as Linh emerged from the bathroom.

Vien set the glass down on the coffee table and surreptitiously indicated her daughter with a darting glance. 'See?' she said, contorting her face into happy and sad masks.

Lexi giggled.

Linh rolled her heavily made-up eyes and said, 'Let's get out of here.'

'You have to eat!' shrieked Vien, aghast. 'I made *bánh xèo*.'

'I don't want that greasy thing; it'll take my lipstick off!'

'Maybe that's a good thing,' muttered Vien. Changing tack, she addressed Lexi. 'You will love it. It's a crispy savoury crepe, wrapped in lettuce and dipped in fish sauce vinaigrette.'

'It sounds delicious,' admitted Lexi.

She flashed an apologetic look towards her friend as she allowed herself to be guided to the kitchen table. Linh shuffled in behind them and sat, looking sullen. Lexi watched Vien pepper her daughter's head with rough kisses before Linh smiled and swatted her away. Lexi thought of her own mother, at the closeness which had eluded them, and a familiar shame rose from the pit of her stomach. She absentmindedly rubbed the Saudi Arabi-shaped scar on the inside of her wrist.

'Are you happy now?' Linh hissed.

Lexi mouthed the word "sorry" as a victorious Vien set down an enormous platter between them. The three ate in silence and, as the contrasting flavours titillated Lexi's taste buds, she didn't feel sorry at all.

~

Although smoking in pubs had been banned for years, the carpet in the Northcote Social Club band room continued to excrete the stale aromas of tobacco and spilled beer from as far back as the 1970s.

'I'll get us some drinks,' Lexi yelled to Linh over the applause as the ragged members of the support act shuffled off stage.

Waiting at the crowded bar, relief washed over Lexi at not being home with Ethan. A chaser of guilt followed. It had just hit 10:30 p.m. and Lexi wondered what he was doing. She knew there were three options. Either he had fallen asleep while putting Lucas to bed, he was lost in a Netflix scrolling wormhole or he had shut himself away in his office again. He did this so often that she had taken to slowly walking past, ear cocked to listen for signs of life.

'What can I get you?'

A bartender appeared wearing a Hawaiian-print Mambo cap that

Lexi could have sworn she had in primary school.

'Two Dark and Stormies, please,' she said.

Lexi watched as the drinks were made, tapped her card to pay and lamented the loss of tips in the digital age. She turned and scanned the crowd for Linh, who was standing beside the stage waiting for her boyfriend's band to start.

The Total Imposters were a five-piece electro synth band with Xavier at the helm. As they took to the stage, the crowd collectively shuffled forward, compressing Lexi and Linh in the throng. They began their set with their most recent track, *Let Down Your Guard*, a universally agreed banger whose pounding drumbeat was accentuated by an epilepsy-inducing light show. Linh's face was pure adoration as she gazed up at the alter ego of her boyfriend dry humping the mic stand. Linh had enthused to Lexi on more than one occasion that she'd had the best sex of her life with Xavier. He was so present, she'd said. So hungry to fulfil her desires and to express his own. Lexi thought of Ethan. How guarded he seemed. How distant. After their first clandestine encounter, things had progressed, but every time they had sex, Lexi couldn't help but feel that his mind was elsewhere. She feared he was thinking of his wife. Could almost feel the shadow of Justine snuffing her own light. What was more, with them now living under the same roof, the tryst of nocturnal texting that had heralded the beginning of their relationship had disappeared, leaving behind a silence she found deafening.

~

After the show, Lexi and Linh found themselves back at Xavier's share-house in Thornbury, where the band and an assortment of friends were spinning old vinyl and smoking weed. Lexi struggled to maintain her posture in a too-soft modular lounge from the 1980s, while a random dude with an insulting moustache talked at her for the sake of his own enjoyment. She had mentally unsubscribed from his monologue but snapped back into awareness when he uttered the words, 'Take you, for instance. You're quite attractive, but you're not perfect. Your eyebrows are asymmetrical, and you have that gap between your front teeth which precludes you from classical beauty.'

Lexi turned her head to gape at him. She prepared to retort and then stopped. She'd experienced negging from guys before and it always left her wondering about those who took the bait. It was in moments like these that she appreciated Ethan's complete lack of bullshit. She reclaimed her body from the sofa, gathered up her belongings and planted a kiss on Linh's forehead where she lay sprawled on a flokati rug next to the turntable.

Back out in the night, Lexi let the fresh, dewy air fill her lungs and wondered if she should walk part way back to Ethan's place in Clifton Hill. Memories of the latest horrific news stories flickered in her mind, so she retrieved her phone and ordered an Uber.

The salmon-hued promise of daybreak was emerging as Lexi quietly unlocked the front door. Shoes in hand, she caught her reflection in the hallway mirror and her cheeks burned. Although she wasn't stoned—she had never had success with weed, despite a few furtive attempts—she was sure that her hair and clothes bore the tell-tale aroma. She thought of her last day in Hamilton ten years prior when, on a morning much like this, her mother had demanded, 'Why can't you leave me in peace to raise my children?'

Lexi had always been careful to arrive home before the little kids awoke, but on this occasion, she had misjudged and snuck in the back door to find her mother, Monique, serving Weet-bix to Mason and Mia. It had been months since her best friend Geoff had fled town, leaving Lexi to bear the guilt that her actions forced his departure. Unable to vanquish profound feelings of loss and regret, Lexi had been floundering. As a fellow misfit, Geoff had been her anchor throughout high school. The only person she had ever truly connected with in her hometown of Hamilton. Looking back through adult eyes, Lexi now understood that her behaviour in the aftermath of his disappearance had been a cry for help. Her responsibilities at the local barbecued chicken shop could have been accomplished post-lobotomy so Lexi spent most of her nights hanging out with whomever was hanging. The sleep deprivation, hangovers and comedowns this induced meant that her only thoughts were of getting through her shift and onto the next party. This deadening of the mind afforded her a reprise from worry over where Geoff was. What fate had befallen him. But instead of alerting Monique to her inner turmoil and uniting them, it had only served as the final cut in the death by a thousand.

The stairs creaked and Lexi looked up to see Ethan descending, crease-faced and shirtless. She braced herself for a scolding.

'Well, good morning!' he said, grinning.

She smiled and accepted his spearmint kiss, self-conscious of her own stale rum breath.

'Come on, I'll make you a cup of tea before you go to bed,' he said, leading the way to the kitchen.

As they sat in the brightening kitchen clutching their mugs, Lexi told Ethan about her night, how great the band was and how tedious the after party.

'Maybe I'll come with you to the next one, get a sitter for Lucas,' he said, tentatively.

Lexi blushed. She hadn't even asked him if he'd like to accompany her, assuming that he'd find the scene juvenile and tiresome. She furrowed her brow and opened her mouth to apologise, but Ethan gave her a small nod that told her he understood.

THREE

LEXI swiped at her wet cheeks and breathed into her pillow, the vision of Geoff's parents' bathroom with its apricot tiles and shaggy toilet seat cover already beginning to fade. She focused her breathing, dispersing with each measured exhalation the image of the sickly red water that filled the tub, Geoff's body slumped and blue-lipped within it, slate-grey eyes open but unseeing. Lexi's nightmares had begun after Geoff fled Hamilton, and were the shadow she couldn't run from, no matter how hard she tried.

The weekend that the Holloway family had moved in across the street was rainy and bleak. Lexi sat at her battered teak desk watching as two boys helped their father unload the moving van. Mr. Holloway's movements were faltering, as though he were annoyed that the rain refused to clear for him. When the elder boy lost his grip on one end of a heavy-looking television cabinet, his father was quick to slap the side of his head. It was at that moment, with tears filling his eyes, that Geoff noticed Lexi gawking at him, open mouthed. She ducked into her book and didn't dare look up again.

The next time she saw him, he was being introduced as the new kid in her homeroom class. Languid and pale with mousy brown hair falling over his face, Geoff seemed braced for the sniggers that followed. A curious combination of protectiveness and repulsion welled up in Lexi. She knew the kids would have a field day with him, but her social standing was so precarious that she feared she'd open herself up to ridicule rather than protect him from it. So, for the first few weeks, all they did was orbit one another with eyes cast down, their trajectories never crossing.

This changed one lunchtime when Lexi arrived at her regular hiding spot—the sheltered doorway of a decommissioned portable classroom—to find it was already occupied.

By and large, the accepted code of conduct at break times was for boys to play football and for girls to flock the side-lines pretending not to notice them. The library was an option but garnered unwanted attention from those who found it inconceivable that a person would willingly be in the presence of both books and teachers longer than necessary. So, it had become a habit of Lexi to hide out in this particular doorway, eating her lunch and reading alone until the school bell beckoned her into fifth period. On this day, she rounded the corner clutching her brand-new copy of *Harry Potter and the Deathly Hallows*—the final in the series—barely able to conceal her excitement over what adventures might lay within, when she all but tripped over a battered pair of Converse high tops. The owner of the shoes let out a startled yelp and stared up at her from behind his own copy of the same book. Although it had been Lexi who'd trodden on him, Geoff let out a string of muttered apologies while scrambling to scoop up his belongings and flee. She halted him by saying, 'Move over and no spoilers.'

Although his mouth remained impassive, Lexi could see a smile glint in his eyes as he shuffled over, making room for her to sit beside him. Their arms were pressed together in the narrow space. The following day, Lexi was surprised by a feeling of disappointment when she arrived to find the doorway unoccupied. Had she been looking forward to seeing him? She shook her head to dispel the thought and sat. A few moments later, a sliver of a face appeared from around the corner. He waited, as if seeking permission, which Lexi gave by moving over. And so began a daily ritual which would last the duration of their final two years of high school.

Lexi's heart rate gradually returned to normal, and she sat up, listening. The house was quiet which, with a three-year-old in residence, could only mean that she was alone. She bypassed the bathroom and found her laptop, transcribing the nightmare before the last wisps of it evaporated from her mind. When she finished, she opened Facebook and for the millionth time in the last ten years, searched the name: Geoff Holloway.

FOUR

AS Lexi headed for the kitchen, thick silence emanated from Ethan's perpetually closed office door. She placed her palm against the wood, as if testing the temperature, before slowly turning the door handle. The click made her flinch, and she looked over her shoulder into the empty house. She padded into the dark room and felt for the light switch, scared that if she opened the curtains Ethan would somehow guess that she had trespassed into his private space.

She approached the desk and sat in the space-age throne of an office chair. It sprung back unexpectedly, throwing Lexi's legs upward. She grabbed the desk to steady herself and emitted a self-conscious laugh, though there was no one there to hear it. She realised that the fingers of her left hand had gained purchase in the slightly open drawer. She eased it open and was confronted with a photograph of a much-younger Ethan, hair longer and styled into a quiff, his cheek pressed against a chestnut-ponytailed woman with a smattering of freckles across her upturned nose. Lexi pressed the drawer shut and sat with her hands splayed on the desk, breathing out her heartbeat. She cocked her ear towards the still-silent house before opening the drawer again and scooping out a stack of dog-eared photographs of varying sizes.

Justine was small and beautiful. The kind of beautiful that is approachable rather than intimidating. As Lexi pored over the images, she guessed that Justine had never been told that *she'd be pretty if she'd just smile*, the way Lexi had countless times. She came across a holiday picture—Bali perhaps, or Thailand—in which Ethan stood with his arm around Justine, her head practically tucked into his armpit, her compact body astonishingly curvaceous in a sporty bikini. Lexi looked upon it with disdain. She became aware of her own body, imagining how hulking she must feel to Ethan with her broad hips and strong arms. For the most part, Lexi didn't notice her above-average height, until the rare occasions she was confronted by her reflection while standing next to a normal-sized woman. The effect would discombobulate her and alter her demeanour, as if shrinking her personality would shrink her stature.

Lexi shuffled slowly through the stack of photos, pausing at each one with an unhealthy fascination, witnessing the couple maturing, their style changing. The warehouse parties gave way to engagement parties. The weddings gave way to christenings. Justine's own belly grew round, Ethan staking claim on the swell with large, encompassing hands, his face radiant with pride.

How disappointed he must be each day, waking up to find her—not Justine—lying next to him. Shame coursed through Lexi's blood—hot and sweet and familiar—until the slamming of a car door roused her. The photos dropped to the desk, the top few sliding off and onto the floor. Lexi dove for them. As she sprang up, she thumped her head on the raw frame of the desk's underside. Emitting a guttural curse, she fought nausea while shoving the stack of photos back in the drawer. She closed it and scurried from the room.

As Lexi power-walked down the hallway she met Ethan and Lucas coming in the front door. She walked to them, head throbbing, wearing something vaguely resembling a smile. As she leaned in to kiss him, he slid a hand behind her head. When he pulled back, he stared in confusion at his palm and then back at her.

'What?' she asked, warmth colouring her cheeks.

Ethan tipped his hand to reveal a smudge of blood. 'Did you hit your head?' he asked.

'Oh, yeah. Just then,' said Lexi, trying to keep her voice even.

Ethan looked at her expectantly.

'I was getting a tampon and I hit my head under the bathroom cabinet,' she added, touching her fingers to where her hair was clumped.

'What's a tampong?' asked Lucas.

'Ahhhh,' began Ethan.

FIVE

'HEY hey, there she is! Sexy Lexi!'

Lexi forced a smile as a pack of slick-haired real estate agents from the office next door strode in.

'Where's lovely Linny today?' asked another.

'She's gone across the street for some avos. Who's the newbie?' said Lexi, noticing an unfamiliar face in the sea of dark suits.

'This is Dennis, he just started with us today, straight outta TAFE. Hasn't even popped his real estate cherry yet.'

At this, the group sniggered and jostled the younger man whose cheap, ill-fitting suit only served to magnify his youth. He stared at her with a stunned expression that reminded her of Geoff's that first day he had arrived at school.

'Okay, so… espresso, espresso, short mac, double shot latte and… what can I get for you, Dennis?' asked Lexi, firing a finger at each man.

Dennis' cheeks pinked. 'Ahhh, j-just a hot chocolate for me please, I don't like coffee,' he stammered.

Thigh slapping and belly laughing ensued along with another round of jostling. Someone yelled, 'Just make him a babyccino, Lex!'

Trying to recover himself, Dennis ventured, 'Be yourself, everyone else is taken—isn't that what they say?'

He warbled a kind of laugh, and Lexi offered him a kind smile.

He'll be drinking espressos in no time.

~

When Linh returned with the avocados, she looked exuberant.

'Successful mission?' asked Lexi.

Linh smiled broadly as she set down the fruit and tied her apron.

'Xavi called. He wants to take me out for dinner tonight, says he's got something really important to talk about.'

Lexi turned to face her. 'Do you think…?'

'Maybe. I hope so,' said Linh, her eyes shining. 'I've been hinting at how much I want to move out of Mum's, get a place of my own. He never really says much about it but, maybe. His place is crazy at the moment, do you know that there's seven of them in the house now?'

'Seven!'

'Eight, including him!'

'Well, rent's a bitch,' said Lexi, turning to rest against the counter.

'Are you still looking for a place?' Linh asked.

'I mean, I *look*,' said Lexi.

'Would it be so bad to stay with Ethan? He's so nice.'

'Nice,' Lexi repeated.

'You don't like nice?' asked Linh, raising her heavily pencilled eyebrows.

'It's not his niceness I don't like. It feels like I've stepped into another woman's life. Her house, her husband, her kid, you know? I'm sleeping in her bed, for Christ's sake. Lying next to a man who is probably wishing I *was* her. If I get out now, then nobody needs to get hurt.'

Linh fixed Lexi with a gaze that told her she was immune to her bullshit. 'You don't know what he's…' Linh began.

'And this is the second time in my life that I've found myself helping to raise someone else's children. Well, child. I made a fucking caterpillar out of an egg carton last night for God's sake!' Lexi interjected.

Linh tried hard to suppress her grin.

Lexi laughed and went on. 'I mean, what did you do last night?'

She asked, thrusting an open palm towards Linh.

'Roller derby,' admitted Linh.

Lexi buried her face in her hands and let out an exaggerated grumble.

~

When Ethan arrived home with Lucas that evening, Lexi was applying the finishing touches to a risotto which she had worked all afternoon to create. After work, she had driven to Preston Market where she procured the three varieties of mushroom and aged pecorino cheese required for the dish.

'It smells wonderful in here,' said Ethan, beaming at her. 'Come on, mate. Let's wash hands and we can sit down for dinner,' he said, addressing Lucas.

The child dropped to his knees and howled, 'Don't wanna wash hands.'

'Come on, mate,' said Ethan, trying to relieve him of the backpack he still wore.

'Nooooooooooo.'

Lexi dished out the risotto, garnished it with extra cheese and added chopped parsley to hers and Ethan's, remembering just in time that Lucas didn't like it. Her eyes darted towards Lucas where he now lay on the floor convulsing, letting out a low gulping moan.

'Please, mate. I know you're tired, but Lexi's made a yummy dinner for us.'

When they sat down fifteen minutes later their "yummy dinner" had transformed into a congealed goo which Lucas poked at with his spoon.

'Eat it, mate,' Ethan said through clenched teeth.

Lucas scooped some and deposited it onto his tongue. 'Blaaaaah,' he exclaimed, ejecting the blob from his mouth. It landed with a *splat* on the table. 'Mushrooms, yuck, slimy.'

Ethan closed his eyes and took a slow, measured breath.

'I might leave you to it,' Lexi said, standing.

'Lex, don't go. I'm sorry, he's tired.'

'It's okay, I know. You can make some toast or something, it's fine. I'll go up and have a bath… read.'

~

Later that night after Lucas had gone to bed, Lexi returned to the living room. She scrunched into one end of the sofa and looked over at Ethan, his face in profile as he scrolled through Netflix. When she had first moved in, she'd playfully teased him about his indecisiveness, but something had changed recently, and she had begun to detest it. *Just choose anything*, she wanted to scream.

Ethan had been a daily visitor to the café where she worked. At first, his pharmacy whites had made him appear older, but once she was able to see past them, she found a not-quite-forty-year-old man whose broad shoulders, glossy brown hair and melancholic hazel eyes became something of an obsession for her. She spent weeks trying to lure him into the type of idle banter that came easily with most customers. But Ethan didn't seem to register her existence, which only served to fuel her increasing desire for him. A sliver of opportunity came when he complimented the double shot latte she had just made him, to which she replied, 'If you think that's good, wait 'til I make you a cocktail.'

His eyes widened, and he appeared momentarily stunned by the intensity of her gaze. Seizing the opportunity, and displaying an initiative she hadn't known she possessed, she scrawled her phone number onto his muscular forearm using the pen she wrote on coffee cups with. His normally impassive face came alive with a glorious smile. He said nothing, just nodded, turned and left. Lexi's heart hammered against her rib cage as if demanding release. The warm glow of her arousal pulsed deliciously from her core as she pulled the next espresso, concentrating her gaze on the slow drip of ebony liquid. That night, he had texted her. And it was here, in the confines of a communication medium cocooned from reality, that he unfurled. He spoke to her via text message in a way that he seemed unable to in person. He told her about his young son, about how his life had pivoted, leaving him the sole-parent of a toddler who had only just weaned from his mother's breast. The story wrung Lexi's heart and she understood why he had seemed so detached. They fell into a surreal rhythm of deep, confessional texting late into the night, followed by furtive glances over frothing milk the following morning.

This split narrative, coupled with Ethan's lack of availability, made Lexi feel as though he were someone off-limits to her. In the early hours of a Sunday morning, after an evening of increasingly intimate texts, Lexi had asked for his address and told him to unlock his front door. She slipped in to find him sitting alone in his lamp-lit living room wearing only pyjama bottoms, a glass of toffee-coloured liquid in hand. She walked to him and, as if possessed, untied her wrap dress and let it fall open to reveal the miniscule shroud of her underwear. His lips parted, but no words came. He rose to meet her lips, running his hands along her bare midriff, and she felt his relief mirror her own as they explored each other's mouths. Pulling away, she turned and led him to the full-length mirror in the hallway. His eyes searched hers, perplexed, and she heard herself say, 'I want you to watch me.' Dropping to her knees, she took him in her mouth. His startled reaction made her feel powerful, and she moved her mouth and hands in rhythmic formations, revelling in the feeling of inspiration, surprised by the creativity of her movements. Finally, he gave a small shudder, pulled out and came into his hand. And, although she felt the hot slick of her own arousal, she rose, cupped his strong, weekend-stubbled jaw and deposited a farewell kiss on his parted lips, leaving him clutching the product of his climax.

She strode the length of his driveway, retying her wrap dress, feeling like an action hero walking from an inferno. Back in the car, she felt faint with exhilaration.

She stared at him now, his face illuminated by the television screen. Sometimes, she had to retrace her steps to comprehend how she had ended up here. Each passing day with Ethan widened the gap between them. What's more, it was as if her grains of creative inspiration were falling into that chasm like a torn bag of rice.

She checked her phone. No word from Linh. She and Xavier were probably in the throes of passion, celebrating moving in together.

SIX

AFTER a string of days which buzzed with the promise of summer, the weather had done an about-face and Melbourne was once again bitten by cold. It was just before 6:00 a.m. when Lexi arrived to open the café, and the sun had not yet emerged to melt the silver frost coating everything. Keeping her coat on, Lexi switched on the heater and coffee machine, and began assembling cups of Bircher muesli and chia pudding. When Paige arrived, she seemed preoccupied, barely acknowledging the latte Lexi set down on her tiny desk in the storeroom. Early morning commuters popped in on their way to the tram stop, and Lexi made small talk while she churned out coffees and handed over breakfasts. By 7:00 a.m. when Linh was due to arrive, Lexi was rushed off her feet. Holding a hand up to pause the next influx of orders, she poked her head into the storeroom to summon Paige, before being sucked back into the tide of customers coming and going.

'Did she text?' Lexi asked, sliding two flat whites over the counter.

'No, nothing. I hope she's okay,' said Paige.

Another hour passed in a blur before a frantic Linh burst through the door. 'I'm so sorry! I forgot to plug my phone in last night. It died and my alarm didn't go off,' she blurted, hurrying to retrieve her apron and take her place next to Lexi.

Lexi shot an inquisitive look at Linh, who knitted her brow and looked away.

When the morning rush petered out, Lexi took in her friend's

34

pallor. Something wasn't right.

'Are you okay?' Lexi asked.

'It depends on what you mean by "okay",' said Linh.

'Should I ask how it went last night?'

Linh let out a weary laugh. 'Well, he didn't ask me to move in with him, if that's what you're asking.'

'Oh, God. He didn't break up with you, did he?' Lexi said, covering her mouth.

'No, nothing like that.'

'What was the important thing that he wanted to talk to you about?'

Linh gave a slow blink as if to centre herself. 'He wants to open the relationship.'

'Open it?'

'To others. Together. With us,' Linh replied.

'What? Like threesomes?'

'Shhh,' hissed Linh, shooting a glance towards the office.

'What did you say to him?' whispered Lexi. But their conversation was interrupted by an elderly woman who shuffled in and requested a "cup of chino".

Thoughts jostled in Lexi's mind as she made the drink and handed it over. Once the woman was out of earshot, she turned to Linh. 'So?'

'I was surprised, obviously. He gave this whole prepared speech about how much he loves me, how he's never felt so comfortable in a relationship before, how we've created this really safe space where we can be authentic. And I'm sitting there thinking, this is it, he's going to ask me.'

Lexi nodded.

'Then he starts talking about how monogamy is a social construct meant to stifle our animalistic desires.'

'He said "animalistic desires" to you?' said Lexi, smirking.

Linh rolled her eyes. 'I know.'

'It wouldn't have been so bad if I hadn't been psyching myself up for something entirely different,' said Linh.

'Of course,' said Lexi, nodding. 'But what will you do? What *did* you do?'

'What I did was gulp my entire glass of wine and tell him I'd have to think about it. Then, I continued gulping wine so I could get through the rest of the night. He was making it sound so idyllic, so non-conformist, you know? Like only the deepest thinkers choose to live this way.'

'Fuck,' said Lexi.

'He's trying to sell it to me as a testament to the strength of our relationship. But my mind keeps telling me that it's because I'm not enough for him.'

Lexi's mind wandered to Ethan, his face illuminated by the television screen, his thoughts a mystery to her.

'Anyway,' said Linh, shaking her head. 'How was your night? How did the risotto turn out?'

SEVEN

WHEN the doorbell chimed Lexi closed her laptop and hurried downstairs. She opened the door to reveal Ethan's sister-in-law, Marija.

'You look beautiful!' said Marija.

Lexi stepped forward to kiss her on the cheek, then fumbled as Marija made to mirror the gesture on the opposite side.

'I'm never ready for the second one,' she laughed, making way for Marija to enter.

'Some habits die hard, I guess.'

They walked into the kitchen where Ethan and Lucas sat hunched over a colouring book, discussing the merits of using blue for grass.

'Look who's here,' said Lexi.

Lucas jumped off his chair and ran over to his aunt, who scooped him onto her hip and planted a kiss on his pudgy cheek.

'Thanks for doing this,' said Ethan, rising and making his way over.

'Are you kidding me? This is the perfect excuse to leave my zoo of a house. And it's nice for Ben to have some time alone with our four.'

'Four,' marvelled Lexi. 'I honestly don't know how you do it.'

'At a certain point they start looking after themselves,' she said, smiling. She looked at Ethan and narrowed her gaze. 'You know you're covered in Texta, right?'

'Oh, what? This shirt is new!'

He made for the stairs and took them two at a time.

'And your face!' Lexi yelled after him.

'We're going to have so much fun,' Marija said to Lucas, setting him back down in his seat.

'Speaking of fun,' said Lexi. 'I have some things for you, for after buddy-boy goes to bed,' she said, eyes indicating Lucas.

She opened the pantry to reveal a box of chocolate-covered macadamias and a little cellophane-wrapped parcel of macarons.

'And there's champagne and strawberries in the fridge,' she said, grinning.

'That's it. It's official. I am doing this every Saturday night,' said Marija, throwing up her hands.

She rounded the island bench towards Lexi, looked over her shoulder at Lucas engrossed in his colouring once more, and said in a low voice, 'This is great, what you're doing.'

'What? The treats?' asked Lexi.

'No,' said Marija, waving away the misunderstanding. 'With Ethan. Taking him out, having time together, having some fun. He was in a bad place when Justine…'

Lexi nodded. 'Oh, I understand,' she said, lowering her gaze as inadequacy swept through her.

'I'm not sure you do. Justine was…'

'What are you two whispering about?' said Ethan, appearing in the doorway, grinning.

'Lexi's showing me all the beautiful things she bought for me,' said Marija, coolly.

~

Lexi led Ethan to a nondescript doorway in the backstreets of Collingwood and pushed it open to reveal a narrow stairwell, lit by a bare hanging bulb. They stepped in, allowing the heavy door to click behind them.

'You're mine now,' said Ethan, adopting a villainous tone.

He slid his arm underneath her biker jacket, around her silk-clad waist, and drew her in. She teetered slightly on her heels before leaning into the steadiness of him and accepting his kiss.

'What is this place anyway?' Ethan asked as they climbed the stairs.

'It's sort of a pop-up restaurant, I guess,' said Lexi, trying to remember what Linh had told her about it. 'It's not exactly legal, I mean, I don't think they have any permits or licenses to operate or anything.'

Ethan laughed. 'It sounds too cool for me. I'm glad I cleaned the Texta off my face.'

He pushed the door open for Lexi to enter and followed behind her.

The expansive warehouse was carpeted with threadbare rugs, and a motley assortment of furniture was arranged for dining. Tea light candles flickered from every available surface, and the sheer volume of indoor plants gave the appearance that nature was reclaiming the building. Above the hum of conversation, Neil Diamond sang about how Shilo always came. Lexi loved it.

Ethan laughed and pointed. 'I think that's my parents' sofa from when I was a kid.'

'Look, if you don't want to....' Lexi began.

Ethan put his hands up in surrender. 'No, this is great, sorry. Where shall we sit?'

Lexi wove through the diners, ducking under macramé pot-hangers and stepping over bags until she arrived at two tatty-velvet armchairs and a gold-framed, marble coffee table which wouldn't have looked out of place at Versailles.

'Here?' she asked.

They sat and Lexi attempted to appear relaxed as her too-high heels conspired with the too-low chair, giving her the posture of a crab. She let out a small laugh and said, 'I think I chose the wrong outfit.'

'You look beautiful,' said Ethan.

Having inadvertently bypassed the entire dating stage of their relationship, the pressure to enjoy themselves weighed down on Lexi.

'What's the deal here?' asked Ethan, looking around for clues.

'I don't really know, I think it's a set menu?' said Lexi.

At this, a young woman with unruly curls and a severe fringe appeared, smiling.

'Hi guys. Have you dined with us before?' she asked, her words a slow drip.

'No, this is our first time,' said Lexi.

'Awesome. So, it's a vegan set menu…'

Lexi stiffened at the word "vegan". She could almost feel Ethan's disappointment emanating from across the table. She focused her gaze on the waiter, trying to suppress the feeling that the entire evening was a write-off. She registered the words "cauliflower", "harissa" and "quinoa". But it was the phrase "biodynamic wine" that roused her.

'…the final fermentation happens in the bottle, so it has kind of a cloudy look to it, but it's amazing,' drawled the waiter.

'It all sounds delightful,' said Lexi. 'And we'll take a bottle of that rosé.'

The waiter turned and walked away.

Ethan leaned in, grinning. 'Promise me we're going for kebabs on the way home.'

Lexi forced a smile as her spirit plummeted. This whole thing felt so unnatural. Here they were in a hive of human interaction and all she could feel was lonely. What was worse, she couldn't think of a single thing to say. She thought of Linh and Xavier's current saga and wondered if she could somehow weave it into a light-hearted anecdote. Wasn't there some sort of code that allowed you to tell other people's secrets to your partner? Lexi was sure that Linh had shared stories about her and Ethan with Xavier. But what would Ethan even make of the bohemian lifestyle of her friends? In the entire duration of their short relationship, Ethan had never even articulated his sexual preferences, let alone his fantasies. What was more, his silence had stifled Lexi's own desire to share hers. She suspected that the product of this silence was a homogenised and lacklustre experience for all. Like every word left unspoken was wedged between them, keeping them apart. Sure, there were orgasms. And, in Lexi's case, sometimes several, but that was more a testament to her expertise with her own body. It amounted to an experience that was fulfilling, on paper only.

'Ground Control to Major Tom.' Ethan's voice cut through Lexi's thoughts, and she realised she was staring into space.

'Okay guys, here's your wine,' said the waiter, setting down two heavy tumblers and filling them with the pink opaque liquid.

Ethan picked up his glass and raised it towards Lexi. She mirrored the gesture.

'Lexi, I know I'm not always easy. I know that my situation… I'm kind of damaged goods and frankly you deserve more. Sometimes I look at you and wonder why on earth you chose me. But…' he trailed off.

Lexi's heart eroded like sandstone in a gale.

'If you're thinking of leaving, I understand. I wouldn't blame you. But…'

Lexi's cheeks pinked.

'…God, I hope you don't,' he finished.

Lexi's eyes filled with tears.

Ethan laughed nervously. 'Worst toast ever,' he said, resuming his regular persona. He took an audible slurp of the wine and forced a self-deprecating laugh.

'It was perfect,' Lexi murmured, her words mute in the din.

EIGHT

'WAIT up!' yelled Lexi, jogging to catch up with Linh on the lamp-lit street.

Although they usually alternated opening the café, on this day Paige had requested they both arrive early. When they entered, the lights were on and the interior warm. At the click of the door, Paige emerged from her office. Lexi and Linh exchanged furtive glances as they took in their boss's demeanour.

'Is everything okay?' asked Lexi, shucking her coat.

She had been summoned to a meeting like this a few years back, in which her then-boss confronted the small team about money going missing from the till. It had been an intensely awkward experience that later revealed a gambling-addicted barista. But it couldn't be anything like that. It was only the three of them working here.

'Take a seat, you two,' said Paige, pulling out three barstools and arranging them into a triangle.

The three women sat perched like flamingos without the anchor of the bench.

Paige took a deep breath and began. 'I'm just going to dive right in here. A couple of weeks back I received a notice to vacate from the landlord. Our lease agreement is coming to an end and, rather than wanting to renew, she wants the space back. Apparently, she's got a daughter who's planning on opening a millinery studio.'

'What is that?' asked Linh, scowling.

'Hats,' said Paige, unable to keep the scorn from her voice.

'Hats?' said Lexi, raising her eyebrows.

'I've been hustling to see if I could persuade her to sell the building to me instead, but she won't even consider it. Says she's promised her daughter already,' said Paige.

Lexi's mind laboured under the burden of the new information. 'So, what? We move to somewhere new?'

Paige looked down at the floor. 'Very new,' she said quietly. 'I have a sister in Perth, she has two kids that I never see and…'

'That's it?' said Linh, an edge creeping into her voice.

'This hasn't been an easy decision. I've lived in Melbourne my whole life but… being close to family seems like the right move now. The café scene is really starting to bloom over there so I figure I'll take a few months off and then start something up again.'

Linh shook her head, but Lexi remained still.

Paige went on, 'For what it's worth, I'd hire you both again in a heartbeat. If you ever decide to go west, there'll always be a job for you.'

'Some consolation prize,' muttered Linh.

When the doorbell chimed announcing the arrival of their first customer, they dragged the stools back into place and shuffled behind the counter. As Linh took the gentleman's order, Lexi looked back towards the storeroom. She could see Paige through the lopsided gap in the uneven sliding door, sitting at her desk with her head in her hands.

The day proceeded in a haze and Lexi couldn't help reflecting on the news of her impending unemployment. She was ashamed to realise that her first thought was about how much harder it would be to leave Ethan now. Living on a barista's salary for her entire adult life had hardly furnished her with any savings, and she'd wasted any possibility of saving in the past few months of living rent-free. She looked down at the $600 RM Williams boots she had justified purchasing because they'd stand the test of time. These boots equated to half the bond on a shitty apartment, and they were currently spattered with milk.

'Can I please have an almond latte and a *pain au chocolat?*' a customer said.

Linh lifted the glass dome on the cake plate, plucked the pastry out and popped it into a brown paper bag as Lexi made a start on the coffee.

'Ten fifty please,' said Linh, handing over the bag.

Lexi watched the crema form in the cup. It undulated as if it were about to reveal all the answers to the mysteries of the universe. She frothed the almond milk, taking care not to overheat it, before pouring it over the espresso in slow, deliberate pulses to create a leaf that she wasn't happy with. *Fucking almond milk.* She pressed on the lid and slid it over the counter. Looking up for the first time, she was confronted by intense, slate-grey eyes that stared at her unblinking.

'Lexi?' the woman asked, her big eyes getting bigger.

All the air drained from Lexi's lungs, rendering her speechless, as her mind struggled to process what she was seeing. Finally, she spoke in a whisper, 'Geoff?'

NINE

FOR the first week of their lunchtime reading sessions, Lexi and Geoff barely spoke to one another. One rainy day, with their feet tucked in to avoid the curtain of fat droplets descending from the roof, they finished the *Harry Potter* novel that had brought them together. They sat, paperbacks clutched to their chests, feeling a strange combination of triumph and regret. The series which had accompanied them through their respective teenagerhoods was over. Lexi's eyes filled with tears; it was like losing all the friends she'd ever had at once. Feeling foolish, she snuck a peek at Geoff. His dipped chin created a veil of hair which concealed his face. Sensing her gaze, he looked up to reveal tear-streaked cheeks. Lexi sniffed comically and Geoff laughed. That day they made a pact to begin the series again, reading in tandem and discussing as they went. During lunch they read in unison, and as the bell tolled, they would agree upon the number of pages to read that night, ensuring they were perfectly aligned the following lunchtime. It was through this shared pursuit that the pair grew to know each other.

Late one night, reading by lamplight, Lexi had received a text from Geoff. They were up to *The Goblet of Fire* and had just reached the point where Cedric Diggory is killed during the Triwizard Tournament. "I knew it was coming but my heart is still breaking. Is it possible to be in love with a fictional character?" he wrote. Lexi blinked at the words. Of course, she had suspected Geoff was gay, but he had never opened up to her about it before. This was her chance to reassure him, to let him know that she wasn't like the intolerant arseholes at their school. She stared at the words on her flip phone, chewing on her thumbnail. She didn't want to make a big deal of this revelation, fearing it may cause him to retreat. "It's probably a good thing he dies, otherwise I'd have to fight you for him," she sent and held her breath. "LOL" was his reply. After that night Geoff seemed to relax around her. Some nights, after their households had gone to bed, Geoff would sneak in through her bedroom window and they would hang out, sharing earbuds to listen to music or having whispered conversations. Geoff always seemed so fascinated by Lexi's possessions, running his hands over things and wanting to know what everything was for.

This period represented the happiest time in Lexi's young life. It was the first inkling she'd had that things might improve. That there could be more for her than being a fifth wheel in her mother's perfect life. But there were nights when Geoff didn't come, when he was too afraid of being caught. When his father seemed poised to pounce.

Bruce Holloway was the kind of man who blamed others for his lot in life. He worked sporadically as an off-the-books farmhand while collecting a disability pension and blaming immigrants for a lack of good jobs. The weeks when Bruce wasn't working were particularly grim at the Holloway residence, with his frustration levels rising as the days tallied, sometimes culminating in violent rage. In a desperate attempt at self-preservation, Geoff's younger brother Peter would deflect Bruce's attention by highlighting Geoff's many deplorable characteristics. Bruce and Peter would then unite to roast the older boy. Most frequently they jibed him about the length of his hair, his bookishness or his lack of a girlfriend. Their mother, Pamela, most likely fearing for her own personal safety, would turn a blind eye to this behaviour, leaving Geoff to weather their taunting alone. One of the insults which had stayed with Lexi even to this day was his father sniggering, 'You can't get any pussy if you are a pussy.'

It was after a particularly long period of Bruce Holloway's

idleness that Geoff took the risk and clamoured through Lexi's bedroom window one night. As he slumped down on the floor to lean against her bed, his face blotchy from crying, Lexi noticed his hair matted with congealed blood.

'Jesus!' Lexi exclaimed, dropping down beside him. 'What the fuck happened?'

He rested his forehead on his bent knees and was quiet for a while. Lexi sat beside him and waited. Eventually, he lifted his head to look at her.

'I'm beginning to think it would be better for me to be nothing than to be this,' he said, his voice pained.

Something about his intensity caused Lexi to become hyperaware of her breathing. Regaining herself, she tried to lighten the mood.

'Well, I'm a big fan of this,' she said, waving her index finger to encircle him. 'Let's get you cleaned up.'

Geoff gritted his teeth and winced as she cleaned the blood from his temple with a warm washcloth. Afterwards, Lexi chattered as if her endless stream of words would somehow fill the cavernous void she detected in him. He sat, lost in his own thoughts, seemingly unaware that she was talking at all. Finally, he stood and muttered, 'I should go.'

Lexi spent the remainder of the night awake, running over Geoff's visit in her mind. How despondent he had been, how dejected. What had he meant by "be nothing"?

The next day was Saturday. Lexi had sat at her desk from daybreak staring at the Holloway house for signs of disturbance. At midmorning, she saw the two boys follow their dad into the family station wagon and drive away. Relief washed over her. She realised how much she had been fearing the worst. If there was even a chance that Geoff was contemplating suicide, something had to be done. She remembered a girl called Erica from her year level who had committed suicide the year prior. At a school memorial for her, Erica's best friend Stacy had stood before the entire school and spoke of how she suspected Erica was depressed but had kept it to herself. She urged the student body to look after their friends. Stacy's detached, steely demeanour had given way to heaving sobs, and she was guided off the stage by the principal. Remembering this, Lexi slipped out of the house without telling her family and made for Geoff's house. His mother answered the door, her grey face all but camouflaged within the raised collar of her tatty bathrobe.

'He's out,' she said, beginning to close the door.

'I know, Mrs. Holloway,' Lexi said, placing a hand on the door. 'I was actually hoping to talk with you.'

When Lexi re-crossed the threshold twenty minutes later, she was convinced she'd made the wrong decision. As she described Geoff's fluctuating moods and his recent descent into despair, Pamela Holloway had rebuffed the evidence with comments about his hypersensitivity and antisocial personality. She seemed inconvenienced by Lexi's presence in her kitchen, spouting phrases like "precious snowflake" and "needs to toughen up" in retaliation. Goosebumps bloomed on Lexi's arms and she pulled her cardigan around her tighter. She had violated her best friend's trust in order to help him and it had all been in vain.

As Lexi accompanied her mother running errands for the remainder of the day, she ran over the facts in her head. Mrs. Holloway had completely dismissed everything she had said. Perhaps she would simply forget about it and Geoff would never even find out about Lexi's visit. But that still left the problem of what to do about Geoff, how to help him and keep him safe.

'For God's sake, Lexi!' Monique shrieked. 'What do I need to do to get a little bit of help?'

Lexi flinched and a can of Diet Coke fell to the ground from the six-pack she was holding. Fizz hissed from an unseen hole.

'Sorry, Mum,' Lexi stammered, bending to retrieve the can.

'Leave it,' Monique spat.

Once in the car, Monique finger-combed her hair in the rear

vision mirror before reversing out of the car space.

'You've been hanging around with that weird kid from across the street too much. You're turning into a freak like him,' said Monique.

When they arrived home, Lexi noticed the Holloway's station wagon in their driveway. She cocked her head, listening. Nothing.

She texted Geoff, "Hey, I hope you're feeling better today, want to come over tonight?"

"How could you?" came his reply.

TEN

GNAWING at a hangnail on her thumb, Lexi tasted blood as she scanned the bustling café.

'You came,' said a familiar, yet unfamiliar voice from over her shoulder.

Lexi turned.

'Ge… Jamie, sorry,' she stammered.

Earlier that day, with her eyes wide and heartbeat in her ears, all Lexi could do was stare. The person who was once her best friend had scrawled something onto a napkin and pressed it to her palm. Linh watched the exchange, her gaze bouncing between the two women as if watching a tennis match.

'Who was that?' Linh asked afterwards.

'It was my best friend from high school,' she said, holding up the napkin. 'Jamie,' she read.

'What, from Hamilton?' said Linh, 'You should have introduced me.'

'Yeah, shit, sorry. I just haven't seen… *her* in ten years or so…' Lexi mumbled.

'Crazy. Anyway, I'm going to go ask Paige if she has any old hospo friends we can hit up for work,' said Linh, walking away.

Lexi had stared at the phone number in her shaking hands.

She retrieved her phone from her back pocket and sent a text. "Am I dreaming? Can we meet up?"

Now, as Jamie took a seat in the chair opposite, Lexi knew she was staring but was powerless to control it. The angular face she had once known was softer now, the edges rounded. The hair, once a mousy mop used to hide behind, was now styled into a sophisticated auburn bob, revealing an open and confident expression. Her posture was elegant, poised. It produced a distorted fun-house effect that Lexi's brain was having trouble processing.

'I know this is a lot to take in,' said Jamie, leaning onto her forearms.

Lexi gave a succession of small nods as her eyes welled. She reached across the table and took Jamie's manicured hands in hers. Lexi closed her eyes and felt her friend's long, familiar fingers give an encouraging squeeze.

'I thought you were dead,' whispered Lexi.

They sat for a time, holding hands in silence.

'I'm sorry,' said Jamie finally. 'I'm sorry I left like that. But I was so confused about who I was. I had never even heard the term "transgender" back then. And I was angry at you. I mean, you were my only friend and when you ratted me out to my mum…'

'Look, I know I did the wrong thing. But I was worried you'd do something crazy; I was terrified of losing you. And then I lost you anyway,' said Lexi.

Jamie gave a sad smile.

'But what happened? Where did you go? When you wouldn't answer my calls, I went over to your parents' house.'

Jamie stiffened at the mention of her parents. 'I'm sure Pamela and Bruce were a big help,' she scoffed.

'They wouldn't even call the police. Said you were eighteen and not their problem anymore.'

They fell into silence again, taking in their surroundings, reflecting on either side of their shared experience.

'It was awful without you,' said Lexi quietly.

'I'm sorry, Lex.'

'I'm sorry too.'

'What can I get you, ladies?' said a waiter, appearing at their table.

'Coffee?' Jamie asked.

'I'm gonna need something stronger. I lost my job today,' confessed Lexi.

'No, really?' said Jamie.

'We've got a special on raspberry mojitos, two for thirty,' offered the waiter.

'Done,' said Jamie, handing back the menu she'd been scanning.

At Lexi's request, Jamie filled in the blanks of the ten years they'd been apart. After jumping on a V/Line train to Melbourne, Jamie had spent the first few nights holed up in a 24-hour McDonalds, trying to conserve the wad of cash she had stolen from the inside panel of her parents' air conditioning unit. On the third night, a zit-faced kid who was cleaning tables had pointed to a "help wanted" sign and said, 'You may as well get paid to be here.'

This position became short lived when one night a glossy, middle-aged man driving a Jaguar handed a business card through the drive-thru window and proclaimed, 'You're too pretty to be working here.'

It was during this time, working as a coat checker at The Peacock's Pride, that the full spectrum of human sexuality and gender was revealed to Jamie.

'One of the bartenders was this trans gay guy. He described feeling like he was born in the wrong body. It was like a switch flicked in my brain. I remember thinking in that moment, *Oh my God, that's me.*'

'What did he say when you told him?' asked Lexi.

'Oh, I didn't tell him. I just carried the idea around with me. It was like a tiny little light glowing inside me that I had to preserve. I started doing research though, joined some online groups. But the real turning point came when one of my online friends invited me along to a trans support group in Carlton.'

Lexi shook her head. In all her years of guessing at what had become of her friend, she could never have imagined this.

'What?' asked Jamie, visibly self-conscious under Lexi's gaze.

'It's just that…' Lexi paused, unsure whether to go on. 'You turned from a caterpillar into a butterfly,' she said.

Jamie rolled her eyes and laughed. 'Are you drunk?' she asked.

'Gosh, I hope not. I have to drive home.' Lexi took a sip of her water and checked the time. 'Shit, I should go,' she said, raising her hand to get the waiter's attention. Jamie leaned over and took Lexi's raised hand in hers, lowering it back onto the table.

'On me,' she said, 'but can we do this again? I spent the entire time jabbering. I want to know about you.'

~

Lexi pulled up in front of Ethan's house as he was helping Lucas out of his car seat.

'Hey!' he exclaimed in surprise. 'I thought you would have been home hours ago.'

'I had a few errands to run,' she said, the lie surprising her.

'Shall we Uber some dinner over from that Japanese place tonight?' asked Ethan, setting Lucas down in the driveway.

'Vegetable pancake!' squealed Lucas.

'Sounds great,' she said. 'I've had a helluva day. Paige told us she's closing down the café and moving to Perth.'

Ethan looked up from the tangle of belongings he was wrangling and said, 'Oh, Lex.' He stepped forward to comfort her but then, realising he had no hands free, gave a self-deprecating laugh instead.

'Here,' she said, extracting Lucas' backpack and water bottle from Ethan's grasp. She took the little boy's hand and guided him up the front steps.

'How was your day, buddy?' she asked, looking down at him.

'I did gardening today,' said Lucas, seeming surprised by this fact.

The evening was mild and fragrant. They dined outside, the crackle of plastic containers jarring in the otherwise peaceful twilight. Lucas, having abandoned his almost untouched *okonomiyaki*, crouched in the buffalo grass observing a procession of tiny creatures beneath the blades.

'It must have been a massive shock,' said Ethan.

Lexi blinked rapidly before realising he was talking about her job. 'Oh! Yeah, it was. I mean, it sounds like Paige did everything she could to keep the place open. But I guess fate had other plans.'

'I don't know how to say this,' began Ethan, tearing at a corner of his paper napkin as if it were of the utmost importance. 'Having you here, the past few months. I know when you moved in it was meant to be temporary, but… I guess what I'm trying to say is that… it doesn't have to be. I'm glad. We're glad you're here.' His eyes flicked toward her before settling on Lucas who was rolling a slater around in his palm. 'Fuck. Why is this so hard?' Ethan said, running a hand through his hair and taking a swig from his beer. 'What I mean to say is that…'

'Thank you. That means a lot,' said Lexi.

Ethan exhaled and leaned into his chair.

Setting down her chopsticks, Lexi took a deep breath. This was her chance to broach the subject of Justine. To confront Ethan about his capacity to invest fully in their relationship and leave his feelings for his wife in the past. She parted her lips.

'Okay, mate. Bath time,' Ethan hollered to Lucas.

Lexi blinked, startled by the volume of Ethan's voice and the severing of their conversation.

Lucas mumbled something inaudible.

'Can't hear you, mate,' Ethan yelled back.

Lucas stood and plodded towards them looking sheepish.

'I want Lexi,' he whispered, eyes cast downward.

Ethan looked at Lexi and she gave a small nod.

'I'm going to teach you a game called "sharky" that I used to play with my little brother and sister,' she said, rising and taking Lucas' hand.

Afterwards, in Lucas' bedroom, Lexi was on her knees attempting to capture Lucas into his pyjama top while the boy evaded her, squealing. Ethan walked in chuckling. 'What a ruckus!' he said.

'This kid is slippery!' exclaimed Lexi, brushing her hair from her face in an exaggerated fashion and diving for him again. She fell onto the carpet in a heap. Lucas fell on top of her giggling.

'I got you!' he said and allowed Lexi to fold him into an embrace.

Ethan grinned down at them. 'Storytime?'

Lucas jumped up like a meerkat and Ethan finished dressing him.

'I'll leave you boys to it,' said Lexi, rising.

As she descended the stairs she heard Lucas say, 'That bath time was the most fun.'

ELEVEN

'ARE they even serious?' Linh asked her phone.

'Huh?' said Lexi. She was also looking at her phone, willing a reply from Jamie.

'Half of these job ads are a joke. The hours are dismal, but they want you to be available all the time, waiting around in case they need you. Who can even do that?' grumbled Linh.

Paige was out, presumably packing up her life for the move across the country.

Linh grabbed her bag and slung it over one shoulder. 'You'll be okay for a minute? I need some air.'

Lexi nodded, pocketing her phone. She stared as Linh strode out the front door and into the dazzling, sun-bathed street. She was having trouble picturing Jamie's face already. Her mind was playing tricks, flitting between past and present incarnations of the same person. She kept combing through her memories, searching for evidence that Jamie had been a girl the whole time. Her best friend had always possessed a simmering angst, but they were teenagers, awkwardness was standard issue.

One of the café's regulars strode in, the cylinder of her yoga mat slung over her back like an archer's quiver.

'Hey, Miriam. Usual?' asked Lexi.

The woman nodded. 'Paige told me about you guys closing down. It's so sad. We're really going to miss you in this strip.'

'You're not excited for the hat shop?' Lexi asked, smirking.

Miriam laughed. 'You know what? There's a café opening near me, in Ivanhoe. They're still doing the renos but, I don't know, maybe you could check them out. Get in contact. It used to be the old post office. Cute little white heritage building across from the supermarket. You can't miss it.'

Lexi capped Miriam's coffee cup and punched the price into the EFTPOS machine for her to tap. 'Hm, I'll check it out, thanks.'

Once Miriam was gone, Lexi pulled her phone out, hating herself for how much she was obsessing. But that feeling was immediately replaced by a rush of excitement at seeing she had received a reply. "Sorry for the delay, worked late last night and slept in. Would love to hang out again. Free this arvo?"

Lexi's fingers hovered over the keypad. She didn't want to risk sounding desperate. She typed, "Wanted to swing by Ivanhoe to see about a job, maybe we could meet after?"

'Sexy Lexi!'

Lexi groaned inwardly and set down her phone. 'Hello, boys,' she greeted the real estate guys, her voice an octave lower.

As they approached the counter, the collective effect of their striped suits made Lexi's eyes jump and skitter. It was like looking at a herd of zebras.

'I hear the café's closing down. We're really going to miss that pretty face of yours around here,' said a slick-haired agent in his thirties. The one they called De Lesi.

Someone towards the back muttered, 'I'm going to miss that arse more.'

A ripple of impressed sniggers jittered the group. Lexi homed in on the speaker, Tony.

'Oh, come on, Tony. If you want to see a grade-A arse, you can always look in the mirror.'

Oh shit, thought Lexi in the beat of silence that followed, *I'm going to get fired all over again.*

Gasps and belly laughs reverberated around the space and Lexi exhaled. She'd gotten away with it. The new kid, Dennis, laughed nervously, a red blush creeping up his newly acquired collar.

'Good one, Lex, put the prick in his place,' said De Lesi.

'The usuals, boys?' Lexi asked, eager to get them out. She would not be missing this part of her day.

'Uh, I might try a coffee today,' said Dennis, in a rasp.

'Sure, how about a cappuccino?'

'Yes please, with sugar.'

'Aww,' gushed Tony slapping Dennis on the back with too much force. 'Our little boy's all grown up.'

As they strode away sipping their coffees, Linh returned. She instinctively lifted her arms in front of her chest as they dispersed around her and out the door.

'Nice of you to join us, Linny,' somebody quipped.

Once they were gone, Linh gave a dramatic shiver. 'Ew.'

'Yep,' agreed Lexi.

'I just spoke to Xavi,' said Linh, her eyes brightening.

'And?' prompted Lexi, knowing full well what she was about to hear.

'I told him I'm up for it. For trying out the open thing. But I've set some ground rules and I've only agreed to a three-month trial.'

'Smart,' said Lexi, nodding.

'I'm kind of excited now,' Linh admitted.

'What are the rules?' asked Lexi.

'Choose the third person together. Don't see anyone on your own unless it's been agreed. And make sure the focus is always on us,' said Linh, counting each point with her fingers.

'What does the last one mean?' asked Lexi, furrowing her brow.

'It just means that you don't get *so* into the third person that you forget about the one you're actually in a relationship with. Like, in a way… anything he does with the other person needs to be like a show for me. Eyes on me. And vice versa,' said Linh.

'It all sounds very pragmatic,' said Lexi.

'I gave it a lot of thought, you know? And I think the reason these things get out of hand is that without any structure, everybody's expectations are different. This way, we all know what's okay and what's a deal breaker.'

'Well,' said Lexi with a decisive nod, 'You're a fucking inspiration.'

Linh laughed. 'Maybe you and Ethan could shake things up a bit, get something of your own going.'

'Oh God, I can't even imagine how I would begin to suggest something that unconventional,' said Lexi. She looked down at her hands and scratched at a cuticle, thinking.

'I don't even know what to do about us, you know? He seems so distant. We literally never talk. After Lucas goes to bed we sit there on the sofa. He scrolls through Netflix, and I think the reason he can't choose anything is that he's not even looking. That he's sitting there thinking of Justine. Plus, if I don't initiate sex, it doesn't happen, like, at all.'

Lexi knew she sounded scattered and unhinged as she gave voice to the worries that had been consuming her since she'd moved into Ethan's house. Tears threatened, but Linh took a step closer and placed a hand on each shoulder, grounding her.

'Look,' said Linh, sternly, 'you don't know what the man is thinking while he's scrolling Netflix. And if you want to talk to him, then talk to him. Maybe he's thinking the same thing about you. You need to spend less time worrying about his heart and more time thinking about your own. How do you actually feel about him? Every relationship needs work but at least Ethan is not a total fuckup. It's a good start! And as for the sex. Has he ever turned you down?'

'Well, no,' Lexi conceded.

'Maybe you're the initiator. Maybe that's your dynamic.'

Lexi pursed her lips.

~

The old Ivanhoe post office was exactly as Miriam had described. Lexi pulled up out front and noted the "Post-Haste Espresso coming soon" sign. Rummaging through her bag, she extracted a pen and paper and scrawled a quick note explaining that she was a barista looking for work. As she climbed out of her car and walked towards the building, she tried to imagine arriving here for work every day. The people she would get to know, shops she might visit on her lunch break. She cupped her hands against the glass-paned door and peered in through a gap of newspaper covering it. Inside, Lexi spied a sweeping dark-wood bar and a gleaming, eagle-topped Berezza Classic espresso machine that rose like a cathedral from the centre. She sighed. This place was the real deal.

'Can I help you?'

Lexi jumped and turned to find a paunchy middle-aged man wearing a t-shirt which read "Don't be sexist, bitches hate that".

'Oh, I was just having a peek inside. I'm a barista, so…' she said, unsure why she was explaining herself to this guy.

'I'm the owner, so…' he said, mocking her.

She gave him a tight-lipped smile. *What a dick.*

'I've already hired a crew but…' He paused to survey her body. 'I could always do with one more. Why don't you give me your details and we'll hook something up?'

Lexi clenched the note in her hand tighter.

'Do you have a business card or something? I'll email you my CV,' she lied.

He pulled a wallet from his back pocket, his eyes never leaving her. Opening it, he thumbed over a condom which crackled under his touch, before extracting a card and pressing it into her palm with a clammy hand. 'Make sure you do,' he said, his touch lingering.

~

'You have a dog!' exclaimed Lexi as an excited greyhound jumped out of Jamie's Mercedes and bounded over to greet her. Lexi crouched to give her a pat.

'This is Ava,' said Jamie, rounding the vehicle.

Lexi rose and stared as Jamie approached. She wore bright,

confetti-print active wear and her hair was pulled back into a sleek, stubby ponytail. Her physique was slender and athletic like that of a ballet dancer.

'Shall we walk?' asked Jamie, clipping a leash to Ava's harness.

Lexi nodded, and they fell into step heading towards the river.

'How was the job interview?' Jamie asked.

'Oh, it wasn't an interview. I was scoping out a new café that someone told me about. But the owner was a slime ball so that's the end of that.'

'What a shame,' said Jamie.

'The place was cool. I felt hopeful for a second, but...' Lexi shrugged. 'What do you do for work? You said you had to work late last night?'

'Well, I didn't *have* to. I set my own hours. It's kind of my own business, you could say.'

'Oh, cool. What's the business?'

Jamie was silent a moment as they crunched along the gravel path.

'I'm a cam model,' she said, shooting Lexi a sideways glance.

'What, you mean like porn?' asked Lexi, eyes widening.

'Well, I don't see it quite that way,' said Jamie, tilting her head.

'But that's what we're talking about, right? You get paid to...' Lexi trailed off, realising she didn't know where to go from here. She changed tack. 'Let's start this again. Jamie, can you please tell me what that means?' she said, her words as punchy as a typewriter.

Jamie matched her tone, smirking, 'Yes, Lexi. I will tell you what that means.'

They laughed.

'I host a chatroom, and anyone online can login and see me,' said Jamie.

'Can you see them? See what they're doing?' asked Lexi, her nose crinkling.

'No, I can't see them, but they can send messages, ask me questions and send tips—the tips are how I make money.'

'But what are you *doing*?' asked Lexi.

'Mainly talking. Telling stories, answering their questions.'

Lexi narrowed her gaze into something sceptical.

Jamie laughed. 'Okay, so I also have a menu where visitors to my room can pay for specific acts.'

'Uh huh!' said Lexi. 'Now we're getting somewhere.'

Jamie rolled her eyes but kept grinning. 'Every cam model has their own menu, things they are willing to do for a price they've set themselves.'

'What's on your menu?' asked Lexi.

'Lots of things. Like, removing an item of clothing, licking a lollipop, dancing to a guest's favourite song, flashing different body parts…'

'And…?' prompted Lexi.

'The most expensive thing is giving myself an orgasm.'

'This is fucking crazy. What world am I in right now?' Lexi howled.

'But it's unusual for one person to tip enough for that.'

'What, do they all chip in instead?' Lexi joked.

'Well, yeah. They're called "countdowns". You set an amount, and everyone sends tips and when the goal is reached. Boom!'

Lexi's eyes became saucers.

They walked in silence for a while, nodding to the occasional passer-by as they traced the meandering flow of the Yarra.

'Are you shocked?' asked Jamie, breaking their silence.

'Not shocked. I mean, surprised maybe. But fuck me if you're not already the most surprising person I've ever known,' said Lexi laughing.

Jamie laughed too.

'But there must be so many creeps sitting there leering at you? How do you deal with that?'

Jamie considered this.

'There are,' she admitted. 'But at least they're online, you know?

You must have creeps who come into the café and leer at you in person all the time.'

Lexi thought of the real estate guys and the sleaze she'd just met at Post-Haste but remained silent.

'At least this is on my own terms, in a safe environment, where I call the shots. My visitors come to be entertained and flirted with and turned on. And if anyone is spoiling the vibe with inappropriate comments or requests then I eject them.'

Lexi let the concept permeate her thoughts. 'To be honest it sounds… fun,' she admitted.

'It actually is. And you'd be surprised how much you get to know people. The regulars I mean. There are so many lonely people out there and this…' she trailed off. 'Sometimes I think I'm the only one waiting for them when they get home.'

TWELVE

'CAN you tell me about a time you went above and beyond for a customer?' asked the juice bar manager, a greasy-haired kid aged no more than twenty. He scratched his scalp, releasing a flurry of dandruff onto his uniformed shoulders. *Well, I have clean hair when I'm at work*, Lexi thought. She forced a smile. It was all so pointless.

'I guess it's about the small things for me. Remembering a customer's coffee order, learning their names, getting to know them a little better each time they come in,' she said.

She thought of what Jamie had said yesterday by the river and went on. 'I guess I make each person feel like I've been waiting all morning, just for them.'

The kid didn't look up from his prepared interview questions. 'Can you tell me what your biggest weakness is?'

Lexi wanted to scream. 'I guess I have a low tolerance for stupid questions,' she said, deadpan.

He blinked rapidly through squinted eyes before continuing. 'Can you tell me what your biggest strength is?'

'I'm really fucking good at making coffee. Which seems like it might be relevant considering you advertised for a barista.'

'Yeah...' said the kid, recoiling slightly so that his chin disappeared into his neck. 'Well, I've got a few more interviews to do and then I'll let you know.'

'Sure,' said Lexi.

She gathered her belongings and clamoured out of the tiny office, knocking over a precarious stack of disposable cups in the process. *See you never.*

~

'Hey, girl! How'd it go?' asked Linh when Lexi arrived for her shift.

Lexi flashed her a look.

'That good huh?'

Lexi banged around in a huff, trying to settle in.

'I have some news,' Linh began tentatively.

'Yeah?' said Lexi, tamping the grounds for a much-needed coffee.

'Did I ever tell you about my Uncle Hung?'

Lexi looked up at the ceiling, scanning her memories. 'Maybe. Is he the barrister?'

'Lawyer, yeah!'

'Okay…'

'My mum was telling him about me losing my job and he said he's been looking for someone to help him out at his firm.'

'Yeah? Doing what?'

'It's kind of a random mix. Some reception and office admin. But he also wants a new website built. I think he's keen to do e-newsletters and socials and stuff.'

'But do you know about any of that stuff?' Lexi asked gently.

'Not really,' admitted Linh. 'But here's the great part. He's going to pay for me to do a TAFE course.'

'Yeah? That's amazing.'

'I know, right?'

Lexi sipped her cortado and leaned back against the bench, thinking. 'Fuck, if I didn't love you so much, I'd be jealous. Your uncle doesn't need someone to clean the toilets, does he?'

Linh sidled up next to Lexi and nudged her gently. 'You'll find something,' she said.

Lexi tried to smile.

THIRTEEN

LEXI had pretended to be asleep when Ethan left that morning. Now, she lay in bed, replaying the reason she couldn't face him.

Woken from sleep by Ethan twitching beside her, she rubbed his back gently to wake him. But when his first unintelligible mutterings became clear, she paused. A single, agitated word was twisting his mouth. 'Justine. Justine. Justine.' She retracted her hand as though his skin was scolding hot and slid back beneath the covers, her eyes wide in the inky darkness. Pulling the pillow around her ears to dull the sound of his lamenting, she wondered at the best course of action. If she had the financial means, would she cut and run now? Lexi wasn't sure. Next to her, Ethan's body stilled, and she felt the warmth of him curl into her. Her body mirrored the gesture of its own volition.

Now, Lexi grabbed her phone and trawled through the job ads. The same sorry selection she'd surveyed yesterday blinked back at her and she groaned. In her final weeks at The Bean & Gone Café, Lexi had interviewed for a string of jobs which ranged from the uninspiring to the soul-destroying. They all bled together in her mind as she lay entangled in the bed sheets on her first official day of unemployment. She sat, took a sad-faced selfie and texted it to Linh with the caption "Day 1 without you" and received an almost instant reply saying, "Miss you too, work-wifey." Lexi's finger hovered over the screen as she considered texting Linh about what had happened with Ethan. Instead, she wrote, "Have a great first day!"

Lexi climbed out of bed, showered, dressed, and padded down to the kitchen for coffee, picking up Lucas' strewn toys as she went.

Lexi had once read a quote which went something like: "If you want to be a writer, then write". Where did this leave her? She told herself that the reason she'd written so little lately was because she no longer lived alone. It was so hard to carve out any time in which to write undisturbed. Even her journaling had gone from sluggish to non-existent. But the truth was, she felt stuck, like her mind was unable to conjure anything interesting. She had nothing to say and no one to say it to.

Sitting at the island bench, she listened to the wall clock tick above her head. The sound was exaggerated in the silence of the empty house. It seemed to be mocking her idleness, counting out each second of her wasted life. Draining her cup, she rose and made for the pantry which she scanned for ingredients and, once satisfied, tied on an apron.

When the brownies were in the oven and the kitchen returned to order, Lexi went to the powder room. As she entered, she caught her mirrored reflection staring back. She still wore the apron, a cocoa powder smudge across her cheek bone. *I'm a fucking housewife.* She tore off the apron and leaned forward to clean her face. 'What the fuck?' she said aloud. She leaned closer to the mirror, squinting at the dark roots of her hairline. The silver stripe of her first grey hair gleamed back at her. The oven timer's shrill ring told her that time was up.

~

Over the past few weeks, Lexi had hung out with Jamie several times. But, after her first omission to Ethan, she had never managed to find a way to tell him about her. She wondered if her secrecy was the result of Jamie being trans. Was her friend too unconventional to share with Ethan? Was this also the reason she kept Linh and Xavier's tallying sexual adventures a secret from him? Maybe deep-down, Lexi thought that divulging these facts would expose her own identity as a societal misfit.

She stared at her reflection in the elevator, which would deposit her on Jamie's floor. When the doors opened, her own image was replaced by Jamie, framed in the doorway opposite.

'Well, hello,' said Jamie, grinning.

'This is amazing,' said Lexi, following Jamie inside. She bent down to pat Ava who was languishing in her dog bed in the corner of the lounge room.

'It's small, but it's mine,' said Jamie.

'You own this?' asked Lexi, straightening to look her friend in the eye.

'Yep. The whole shoebox,' said Jamie.

'Gonna give me a tour?' Lexi set her bag down on the coffee table.

'This is the tour.' Jamie laughed.

'And is this where the magic happens?' asked Lexi, walking towards the bedroom. An unexpected skipping sensation entered her stomach as she walked through the door.

Jamie laughed. 'No, I don't work from home.'

'You don't?' said Lexi, turning.

'The site I cam for has a house out in Eltham, it's about twenty minutes away.'

'Really?' said Lexi, nodding slowly.

'Come on, I'll make us some tea.'

Lexi followed Jamie out of the bedroom. She sat on the sofa, scratching Ava behind the ear and watching Jamie fill the kettle and place teabags into mugs.

'How's the job hunt going?' asked Jamie, over the bubble of the water.

Lexi closed her eyes and shook her head.

'Want some biccies?' asked Jamie, pouring the water.

'Oh, I almost forgot. I made brownies,' said Lexi, retrieving the container from her handbag and handing them over.

'Thanks, Martha Stewart.'

'Shut up and give me my tea,' said Lexi.

When Jamie joined her on the sofa, Lexi asked, 'Do you think I could do it?'

'Do what? Oh, these are amazing,' said Jamie, between bites.

'Camming.'

Jamie smirked into her teacup, her eyes peeking out from above as she sipped. 'The best cam models are attractive, sexy and intelligent,' she said.

Lexi held her breath.

'So, yeah. You'd be amazing at it.'

~

'I have a job interview tomorrow,' said Lexi, trying to sound casual.

'Oh, nice. Where at?' said Ethan. 'Mate, use your fork, okay?'

They were seated at the dining table eating the fettuccine carbonara Lexi had prepared.

'A café in Ivanhoe. It's called Post-Haste. It used to be the old post-office building. It's really cool. One of our regulars told me about it—Miriam—she lives out that way.'

Lexi could hear herself offering too many details to authenticate her lie and halted her words.

'Mate, that's enough parmesan, okay? You're going to make it inedible,' said Ethan, extracting Lucas' hand from the bowl of cheese and shaking it off. 'That's great, Lex. Lucas, I said no more!'

FOURTEEN

AS the Mini crept along the narrow, tree-lined road, Lexi craned and squinted looking for houses. They were all set so far back from the road that she could only just make out the occasional rooftop nestled on the sloping hillside beyond the thicket. 'Shit,' she said aloud, driving past the number she was scanning for. Gravel crunched under the tyres as she eased her car onto the road's shoulder to make a U-turn. Entering the driveway, she was confronted with an iron gate set into a stone wall. She cranked down the window which groaned at the disturbance and leaned out to press the intercom button.

'Yes?'

'Hi, this is Lexi Karras. I'm here to see…'

She faltered, momentarily forgetting the name she'd been chanting over and over in her mind for the entire journey. '… Margot Scheringer of Camnation,' she finished.

The intercom buzzed and the gate opened.

Lexi followed the meandering driveway and pulled in next to an assortment of glossy cars. Her little Mini was like a broken tooth in an otherwise perfect smile.

She took a deep breath and smoothed her pencil skirt before clip-clopping to the front door.

As she raised her fist to knock, the door opened to reveal a petite, raven-quiffed woman who Lexi would have guessed to be in her early forties, but Jamie had said was fifty.

'Well, you're certainly beautiful. Come in.'

Lexi stood, stunned for a moment, before crossing the threshold into a bright, open-plan living area overlooking a lush expanse of eucalypts.

'Sit,' said Margot, motioning to the dining suite.

Lexi extracted a heavy, white leather chair and sat. Margot reciprocated and leaned forward, resting her steepled fingers against her lips. Lexi's heartbeat quickened as the older woman appraised her, unblinking. *She's trying to psych me out.* Lexi eased herself back in the chair, clasped her freshly manicured hands together and crossed her legs, never dropping the woman's gaze. Finally, she allowed her face to open into an enigmatic smile. Margot gave a small nod and leaned back.

'What makes you think you'd be a successful cam model, Lexi?'

'Well…' Lexi began. Her eyes were drawn to a pair of bronzed legs bounding down the stairs.

'How's your day going, Sienna?' asked Margot, following Lexi's gaze.

'Great, such a good vibe going,' drawled the blonde. She extracted a bottle of water from the fridge. 'I gotta run though, Tokyo's about to go on lunch break.'

Lexi watched in amazement as the woman hurried back upstairs, her flouncy dress fluttering like waving hands in her wake.

'Who's Tokyo?' asked Lexi.

Margot laughed. 'Tokyo. The city.'

~

Ethan let out a low whistle as he walked into the kitchen to find Lexi, still in her interview attire, drinking a glass of wine.

'How'd it go?' he asked.

'I got it.'

'Yeah, ya did!' he said, leaning in to kiss her.

He sat beside her, pouring wine into the glass she had waiting for him.

Lucas appeared flying a toilet-roll rocket ship in the air. 'Zoom.

71

Zoom. Ah zoom ah zoom zoom,' he sang.

'Hi, buddy,' said Lexi and received no reply.

'So… tell me,' prompted Ethan, taking a sip of wine.

Lexi's neck grew warm and she swallowed. 'The owner, Margot, interviewed me. She was kind of intense but very smart. I think she'll be a good boss. No nonsense, you know?' said Lexi, leading with some semblance of the truth.

'Great,' said Ethan.

'She got me to do a kind of customer role play exercise that was a little confronting. I felt like kind of a dickhead,' she said, whispering the curse word, her eyes darting towards an oblivious Lucas still piloting his aircraft. 'But I pretended to be cool with it.'

'Oh, I hate that sort of thing. I've always sucked at it,' admitted Ethan.

You have no idea, thought Lexi, remembering the moment Margot asked if she'd step into one of the rooms and simulate a chat scenario.

From her office, Margot live-chatted Lexi, initiating topics of conversation and making requests under three different usernames. Shy_Guy showered her with clichéd compliments and Lexi had to curtail her eye-roll impulse to graciously accept them. HomeBoy29 tried to lure her into sexy topics of conversation without tipping. Remembering Jamie's advice, she employed the "Won't you at least buy me a drink first?" technique. A tried and tested way of asking for money, without asking for money. Overtly requesting tips was the most unforgivable sin in the world of camming. This must be a dance, not a shakedown, Jamie had insisted. The final persona was Rev_Head_69 whose opener was, "Your mouth would be even more beautiful with my cock in it". He had to be managed firmly and swiftly without bringing down the mood of the other chatroom guests. When he refused to desist trolling, she blocked him without getting outwardly flustered. She was the ultimate hostess, discreetly ushering an inebriated party guest into an Uber home.

'When do you start?'

'I have a training shift this week before officially starting next week,' said Lexi.

'And the hours?'

'Similar to The Bean & Gone, mornings, no weekends.'

After the chatroom simulation, seated in Margot's office, Lexi had tentatively proposed the café hours to align with her alibi.

'Fine,' she'd said. We'll market you to Europe and the Americas.'

Lexi had laughed. 'At least I won't have my mechanic or dentist recognising me.'

'We'll block users from Victoria, if that's a concern for you,' Margot intoned. 'And some models choose to use an alias, rather than their real names.'

Lexi remained outwardly unfazed, although she was relieved.

Margot had extracted a contract for her to sign and slid it over the desk with a binder containing procedures for securing personal social media accounts and setting up fan pages. Twitter was a must, for communicating with regulars about special events and scheduling changes, while Snapchat could be used as an additional revenue stream. Lexi felt overwhelmed, there was so much she didn't know.

'Are you feeling okay about it?' asked Ethan, breaking into her thoughts.

'Yeah, I feel a little nervous starting something new after so long,' she said.

'Someone once told me that it's in that feeling that the living happens.'

Lexi smiled. 'I hope you're right.'

FIFTEEN

'JOJO Cortado,' said Lexi to her mirrored reflection. 'Jojo Cortado. Hi, I'm Jojo. Hey! Jojo here.'

The doorbell chimed and Lexi hurried downstairs. She flung open the door to find Jamie and threw her back against the jamb, chin raised, lips pouting. 'Why, hello there, I'm Jojo Cortado,' she said, her voice breathy and low.

'More like Crazy McCray Cray,' said Jamie, laughing.

'Get in here.' Lexi pulled her in and closed the door behind them.

'This place is amazing.' Jamie took in her surrounds.

'Oh, it's Ethan's,' said Lexi, dismissively, leading Jamie to the kitchen. 'Thanks for helping me with this, I had a little freak out over it when I read through all Margot's info.'

'She is nothing if not thorough.' Jamie grinned. 'Tell me about the name.'

'Well, Cortado is my favourite type of coffee and Jojo as in "Cup of Joe",' Lexi explained.

'Cortado? Is that a brand name or something?' asked Jamie.

'No, it's a beverage. It's like a flat white but with less milk, so it's stronger.'

'You're such a nerd.'

'I know you are, but what am I?' said Lexi, throwing back to high school.

Once they were seated at the island bench with coffees, Jamie spoke. 'What are you having trouble with?'

'I guess, the menu. I don't really know where to start. I mean, will anyone even visit my chatroom and if they do, what will they like?'

Jamie took a breath, seeming to consider where to begin.

'The key is to think about yourself, not them. What do you like? What is natural for you? You are the honey, the right flies will come,' she said. 'You should think about what you feel comfortable with, how far you're willing to go. For instance, I know women that don't ever get fully nude. On the other hand, I know some that will do double dildo self-penetration like it's flossing their teeth.'

Lexi snorted, spraying a fine mist of coffee across the white benchtop. She dove for a nearby cloth to mop it up as Jamie let out a raucous laugh.

'I guess I'm somewhere in between those two,' said Lexi, between gasps.

'The other thing that's good to remember is that you'll be changing the menu up, it won't stay the same forever. And it's much easier to increase how provocative you are. It's way more difficult to go backwards,' said Jamie. 'Well, at least not without losing regular visitors,' she added.

'You need to write a training manual,' said Lexi.

Jamie laughed.

Lexi regarded her friend and narrowed her gaze.

'What?' asked Jamie, shifting in her seat.

'No, nothing. I don't even know if I should. I mean, it's completely inappropriate to ask.'

'Spit it out,' said Jamie.

'Your customers. Are they into… I mean… is it a transgender thing?'

Jamie let out a small snigger.

'I'm sorry, just forget it,' blurted Lexi.

'No, no, it's okay,' said Jamie, crossing her legs and draining her coffee cup. 'It's not a trans thing. Margot knows, and of course all my friends know but when I first met with Margot, she told me I could go either way. She said that seeing as I pass for cis…'

'Cis?' asked Lexi.

'Cisgender,' Jamie offered.

Lexi's face became quizzical.

'For instance, you're cisgender. You were assigned female at birth and you identify as a woman. It means that I look like I was born female, not that I transitioned.'

'Oh,' said Lexi. She felt like an idiot. Why hadn't she googled any of this beforehand?

Jamie was quiet for a moment, pensive.

'You know, I think in the beginning the reason I chose to market myself as cis was to win at something. Like, if I could have all those intolerant jerks we grew up with lusting after me then I'd be having the last laugh. I mean, not them literally. Just guys *like* them. The ones that think that anyone trans is an affront to their masculinity or something. But it hasn't been like that at all. I used to imagine the guys who use cam-sites as a mob of blockheads, fair game, but then… don't get me wrong, those guys do exist but there's so many who… Once you start seeing past the veneer there's so much nuance. So much pain and tenderness and… need.'

Lexi looked down at her hands. 'I'm sorry, I didn't mean to…' she said, trailing off.

'Lex, it's okay. Of course, you have questions.'

They sat in silence for a while, clutching their empty coffee cups.

'Anyway,' said Jamie, breaking the silence. 'How are you feeling about our broadcast tomorrow?'

Lexi considered this.

'Excited, nervous, terrified,' she said.

Jamie smiled. 'Okay, let's make a plan.'

SIXTEEN

LEXI stepped into the pantry and surreptitiously checked her phone. Ahead of her guest appearance on Jamie's broadcast, Lexi had set up her Twitter and Snapchat accounts as per Margot's instructions. Now, her silent phone was vibrating with every new follower and comment she received. *How the fuck do you disable notifications?* She banged about in Settings.

Earlier today, when Lexi had joined Jamie's broadcast, her heart was playing a techno track beneath her ribs. She had hoped to embody the invented persona of Jojo Cortado—a woman like her, only better, more confident—but all she felt was nauseous. Despite her inner voice screaming for her to flee, her legs had carried her, seemingly of their own volition, towards Jamie. As Lexi came into the webcam's frame, she had been astonished to find Jojo Cortado waiting for her there. 'You need to stop changing the subject and get ready,' she had said to Jamie. 'See, I'm ready to go out and you're not even dressed.'

The thrill had been intoxicating.

After the transmission had ended, she and Jamie had dressed in silence and gathered up their props and decor so the next model could begin. Jamie opened the door to reveal a woman in her late forties, with grey-streaked, tight-curled, chestnut hair and a nose ring. She wore a sheer burgundy dress, her black lace lingerie visible beneath.

'Hi, Jamie,' she said, tossing pillows and a throw blanket onto the bed to redress the space.

'Hey, Karma, this is Jojo, an old friend. She's new.'

'First show huh? How'd it go?' asked Karma, her voice husky.

'Good. I think. I mean… was I okay?' Lexi said, turning to Jamie.

'You're a natural. But remember, never give something away for free that you can charge for.'

'Fuck,' she said, realising that offering to strip down to her lingerie alongside Jamie, without asking for tips, was a mistake.

Karma let out a gravelly laugh. 'Rookie error. You'll get the hang of it.'

Down in the kitchen, Margot had been waiting.

'She did great!' said Jamie, retrieving a jug of water from the fridge and filling two glasses.

'She did,' agreed Margot, 'except for giving away freebies.'

Lexi blushed. 'Rookie error,' she said, parroting Karma. She should have known Margot would be watching.

'It's a quick lesson to learn,' said Margot. 'But you have a natural on-screen presence. You know how to move; you know your angles.' She paused, regarding her. 'How did it feel?'

Lexi had thought for a moment. 'Truthfully? It was exhilarating.'

Now, Ethan walked into the kitchen and asked, 'Do you need any help, Lex?'

Lexi fumbled with her phone, almost dropping it as she slid it back into her pocket. She poked her head out of the pantry. 'Do you have any paprika?' she asked, breathlessly.

'Umm, I think so. Somewhere…' he said, pressing himself into the tiny space beside her.

Buzz buzz buzz. Her phone continued to vibrate with notifications as Ethan retrieved the jar.

'Thanks,' she said.

The sound of a plastic cup crashing to the floor, rang out from the dining area. 'Oh no!' exclaimed Lucas. 'Mess! Big mess! Halp!'

Ethan exhaled and strode towards the disturbance, grabbing a cloth on his way.

Lexi extracted her phone once more and successfully disabled notifications. She took a deep breath and regained her composure before stepping out of the pantry.

As she rubbed spices into chicken fillets, her mind wandered to the afternoon spent in Jamie's chatroom. What had started out as a curiosity, an abstract interest, had burst into a fully-fledged visceral obsession. Not only did she now understand the appeal of the cam experience for users, but she had been bewitched by it herself, albeit from the other side of the screen. She suspected that the reason she was so enraptured by it reflected narcissism or some other equally unfavourable quality. She had been as aroused by her own image on the laptop screen as she was by Jamie in the flesh. How could she explain to anyone that seeing herself as Jojo had solidified her own sexuality? It was like an out of body experience. It had disconnected her from reality and, in the next heartbeat, reconnected her with an entirely new perspective. For all the years she had spent hunched over a coffee machine, brow perspiring, spattered with milk, she had never appreciated her own sensuality. But today, stealing glances at her own reflection, reading the lustful comments, she had unlocked a part of herself that, up until now, had only made fleeting appearances. An unearthed shadowy part was now being brought into the light. It felt primal, and it felt good.

~

Ethan plonked onto the sofa next to Lexi, making her jump.

'I know one day I'll miss it,' he said. 'But sometimes, I wish I could read him a story, kiss him goodnight and be done with it.'

He had been gone the better part of an hour. Lexi knew he had been laying cramped in Lucas' single bed, cuddling him and muttering made up stories until the boy drifted off to sleep. Meanwhile, Lexi had been captivated by her growing number of Twitter fans and the messages of support they brought with them. Since her account had been shared by Camnation and Jamie, her followers had soared to hundreds in a matter of hours. She stared at the profile picture Jamie had taken for her. In it she wore a figure-hugging, high-waisted black skirt that barely covered her bottom. She'd paired it with a white cropped tank that was so short it revealed the alabaster orbs of her breasts. Her face was partially cropped out, cherry-coloured lips open and expectant. She knew this was a picture of herself. She remembered the moment she arched her back, twisted her shoulders and tilted her chin. And yet, sitting here staring at the image, she couldn't help feeling envious of this woman. Her body, her confidence, her self-possession. One new fan had commented "You are beyond beautiful. You're not real". She stared at the words. Read them over and over as if they would cease to exist if she took her eyes off them. Lexi clicked out of the image, pulled from her fantasy world by Ethan's sudden appearance. He was saying something to her, but what? She looked over at him, hoping to pick up the tread from his next utterance. But instead, he sat in silence and began his scrolling ritual. She stared at him, marvelling at the contrast between her two worlds. She had hundreds of men in her back pocket who were lusting after her and a single man, sitting close enough to touch her, who couldn't seem to see her.

SEVENTEEN

LEXI pressed her fob to the door. It hummed her admission and yielded to a shove. While she had access to the communal wardrobe at Camnation and would be dressing for her new role as technological temptress, this morning she was compelled to dress differently than she ordinarily would, even if it was just for the commute. She recalled Jamie describing how her transition had magnified her already intense obsession with clothes and make-up. How as her body began to align with who she really was, she'd felt like a kid playing with a highly anticipated new toy. Lexi's new toy wasn't her body, exactly, but how she felt about it. She strode down the glossy tiled hallway in heels which made her feel powerful and self-possessed. As she moved, her silk blouse brushed against her skin like fingertips. Her breasts, normally contained, were free to bounce with each purposeful step. Her nipples responded to the fabric, her movements, and the changes in temperature. She knew the evidence of this was on show, but she also knew that it would only be to the other cam models. She headed into the kitchen to fill her bottle from the water in the fridge, lingering in the frosty air and enjoying the nervous anticipation coursing through her body. Before leaving home, she had tweeted to her growing fan base and received countless messages of support and promises to login at the appointed time. Now, she clutched her water bottle, wrapping her lips around the neck. Pulling out her phone, she snapped a selfie capturing her suggestive pout, elongated neck, and the protrusion of her nipples just visible through her white silk shirt. Her hands shook as she posted it with the caption "Getting hydrated for my first show". Almost immediately, her phone lit up in approval. While Melbourne yawned and stretched to life under a rising sun, her largely European followers seemed to be slipping into the delightful possibility of nocturnal escapades. Lexi's heart hammered and she tried to quiet her self-doubt. She had prepared as best she could. She'd studied the Camnation model interface and even posed as a chatroom visitor thanks to a fake email address and the alias ShortMac. But she was acutely aware of how unpredictable the environment would be, how unscripted. What would they say to her? What would they ask of her? Would they respond favourably to her on-screen persona, or would she be vilified as the hack she suspected she was? Her mind wandered to Ethan, in his pharmacy whites, dropping Lucas off at childcare and was thankful for even the terror that punctuated her excitement. For better or worse, this was living.

'All set?'

Lexi turned to see Margot framed in the doorway and arranged her face into a confident smile. 'Ready as I'll ever be,' she said.

'Well, break a leg, as they say. Come and see me after?'

'Sure.'

Lexi picked up her bulging tote bag, embarrassed about the Peace Lily she'd brought. The leafy plumage poked out at odd angles tickling her cheek and neck as she walked out of the kitchen. Each model was required to dress the rooms according to their personal style, lending an element of authenticity to what was essentially an artificial environment. Lexi had taken great care in selecting her decor, but now that she was here, under Margot's scrutiny, her selections felt juvenile. She straightened and climbed the stairs.

The Camnation wardrobe was a full-sized bedroom converted into a closet. Industrial fashion racks lined the walls, displaying a colour-coded selection of garments, while shoes sat below in neat pairs. Lingerie was the responsibility of each model but everything else could be borrowed and shared.

Lexi ran a hand over the fabrics, unsure what to wear. She had some firm opinions on what she didn't want to wear as she paused to grimace at a sequined gown, whose plunging neckline met an outrageously high split at crotch level. 'Yikes,' she said, smirking to herself as she flicked through the hangers.

'Morning.'

Lexi turned to see a stout redhead clothed in a confection of polka dots and lace. Her set hair bounced as she threw herself onto an ottoman to remove her Mary Jane heels.

'Hi, I'm… Jojo. I'm new,' Lexi said, almost forgetting to use her alias.

'I'm Cherry. Obviously,' she said, indicating her dyed hair.

Cherry grinned and her eyes all but disappeared into her powdered cheeks. Lexi couldn't help grinning back. Cherry stood to remove her dress, revealing pale flesh as soft and doughy as unbaked bread. Lexi looked away and studied a nearby dress. It was black linen with a midi-hemline and mother-of-pearl buttons running down the centre.

'That'd be gorgeous on you,' said Cherry, pulling a David Bowie t-shirt over her sizable breasts. Lexi watched as the Thin White Duke expanded under the strain. Cherry extracted the dress and handed it to Lexi. 'Only one way to find out.'

Lexi unbuttoned and shucked her blouse before rummaging around through her lingerie for a bra, as if being partially nude in front of a total stranger was commonplace.

'How are you finding it so far?' asked Cherry, pulling on her jeans. She dropped to the floor, pulled on a pair of Dr. Martens boots, and looked up at Lexi.

'Oh, ah. This is my first solo broadcast,' she said, feeling the morning's bravado seeping away.

'Well, I'll tell you what someone told me when I started,' said Cherry, tying her laces. 'What you need is layers and accessories.'

Lexi blinked; she hadn't expected Cherry's words of wisdom to be fashion advice.

Cherry smiled, clearly amused by Lexi's stunned expression. She went on, 'Layers so it takes longer for you to get down to nothing, and more tips to get there…'

'And accessories?' prompted Lexi.

'Accessories are great for fiddling with. The most boring thing a cam model can do is just sit there, you know? If you've got a necklace on or bracelets—anything—a silk scarf around your neck, you can fiddle with it. Gets your hands moving. So, while you're sitting there waiting for something to happen, for someone to jump in and interact with you, you won't look like a stunned mullet.'

Lexi laughed. 'Accessories,' she repeated, nodding.

She thought of Jamie's make-up routine, how her movements had been subtle and slow, how she never stopped moving.

Cherry rose and opened a nearby drawer. She rummaged around and pulled out a white mesh negligee trimmed in black lace. 'Here,' she said, handing it to Lexi. She let out a luxurious yawn, shrugged on her vinyl Pan Am airline satchel and wiggled out of the room with a 'Good luck, you'll be great.'

'Thank you,' Lexi called after her.

~

Waiting in the hallway dressed and ready, Lexi pressed a palm to her belly to quell the roiling. She tried not to look in the mirror opposite, but every now and then the temptation would prove too great, and she would steal a furtive glance. The woman looking back at her appeared frightened and overdressed for this hour of the morning. She looked down at her shoes, trying to recover any shred of the confidence she had felt upon her arrival. The door opened suddenly, tipping her slightly off balance.

'Hey, you must be Jojo, come in.'

Lexi picked up her bag with the ridiculous plant sprouting from it and stepped into the room. 'Veronica, right?' she asked.

'Yeah, hi. Nice to meet you,' she said, winding up her thick blonde hair and tying it into a top knot. The heavy mass bobbed to one side as she buzzed around the room tidying. She flung open a storage chest and indicated an empty compartment. 'You can store your room stuff here,' she said. 'Although, I'm not sure your plant baby will survive.'

Lexi forced a self-deprecating laugh. 'It seemed like a good idea at the time,' she said.

'I think it's nice. Keep it in the ensuite, there's loads of natural light in there. I'm sure the others won't mind. So, I've logged off, make sure you do that at the end. And the desk is on wheels. We tend to choose a different angle to shoot from, make sure the room looks different enough for each girl.'

'Right, thanks.'

As Veronica made to leave, fear rushed through Lexi. As soon as she was gone, there would be no more stalling. She thought of Cherry's guidance and blurted, 'Got any parting advice?'

Veronica stopped and tilted her head, the weight of her hair threatening to topple her petite frame. 'Just be yourself. Be yourself as you are on your best, happiest day. That's all.'

And with that, she left, closing the door behind her.

Lexi extracted the plant, careful not to spill any potting mix. She placed it on one of the nondescript bedside tables, turning it this way and that to ensure its glossiest leaves were displayed. Next, she pulled out a tasselled bedspread and threw it over the bed. She piled on an assortment of cushions, all the while not looking at the laptop which sat on the desk. The final touch was a collection of battery-operated candles which flickered in the dimly lit space. She wheeled the desk to a corner of the bed, sat and logged in. The sudden appearance of her image on screen startled her. Her expression was grave, the angle exaggerating her chin and nostrils. She grimaced. Adjusting the angle of the webcam, she sat further back on the bed and leaned in so that just her lips and the outline of her breasts were framed. Taking a deep breath to centre herself, she clicked the broadcast button.

EIGHTEEN

THE supermarket lights buzzed overhead as Lexi ran her hands over a large, red-blushed mango. She lifted the fruit to her nose and breathed in deeply, the fragrance causing her mouth to salivate. The scent was sweet and floral. It transported her back to countless summer afternoons spent leaning over the kitchen sink as thick nectar dripped from her chin, splattering onto the metal basin. The thought of sucking away the soft flesh made her feel sultry. She grinned as she placed the fruit in her basket, deciding in that moment that she would incorporate this into her act. *They're going to pay me to eat fruit tomorrow.*

Lexi knew she was wearing a grin that probably made her look a little unhinged as she glided around the supermarket. It was mid-afternoon and the store was filled with frantic women buying dinner ingredients, post school pick up. Their children, wired and hungry, grabbed at junk foods and rattled off machine-gun fired questions as their mothers tried to keep the fraught mission on course. The figs, plump and warm, reminded Lexi of human flesh. As she made her selection, she reflected on her day. Her nervousness seemed to belong to someone else now.

When Lexi had asked Jamie for a detailed description of the camming process, she had likened it to fishing. 'In the beginning, all you are doing is waiting for someone to swim by and take a nibble.' Lexi had laughed at this. It was the last analogy she had expected to hear. But it hadn't been like that for her. After she had clicked the broadcast button and swivelled the assortment of bracelets around her wrist, visitors to her chatroom had arrived *en masse*. Lexi had laughed as the computer screen lit up. 'You really know how to make a girl feel welcome,' was the first thing she said.

She acknowledged each user who sent a tip and ignored those who could not be persuaded to contribute, as Jamie had instructed her to do. All the while toying with her accessories and shifting her position as if sitting on a sun-warmed slab.

When a visitor by the name of ChivalryAlive sent a substantial tip and asked about her pastimes, Lexi surprised herself by confessing she was an aspiring writer.

Predictably, the next question from a user called DeadLiftPhil was, 'Written any erotica?'

She gave a sly smile, seeming to consider if she should reveal a secret, before admitting, 'I have been known to.' Even though she had never written anything erotic in her life. ChivalryAlive's response was immediate. 'Will you regale us sometime?'

She had clasped a small silver charm and ran it along the chain around her neck, listening to it purr. Cocking her head, she considered the question as her screen flashed with comment after comment asking to hear her work. 'Well, how could I say no when you've all gotten so excited about it?' Then, remembering Jamie's advice about never giving anything away, she added, 'How about we do a countdown tomorrow and if we reach our target, I'll read you something nice and saucy? That is… if you'll all come back and visit me tomorrow.'

After that, RagazzoEccitato tipped for her to take her dress off. Her hands trembled visibly as she undid each button which only served to further tantalise her audience. There was something thrilling about having so many eyes on her, about submitting to the desires of anonymous onlookers. As she let her dress fall to the floor, her body grew warm. She wanted them to ask for more. Her fingers tugged at the white mesh negligee that Cherry had selected for her. She ran her thumbs under the straps and smoothed the tight fabric over her hips.

Leaning forward, she pulled down the bodice to reveal her overflowing bra line and pouted. 'This thing is so uncomfortable. Will someone help me out of it?'

RagazzoEccitato rallied the other users. "Come on, boys, help the lady out," he wrote.

Lexi laughed as small, attention-grabbing tips from Casse_Couilles_11 filled the screen, finally culminating in him purchasing the menu item for her to remove the offending garment. After thanking him and conducting a monologue as to the best course of action, Lexi wriggled out of the slip, peeling it down before kicking it off. Down to her bra and underwear, she threw herself back onto the bed with a flourish. 'What a relief,' she sighed.

Comments filled the screen complimenting her on the shape of her legs, the smoothness of her skin, the curve of her back. Lexi became more attractive with each flickering line of text. But when Bon3rBoy said he'd like to "…cum all over that big ass", Lexi's colour drained. 'Come now, Boner Boy, that's no way to talk to a lady,' she said. When he replied that he wasn't looking at a lady, she swiftly blocked him, all the while smiling sweetly at the webcam. Although she appeared to remain nonplussed, the experience had unnerved her. She no longer felt as powerful as she did just moments prior. So, when ChivalryAlive tipped for private messaging, condemned Bon3rBoy's deplorable manners and beseeched her not to be disheartened, she was grateful. She thanked him for his concern, and admitted how nervous she was about reading her work tomorrow as she'd never shared her writing. "Courage has the capacity to yield great rewards, Jojo," he replied.

After steering the show back on track, the remainder of her broadcast followed on as before. Lexi answered questions and flashed body parts, when the appropriate tokens were tipped, all the while feeling nervous and excited at the possibility that someone could swoop in and purchase her most expensive menu item—giving herself an orgasm. When someone paid her to get naked and rub lotion all over her body she took her time, watching her image on screen to ensure that every movement would elicit desire in her audience. She started with her legs, alternately placing a foot on the bed to caress her skin in slow, sweeping strokes. Next was her stomach which she circled, occasionally letting her hand stray down to her pubic bone and beyond. When she did this, she flicked her gaze towards the webcam as if to say, 'I'm so tempted to keep going.' Then, turning her back on the tallying comments, likening her to a goddess and calling her a dream come true, she encircled her buttocks, pulling them slightly apart as she arched her back, affording her audience tantalising glimpses of what they craved. She turned once more, tracing each arm like a burlesque performer peeling off gloves, and then began the most thorough moisturising her breasts had ever received. It was during this, that Lexi confessed her desire to continue pleasuring herself. Inwardly, she regretted not starting a countdown to which multiple users could contribute. As it stood, the highest tippers tried in vain to rally the other chatroom guests to buy the coveted menu item but to no avail. The broadcast ended with Lexi thanking her audience for their generosity and inviting them to join her again tomorrow. When the transmission ended, she did a quick calculation of her tips, making sure to mentally deduct Camnation's cut. She had made thousands and it wasn't even midday. A laugh escaped her open mouth as she sat disbelieving on the edge of the bed.

After changing back into her own clothes, Lexi had bounded into Margot's office without knocking and all but collided with a wall of a man who was standing to leave.

'Sorry,' she blurted, 'I should have knocked.'

His dark, wavy hair was cropped short, and his jawline still retained the last traces of boyhood. Her cheeks grew warm, wondering if the remnants of her self-induced arousal were perceptible to him. He looked down at her, amused.

'This is Senior Constable Nolan, we're assisting him with some federal investigations into cybercrime,' said Margot, sounding disinterested.

'Jojo,' said Lexi, extending her hand. She watched as it disappeared inside his, noticing his gaze stray to her slightly transparent shirt.

He turned back to Margot. 'I'll be in touch,' he said, his voice booming in the small office.

Lexi watched him leave and then turned to find Margot's inscrutable eyes locked on her. 'Sit,' she instructed.

Still at the supermarket, Lexi looked into her shopping basket and realised she had been aimlessly wandering the aisles. What she needed to do was get home and write an erotic short story for her broadcast tomorrow. She made a hasty selection for dinner and headed for the self-checkout.

As Lexi crossed the carpark, her phone rang. 'Hi, Jamie,' she answered.

'How'd it go today?' Jamie asked.

Lexi grinned. 'It was kind of amazing.'

'Tell!'

'Margot said it was "one of the most fruitful maiden voyages of all time". Her words, not mine, obviously,' said Lexi laughing.

'That's my girl,' said Jamie.

Lexi could hear the smile in her voice.

'Obviously it was because of you,' said Lexi.

'I'm like your sexual fairy godmother,' said Jamie, laughing.

'Bibbidi bobbidi boobs?'

They howled with laughter.

'What are you doing this afternoon, want to hang out before I start work?' Jamie asked.

'Oh, I wish I could. I have some…' Lexi faltered. She closed her eyes, wondering how she should proceed.

'Hello?' asked Jamie in the silence.

'Yeah sorry. It's, um… I actually have some writing to do this afternoon.'

'Writing? What kind of writing?'

Lexi thought of all that Jamie had confessed to her. How, instead of fleeing at the sight of her, that day in the café, she had been brave enough to meet up and tell the entire story of her life. Jamie had described the first tentative realisations that she was trans. How difficult it had been to muster the courage required to embark upon her transition. About the hormone therapies and surgeries she had to endure to achieve what most people were lucky enough to have been born with in the first place.

'I usually write short stories but I'm going to try my hand at erotic fiction. I thought I could read it in my chatroom,' she said.

Lexi held her breath, braced for Jamie's reaction.

'That's so cool. I didn't know you were a writer!'

'Well, aspiring,' Lexi corrected.

'I once read somewhere that "aspiring" writers are the ones who only talk about writing. If you write, you're a writer. By definition.'

Lexi let out a husky laugh as she unlocked her car. 'You always were smarter than me,' she said, smiling into the phone.

The line remained silent for a while until Jamie spoke. 'Maybe tomorrow then? I can always get to work early if you want to hang around after your shift. Margot's happy for us to use the pool and the weather's looking good.'

'Yeah? That sounds amazing,' said Lexi.

'Okay great, I'll aim for midday.'

~

Lexi tried not to think about how she would explain to her audience tomorrow if she couldn't come up with a story. As she manoeuvred the Mini through the traffic, she tried to grab at the wisps of an idea that flitted into the edge of her thoughts. She knew the protagonist should resemble her and that sensitivity was required when describing the suitor. Describing a perfect man had the potential to alienate her chatroom visitors who, for reasons that Lexi guessed were many and varied, chose to derive their sexual and interpersonal pleasure online. By the time she pulled up in front of Ethan's house, she had decided that the story would centre on a young woman putting herself through a neuroscience doctorate by camming. When the conflicting hours begin to take their toll, she develops an experimental technology which allows subscribers to create an avatar and enter her dreams as she sleeps. Lexi knew that she was typecasting her audience by choosing to play in science fiction, but it was the only shred of an idea she'd had all afternoon. She hurried into the house, shoved the bag of groceries in the fridge without unpacking it and sat down in front of her laptop.

NINETEEN

'WHERE'D you go? You're going to set the backyard on fire!' shrieked Ethan.

'Shit, sorry. I forgot I had to… do something upstairs,' Lexi muttered.

After tearing herself away from writing just long enough to fire up the grill and rip open the bag of salad she'd bought, Lexi raced upstairs to bang out a few more lines of story that had sprung into her mind. She returned outside to find Ethan, still with his satchel draped across his body, hissing more than the burning sausages he was saving.

He leaned in to kiss her before gathering up the loaded plate and heading inside. 'Snags tonight, mate!' he called to Lucas, who yelled 'Yay!' from an unknown pocket of the house.

While Ethan extracted Lucas from his cushion fort and ushered him to the bathroom to wash up for dinner, Lexi snuck into the pantry with her phone. Here, she typed out a hasty tweet telling her followers that they were in for a treat. She was working on a story just for them. If Margot was right, and her audience really was in a different time zone, then they would have an entire workday to look forward to it.

'Grab the sauce?' said Ethan, appearing in the doorway.

Lexi jumped and fumbled with her phone, almost dropping it.

'Everything okay?' said Ethan, his eyes narrowing.

'Yeah, sorry. I came in for the sauce, but I got distracted by a text from Linh, she's having some dramas with Xavier,' said Lexi, shocked at the swiftness of her lie.

'Yeah, well… he's a strange cat,' said Ethan, smirking.

Lexi cursed herself, she really had to be more careful.

When they sat down at the table, Ethan asked, 'How'd it go today?'

Lexi had been so deep in thought about the story she was writing that it took her a moment to register she was being addressed. She blinked back into reality and asked him to repeat the question.

'Margot was really pleased,' Lexi answered truthfully, loading her fork with greens and folding them into her mouth.

'And the customers? What kind of crowd do they have coming through that strip?'

'I'm not sure yet, to be honest. It's difficult to form any opinions from one day. I don't know who my regulars are yet, you know?' said Lexi, munching.

She was beginning to find the ambiguity of the conversation very entertaining.

'There was one guy who was kind of a jerk, but there's always going to be one or two. Everyone else was nice… and I met another couple of staff members today who seemed kind of great.'

'What is it they say about one door closing and another opening?' Ethan asked. 'Seems like The Bean & Gone closing was the best thing that could have happened for you.'

'I had the exact same thought today,' said Lexi, popping a cherry tomato into her mouth.

~

The carpeted stairs creaked as Lexi tiptoed up them, head cocked, listening. While Ethan was bathing Lucas, she had snuck her laptop downstairs to continue working on the story. She'd sat at the island bench in the kitchen, facing the door ready to conceal her screen if Ethan returned. Lexi wasn't sure how long she had been sitting there but after feeling satisfied with her final edits, she looked around to realise that she was in the only illuminated room of the house, the glow of dusk long disappeared over the neighbours' rooftops. Reaching the top of the stairs, Lexi's eyes darted from Lucas' bedroom door to the room she shared with Ethan, trying to ascertain where he had fallen asleep. The culmination of today's cam-session and the penning of her first erotic story had left Lexi feeling concupiscent and squirrelly. Something needed to be done. The question was, would she need to take matters into her own hands, or could she persuade the involvement of the only man in the house? She tiptoed towards the slightly ajar door to Lucas' room and peered in to see Ethan asleep, curled around the boy, a brightly coloured picture book blanketing them. Relief and disappointment swirled through Lexi, the juxtaposition confusing her. She crept to her own bedroom, entered the ensuite and switched on the make-up mirror. Undressing in the cool low-light, she enjoyed the otherworldly, smooth-marble appearance that it gave her body. It was how she envisioned the fantasy dream sequences in the story she'd just written. Her fingers sought her molten centre. At first, her movements were flat and sweeping. She thought back over her day, imagining the webcam was focused on her now. She knew that her chatroom guests had been sitting in their homes, bringing themselves to climax as they watched her. Bursting spontaneously like fireworks throughout her broadcast. The idea of that had aroused her then, and now she recalled the feeling. Resisting the impulse to close her eyes, she focused her gaze on her reflection, the act of practicing her on-screen skills adding a layer to her pleasure. She leaned her breasts forward into her left hand, enjoying the weight of them, the way they felt as heavy as ripening fruit. Meanwhile, her right hand worked with purposeful pressure, fingers darting inside at rhythmic intervals. *I need more hands.* She wondered if she'd made the wrong choice by not waking Ethan. Releasing her grasp on her breasts, she plunged both hands downwards, fingers swirling, rubbing, thrusting. In a moment of inspiration she turned, pressing her breasts against the bathroom tiles. The startling cold made her gasp, and she threw her head back with the pleasure of it before resuming the practiced movements of her fingers. On and on her fingers danced until, moments from climaxing, her mind was inhabited by an unexpected figure. She could almost feel his presence in the bathroom behind her. 'You've been a bad girl, Jojo,' he'd say, his deep voice husky as he leaned down to whisper in her ear. She shuddered pleasurably before being pulled under by the unstoppable current of her orgasm. The face of Senior Constable Nolan vivid in her mind as she peaked.

TWENTY

"'HIS lips hovered just above hers, hot breath rousing her from sleep. Blinking awake, she smiled into his kiss and raised her hands above her head, giving him permission to bind them together with the silk kerchief he was pulling from his neck.'"

Having reached her countdown goal in the final hour of the broadcast, Lexi now sat on the edge of the bed, her laptop perched on her crossed legs. She wore a black, striped lace peignoir, loosely tied to reveal her breasts and navel. Keeping her voice low, she ignored the mounting comments which flickered in her peripheral vision on the Camnation laptop, terrified that the response might be less than favourable. As the story ended, Lexi closed her eyes, reciting the last sentence by heart. She sat like this for a moment, extending the time she remained ignorant of the reactions. Opening her eyes, she set her laptop down and leaned closer to the other screen. Her mouth opened into an unabashed smile as she tried in vain to read through the past five minutes of comments, as more continued to arrive. She threw her head back and let out a pleasure-filled laugh, giddy with the sensation of overcoming her greatest fear.

'I hope it's not too soon to say this,' she said to the webcam. 'But I think I'm in love with you.'

Reciprocal feelings and tips of appreciation followed along with requests for more stories. *Can I do it again?*

Like the day before, ChivalryAlive tipped for private messaging. This time he complimented her story and asked where she had studied writing. When Lexi admitted that she'd never had the opportunity and it was her biggest regret, he told her he was a senior editor, now retired after thirty years working at the Billbury Publishing House in Yorkshire. Lexi kept her face impassive as her mind was engulfed by suspicion. Was this some kind of line? And if so, to what end? Shifting the conversation away from writing, she asked how he was spending his retirement. When he answered that his time was spent caring for his wife who was suffering from advanced dementia, Lexi felt ashamed. Her fingers hovered over the keyboard. "That must be incredibly difficult," she wrote, though the words felt grossly inadequate. "She has good days and bad days. Today was a bad day, if I'm honest. But the thought of logging in to spend time with you got me through it." Lexi smiled, knowing he was watching her reading the message. "Chivalry is alive indeed," she wrote.

Lexi's eyes flicked back to the comments feed, and she read out the names of those who had tipped while she was focused on the private messages.

'You've only got twenty more minutes with me, boys. After this I'm going swimming with a friend. Well, I doubt we'll do any swimming, more like lounging by the pool,' she said, tilting her head so that her hair brushed her shoulder. 'I brought a few different bikinis, want to help me choose what to wear?' she asked.

~

'Hey, Sienna,' said Lexi, throwing open the door.

'Hi, Jojo, theme today?' said Sienna, taking in her swimming attire.

'What? Oh! No, nothing like that. I'm meeting Jamie at the pool; she said that Margot doesn't mind if we use it.'

'Oh,' said Sienna, walking into the room.

'It's a great idea though. Theme days,' said Lexi, turning the idea over.

'Oh yeah, I do things all the time. Christmas will be soon and after that I like to do stuff for the Australian Open.'

'Double entendre city for that one.' Lexi smirked.

Sienna stared at her blankly.

~

Lexi reached the foot of the stairs and took a couple of tentative steps off course, towards Margot's office. The thought of running into Senior Constable Nolan both exhilarated and terrified her. She peered at the closed office door, leaning into the silence emanating from it.

'Jojo, isn't it?'

Lexi closed her eyes, still as a cornered animal. She breathed in courage and turned. 'Senior Constable Puffnstuff, right?'

She lifted her chin in a display of defiance.

'Only when they're paying me,' he said, the slight curl of his lip compromising his otherwise steely expression.

'And if they're not?'

She knew she was flirting but the absurdness of it was so entertaining that Lexi couldn't resist.

'Travis,' he said.

They stood for a long moment in the dimly lit hallway, staring at each other, waiting for the other to speak. Lexi became hyper aware that she was wearing a bikini covered only by a wisp of a kaftan, her overflowing breasts rising and falling with every measured breath.

'Well,' said Lexi, breaking the silence, 'I have a date with a swimming pool.'

She made to leave but was stopped by his baseball mitt of a hand on her upper arm. 'Is there some way I can reach you?' he said.

She looked up at him with sceptical eyes.

'In case I have any questions, pertaining to the…'

Lexi turned away. 'Goodbye, Senior Constable,' she said over her shoulder, revelling in the certainty that he was watching her leave.

TWENTY-ONE

'MARCO?'

   'Polo!'

   'Marco?'

   'Polo!'

Lexi glided around the swimming pool, straddling an inflatable flamingo, eyes closed under her Ray Bans.

When Lexi had arrived at the pool, she found Jamie chatting with a dark-haired beauty of Amazonian proportions who she introduced as Ali. Ali, Jamie explained, was camming to fund the launch of an activewear label whose garments were made exclusively from recycled plastic waste. At first Ali seemed shy, but her reservation soon gave way to a passionate explanation of her concept and brand values. It culminated in an outraged sermon about the desperate need for sustainable practices in the fashion industry and Lexi and Jamie nodding in firm agreement. Seeming to realise that she had ventured into the righteous, Ali emitted a self-deprecating laugh before suggesting that they play a game.

'Marco,' Lexi called again, this time straining her ears to determine the location of her friends.

'Polo!' Came two giggled replies.

Lexi threw out a hand in the direction of one of the voices. Her hand fumbled to grasp a slick limb and she plunged into the cool salt water. She opened her eyes in an underwater flurry and kicked to the surface to find Jamie and Ali quaking with laughter. She blew out a spray of water, her sunglasses comically skewed.

Back on dry land, the three sat on the blue-tiled edge, heaving.

'Do you need more sunscreen?' Jamie asked, poking at Ali's reddening thigh.

'Oh, I'm okay. I've been using some fuck-all SPF coconut thing. My chatroom can't get enough of tan lines; I don't know what it is,' Ali said, laughing.

'You think that's weird? Jojo's got hers turning to literature!'

'You what?' shrieked Ali.

Lexi laughed, her head dipped, as Jamie explained.

'I might have to tune in for these stories of eroticism,' said Ali.

'Ha! Well, Margot has hidden me from Victorian users, so you can't,' Lexi baulked.

Jamie and Ali exchanged a look.

'What?' asked Lexi, looking between the two.

'Is she serious?' Ali asked Jamie.

Jamie, ignoring her, leaned in and placed a hand on Lexi's knee.

'What?' Lexi demanded.

'Blocking does work,' began Jamie, tentatively. 'Unless the user connects via a VPN.'

Lexi's eyes narrowed, scanning her knowledge for what this meant.

'Virtual Private Network,' offered Ali.

'It means that a Victorian user can appear to be from somewhere else in the world. If Ali wanted to tune in and watch you, she could,' said Jamie.

'Easily,' added Ali.

~

As Lexi manoeuvred the Mini down the winding driveway, she held her body in the same forced display of nonchalance she had adopted poolside. Now, on the open road, she hunched over the wheel and began to synthesise her feelings.

She thought over the implications of Ali's revelation. Lexi had embarked on her camming journey assuming that what she was doing could be discovered by anyone. But Margot's assurance that she could remain anonymous, at least in her pocket of the world, had come as a relief. Now that the illusion was shattered, she could see that she had been conceited. Enamoured by her ability to outsmart the system. The realisation of her foolishness stung but she decided that this new information didn't change anything. She was enjoying what she was doing, was making the type of money that could buy her independence, and in an unforeseen twist, was inspired to write again. The gains far outweighed the risk of being discovered. Worrying over "what-ifs" was a waste of her energy, especially when she had to work on the premise for tomorrow's story.

TWENTY-TWO

LEXI inserted a newly-manicured hand into the brass vase she was clutching in the crook of her arm. Outside, the temperature clawed its way towards a predicted forty-two degrees while inside the air conditioning laboured. She rustled through the knots of paper she had crafted moments before.

'Bisous69, you've won! What word would you like included in tomorrow's story?' asked Lexi.

She trained her eyes on the webcam, face effervescent, awaiting his response.

After Lexi's veneer of anonymity had been shattered poolside, she returned to Ethan's house feeling dejected. As she prepared dinner—a dismally suburban arrangement that was barely more interesting than the meat and three veg she was raised on—Lexi stole upstairs to gather her thoughts. Although she had never intended it, Lexi had type-cast herself as the bookish nymphomaniac and now, in two short days, she was beginning to feel stifled by her self-imposed persona. Which was why, to keep things light and more in line with the tone of her peers, she had devised a fun and frivolous activity which involved her chatroom visitors purchasing low-cost raffle tickets to win the ability to request words in her next story.

She told herself that her audience wasn't tuning in for great literature. That the punters would be happy if she was reading the horoscopes from the *Herald Sun* if she had her tits out. And so, she concocted this little bit of pageantry to extract herself from her own stifling perfectionism and have some fun with it.

She waited for Bisous69 to respond. "My word is fingerbang. LOL!"

Lexi closed her eyes to dissuade her eye-roll reaction and forced a bubbly laugh. 'Technically Bisous, that is two words, but I'll let it slide this time,' she said.

A few comments appeared, teasing Bisous69 or praising him for his choice. Lexi arranged her face into something thoughtful. 'Fingerbang, rhymes with wang. Maybe I should do a poem instead?' she said. She laughed and the sound was so candied that she almost hated herself for it. 'We've almost reached our countdown goal, guys. I'm so excited to read this story to you. It's kind of a naughty one, set at a party.'

Lexi dipped her chin and glanced upwards, feeling her long eyelashes caress her upper lids. 'Does anyone want to go to a party with me tonight?' she asked the webcam. 'And we're going so well with time today that I was hoping, maybe…' she paused for effect, expressing a bashfulness that wasn't entirely fabricated, 'I might get to have an orgasm today.'

If Lexi could encourage her audience to contribute to two countdowns, as well as her regular menu and tips, she was set to double what she had earned the day before.

'Seeing as it's a party theme today, maybe I could start a dance floor while we wait for the countdown to finish? Anyone want to request a song for me to dance to?'

Before anyone had the chance to respond with the appropriate tip, Lexi's screen lit up to announce that someone had contributed the balance of the reading countdown. Lexi's mouth fell open but she recovered swiftly.

'No time for dancing boys, TheBiggestApple wants us all to read a story. That was *very* generous, thank you,' she said.

Lexi retrieved her laptop and lay on her stomach, propped up on her elbows. She checked her reflection and adjusted her angle to ensure her pushed-together cleavage was visible in the window between her arms and that the lace-trimmed curve of her bottom peeked over the horizon of her body. Offering a conspiratorial smile to the webcam, she began to read the story. The protagonist, Jojo, is visited in her dreams and whisked to a party where she and her suitor are so enraptured with one another, they dare to consummate their desire on a crowded dance floor. All but one of the revellers remain ignorant of the act happening in their midst. The sole witness, a young woman who had found the gathering tedious, is so overcome with arousal that she wordlessly approaches, helping to bring Jojo to climax, eyes fixed on the suitor before disappearing into the crowd.

As her reading ended, Lexi once again took pause. It was very possible that yesterday's positive reception was a fluke, and a mild panic rose in anticipation of a negative response. If these stories weren't her point of difference, what on earth would replace them? She gazed cautiously up at the screen and was rewarded with the exuberant approbation of her audience. She sat up, thanking them profusely for their praise, genuinely appreciative and more than a little relieved. Of course, the comments were peppered with poorly expressed recounts of arousal and climax, but Lexi was so thankful for the lack of criticism that even those comments pleased her.

Again, ChivalryAlive tipped and sent her a private message. "A very good effort, my dear," he wrote, and Lexi's heart swelled.

"I know I shouldn't admit to having favourites," she wrote. "But your opinion matters most to me."

"I'm glad to hear it. I hope this isn't too presumptuous of me, but I would like to offer you my services as a critique partner and editor."

Lexi paused to address the comments in her feed as her mind raced. Was this offer a reflection of her talent or lack of it? Feeling emboldened, she asked.

"Now is no time to think of what you do not have. Think of what you can do with what there is," came his immediate reply.

Lexi's shoulders jiggled as she laughed silently to herself. "Well, who am I to attempt an argument with the logic of Papa Hemingway?" she wrote.

Lexi agreed to send him her next story and received his personal email address in reply.

"It's lovely to officially meet you, Clive," she wrote.

Turning her attention to the webcam once more and running her hands provocatively over her lace underwear, Lexi asked, 'Shall we begin that countdown we talked about? I really need a release.'

~

Lexi made her way into the searing midday heat, dipping her face into her sunglasses and cursing her beloved car for its lack of air conditioning. The drive home was going to bake her. As she rounded the vehicle, she caught sight of a scrap of paper flapping under the windscreen wiper. It crackled under her touch as she extracted it and replaced the wiper with a *thud*. The scrawl, tight and juvenile, was difficult to make out. She cocked her head to the side before realisation smoothed her brow and sent a flutter through her. It was Senior Constable Travis Nolan's phone number. She glanced around the secluded driveway before throwing her belongings into the car and climbing in after them.

TWENTY-THREE

LEXI rapped on Jamie's door, which immediately flung open.

'Oh!' said Lexi, faltering at the sight of Ali.

'Hey, she's in the bathroom, come in,' said Ali, turning.

'I didn't know you…' Lexi began, unsure how to finish the sentence without coming off as rude.

'Yeah, I popped over to borrow a cup of sugar,' said Ali, flashing a look at Jamie who was entering the room holding a set of hair straighteners.

Jamie laughed and handed the straighteners to Ali. 'Ali's moved into the building,' she said.

'Upstairs,' added Ali.

'Oh. That's cool,' said Lexi, taking a seat on the sofa and leaning down to give Ava a scratch behind the ear. The dog opened her eyes lazily before resettling herself.

'Anyway, thanks for these,' said Ali, giving the straighteners a shake and making for the door. She turned. 'Are you sure you won't come by for one?'

'You know there's no such thing as one for me,' said Jamie wearing a wry smile, 'And I have to work this afternoon.'

'How about you, Jojo?' asked Ali. 'I'm having a few friends over for drinks, a last-minute housewarming party, although I haven't unpacked a single box.'

'Oh,' said Lexi, unsure how to respond. She barely knew Ali and had never met any of her friends. If Jamie wasn't going, it sounded like an energy drain.

'Well, I'm up on three. Apartment four, come by if you want.'

'Thanks, maybe,' said Lexi as Ali disappeared out the door.

Lexi's first week of camming had been rewarding in more ways than one, but she was looking forward to having a break over the weekend. All she wanted to do tonight was chill out with a glass of wine and a book.

'Tea?' asked Jamie. 'Or maybe we should have a glass of wine, seeing as it's Friday afternoon and we're work colleagues now.'

Lexi smiled broadly. 'I thought you said there was no such thing as one drink?' she said.

'Oh, that was just an excuse. I really can't be bothered with small talk right now. I do enough of that at work.'

Lexi nodded.

'Wine then?' coaxed Jamie, eyes bright.

'Wine,' agreed Lexi.

The friends sat on the sofa, debriefing about their week. Lexi choked on a mouthful of Pinot Gris as she listened to Jamie's recount of a foot-fetishist who paid an exorbitant sum for Jamie to give a private show of licking her own toes.

'What time do you need to leave?' Lexi asked, polishing off her last sip of wine.

Jamie looked at her phone. 'I should head off soon,' she said. 'I wish I didn't have to go now.'

Lexi nodded placidly, feeling the unfurling effects of the wine. 'Did I mention lately how glad I am that you're back?' she said.

'Once or twice,' said Jamie, grinning. 'What are you doing tonight?'

'Blissful nothing,' said Lexi.

'Well,' began Jamie, suddenly sheepish, 'maybe one day soon me and my guy can go on a date with you and yours?'

Guilt sunk its teeth into Lexi. Ethan didn't even know that Jamie existed.

'Your guy? I didn't know you were seeing someone!' she said, slapping her amiably on the knee.

'It's early days. I don't want to jinx it.'

~

Lexi and Jamie rode the elevator together, saying a hasty farewell on the ground floor before Jamie continued to the underground carpark. Once Lexi was settled in her car, poised to start the engine, her phone chimed with an incoming text from Ethan.

"Kate texted to say she's doing some last-minute thing for Michael's birthday tonight. Are you around? Shall we go?"

Lexi groaned. Heading over to the back blocks of nowhere to eat some four-dollar supermarket mud cake served up by Ethan's sister-in-law was not what she had in mind for her Friday. She stared at the phone in her hands and then back up at Jamie's building.

"Oh, that sounds so fun, but I've been invited along to drinks by one of the women from the café. See you later at home. x"

Once Lexi had ducked over to the supermarket to procure a bottle of prosecco and some nibbles, she once again entered the apartment building, this time riding the elevator up to the third floor. At Ali's door she paused, listening to the thump of non-descript bass and the low murmur of voices. She knocked.

Ali flung the door open.

'Jojo!' she exclaimed, launching into a funny little hop, the cuteness of which seemed at odds with her stature. 'Jojo's here!' she called out to no one in particular.

She pulled Lexi into an embrace then squealed as the cold prosecco kissed her bare midriff.

'Sorry,' said Lexi, holding up the offending bottle and handing it over along with the food.

'Oh, you're sweet,' said Ali, making way for her to enter.

The apartment was a mirror image of Jamie's, which had a curious, mind-bending effect on Lexi. *I better not drink too much or I'll end up taking a pee in the linen closet.*

Moving boxes lay scattered around the living area like a cardboard Stonehenge.

'Everyone, this is Jojo. Jojo, this is Antony, we studied at RMIT together,' said Ali, indicating a waif-like boy dressed in black who grinned at her with an endearing crooked-toothed smile. 'This is Jess, my old housemate. Clearly still distraught over my departure,' said Ali, leaning in conspiratorially.

'Shut up, Al. Nice to meet you, Jojo,' said Jess.

'And this is Jess's girlfriend -'

'Cherry,' finished Lexi.

Cherry beamed her lunar grin at Lexi and waved, causing her red curls to bounce.

'I was wondering if you two had met,' said Ali. 'Shall we open the bubbles? My brother's on a run to the bottle-o.'

She opened a box in the kitchen and unwrapped the newspaper from a mismatched assortment of glasses. Lexi, still standing in the doorway, looked around for somewhere to sit. The small sofa was already bursting with Ali's three guests and there wasn't any other furniture in the room.

'Here,' said Antony, reading her thoughts, 'you sit here. I'll sit on a box.'

Lexi was about to refuse when there was a loud knock on the door behind her. She glanced over at Ali, now handwashing the glasses.

'Would you mind?' she said, indicating the door.

Lexi opened the door to reveal Travis Nolan filling the entrance. His eyes momentarily belied his surprise before he emitted a low laugh that caused his brimming box full of bottles to clink.

'What took you so long?' asked Ali, appearing at Lexi's side and relieving Travis of his encumberment.

'Jojo, this is Travis. I unfortunately share a mother with him,' she said dryly.

'Nice to meet you, Jojo,' said Travis. He stared at her intently, eyes sparkling as Lexi's mouth fell slightly open at his omission that they'd met before.

Recovering herself, she muttered, 'Nice to meet you too.'

Antony sprung up from the sofa as Ali pulled a bottle of Aperol from the box.

'I'll make Spritzes,' he sang.

'Just a beer for me,' said Travis, his eyes still locked on Lexi.

His voice was so deep it reverberated around her body.

'I'm going to pop to the…' Lexi said, vaguely indicating in the direction of the bathroom.

On the other side of the bathroom door, she stared at her reflection in the mirror, rubbing at the faint mascara smudges which had formed under her lower lashes. Fussing with her shirt dress, she untied and retied the belt before undoing a couple of buttons and scooping her breasts more securely into her bra. She flushed the toilet for effect and washed her hands, realising too late that there were no towels. When she emerged, Antony handed her a drink and reclaimed his position on the sofa. Travis, looking even taller than usual, sat spread-legged on a box marked "books". Wordlessly, he repositioned himself to the floor, indicating the newly vacated box with his eyes. She sat and as he glanced up at her she had an involuntary premonition of him going down on her. She blushed and, as if reading her thoughts, his eyes once again shone with amusement, lingering knowingly on her newly revealed cleavage.

'Jojo?' he prompted.

'Yes, Travis,' she said, in a voice too breathless.

'Jess was asking what you did before you started camming.'

Lexi looked around to find all eyes were on her, waiting for her to respond. 'Oh, I was a barista,' she blurted.

'It's not what she used to be that you want to hear about. It's what she's going to be!' said Ali, sitting at Antony's feet.

Lexi gave her a quizzical look. She had no idea what she was going to be.

'You're a writer...' Ali prompted.

Lexi's cheeks grew warm. 'Oh,' she said. 'No, the writing I do is silly. Really, it's something to kill time while camming.'

'You write while you're camming?' asked Cherry, cocking her head to one side.

Lexi laughed. 'No, sorry. I mean, I write erotic stories at home and then read them during the broadcast.'

'She'll have a book full if she keeps it up. And I heard they're good. Margot was talking about it with Jamie yesterday.'

Travis let out a low growl that only Lexi could hear. She was annoyed by how much he was getting to her. She ignored him and tried to shift the focus of the conversation away from her.

'What do you do for work, Jess?' she asked.

'I'm a freelance bookkeeper,' said Jess.

Lexi took a large gulp of her drink. 'And you, Antony?'

'Oh, well I just...' Antony began.

'Antony is a fashion designer,' Ali answered, then addressing Antony she said, 'Don't play it down.'

He smiled his crooked grin and looked down at his glass.

Travis had shifted his weight so his shoulder was brushing against her outer thigh. Lexi's nerve-endings buzzed as she tried to keep her focus on what Ali was saying.

'...one of the oldest fashion labels in Melbourne. They were about to go belly up with their tired old aesthetic and then Antony single-handedly turned it all around. He was featured in Vogue last month.'

'That is seriously impressive,' said Lexi.

'Ali is my unofficial public relations representative,' said Antony, peering up through his fringe. 'She's the really impressive one though. Starting your own label is bold,' he said, giving her shoulder an affectionate rub.

Lexi could still feel the bulge of Travis' deltoid pressing into her. She crossed her legs, leaning her weight on the opposite side, and snapped her attention to him.

'And Travis, what is it that you do?'

Travis, mid-sip, gulped down his beer. 'I'm a federal cop,' he said.

'How exciting,' said Lexi. 'Caught any bad guys lately?'

'We're trying. Actually, Margot has been helping with our latest case. I've been out to Camnation a couple of times to chat with her about the financial mechanics of what you do over there,' he said.

'He's trying to catch some mafia dudes laundering money through their own cam site,' said Ali.

Travis shook his head. 'I don't know why I tell you anything.'

'Oooooh which site is it?' asked Cherry, leaning forward.

'I am not at liberty to say,' said Travis, in a terrible American accent.

They all laughed.

After that, Lexi slipped easily into the evening. When she snuck a look at a text from Linh asking if she was out tonight, Travis eyed her phone and asked, 'From your boyfriend?'

'Friend,' she replied, allowing the opportunity to disclose her dating status to pass by.

Lexi's head spun, and she realised she hadn't eaten anything since breakfast.

'Mind if I put the food out?' Lexi asked, rising from her perch on the box.

'Oh, I like her,' said Jess, softly nudging Ali with her knee.

Lexi grinned.

'I'll help. Gotta stretch my legs,' said Travis, heaving himself up from the floor.

She strode the short distance to the kitchenette, aware of him shadowing her. She turned, ignoring him to address Ali. 'Any idea where I might find a platter or serving board?' she asked.

'Try the box by the sink,' said Ali.

Lexi opened the fridge and removed the bag she had brought, noting it was the only thing other than alcohol stored within.

'Will this do?' Travis asked, clanging through saucepans to extract a battered wooden chopping board.

'Sure will,' she said, unpacking the bag's contents onto the bench.

Travis sidled up next to her and gave her a sideways glance. 'What would you like me to do?' he asked.

Lexi shot a glance over her shoulder at the others, locked in conversation. Her heartbeat quickened and she wondered if he could feel the thudding. 'Drain the bocconcini please,' she said, haughtily.

'Sure thing,' he said nodding. 'What's bocconcini?'

She threw her head back and laughed loudly, drawing everyone's attention.

'Sounds like Lexi's just realised how useless you are,' Ali called out to Travis.

'I could think of some uses for you,' Lexi said under her breath.

He turned sharply towards her, and she pressed the container of cheese into his chest. Catching her hands inside his, he paused a moment, before releasing them and stepping around her to the sink.

Once Lexi had finished plating the antipasto, she instructed Travis to rearrange some boxes into a makeshift coffee table in front of the sofa. She stood, holding the brimming board, watching. Sensing her gaze, he looked up at her as he was heaving the final box into place and smirked. As she bent over to place the board down her dress gaped, allowing a gust of cool air from the split system to rush down the length of her body. She straightened to find Travis' eyes locked on her, while Ali and her friends fell upon the food.

Long after the food had been cleared away and the volume of the music had been increased, Lexi and Travis sat with Jess on the sofa, watching Ali, Antony and Cherry jump around excitedly to the music while singing off key. When Jess excused herself to go to the bathroom, Travis scooted his body down to lean his neck against the back of the sofa. He turned his face up towards Lexi who peered down at him with wry eyes.

'You didn't call me,' he said.

He was so close to her that she could smell the crisp oceanic scent of his aftershave.

'I didn't,' she agreed.

He waited for her to elaborate and, when she didn't, asked, 'Is there a reason for that?'

She thought for a moment. Lexi was enjoying how his light shone on her and feared that it would be abruptly switched off the moment he learned that she was attached. The thought of that moment felt sharp and steely, a severing of something alive.

Lexi's relationship with Ethan was such a source of heartache. She wanted to connect with him but there didn't seem to be a way. How could he be free to love her when his heart still belonged to someone else? And as much as she had a great affection for Lucas, he was hardly a bonus prize in the equation. Here was a man, her own age, unattached and looking at her as though she could outshine the sun itself.

Travis raised an expectant eyebrow.

'It's complicated,' she said, feebly.

He nodded for a long moment. 'We're friends then,' he said.

'Mates from way back,' she said, echoing his tone.

'So, a couple of good mates like us could definitely catch up for a drink sometime.'

Lexi felt relief and excitement dance through her. 'Friends do like to hang out sometimes, I suppose,' said Lexi, grasping her chin between thumb and forefinger.

When Travis suppressed a grin and head-butted her shoulder gently, Lexi felt an overwhelming urge to cup his face. Jess returned and stumbled over Travis' giant boots, falling into her seat in a fit of giggles. 'Whoops! I think it's time we head off,' said Cherry, laughing along.

'Nooooo!' wailed Ali.

Lexi stood, feeling tipsy. 'I'll walk out with you,' she said, pulling out her phone to order an Uber.

Travis stood and towered over her.

'It was nice meeting you, Travis,' she said, pulling him down into a one-armed hug.

He put both arms around her and squeezed, lifting her partially off the ground. Lexi's bones suddenly felt fragile.

'Text me, mate,' he said into her neck, sending a shudder down her spine.

TWENTY-FOUR

AS Lexi scaled the stairs, she could hear the faint sound of whimpering. Light poured from the bedrooms. Reaching the landing, she was confronted by an acrid stench which contorted her face and she recoiled. She peered into Lucas' bedroom to find Ethan stripping vomit-soaked sheets off the bed. Lucas sat on the floor, clutching a stuffed lemur, a blanket wrapped around his bare shoulders. They both turned towards her as she nudged the door open.

'Hey, Lex,' said Ethan, wearily.

'Too much cake,' muttered Lucas.

'Too much cake,' Lexi agreed, crouching down to pat Lucas' smeared cheek. 'Want me to take you for a quick wash while Daddy makes the bed all fresh?'

'Oh, no, you don't have to…' began Ethan.

Lexi held up a hand to silence him.

'Thank you,' he conceded.

She helped Lucas to his feet and led him out of the room. 'Would you like to try some of my special body wash? It smells like pomegranate.'

'What's pomegramit?'

'It's this really yummy fruit and when you cut it open it looks like it's made of sparkly red jewels.'

'Treasure fruit,' he whispered.

~

The next morning, Lexi sat by Ethan's pool, sipping her coffee and opening her mind to allow in the flow of story ideas. On her laptop, the cursor blinked at her expectantly. Ethan had taken Lucas to his Saturday morning swimming lesson, leaving her with a block of time in which to compose her next story, but all she could think about was Travis. And how in Ali's crowded living room it had felt as though they were alone. She thought about the case he had mentioned, the idea of it sparking something unformed in her mind. Leaving it on the back burner, she instead proceeded with another idea which she had been discussing over email with Clive. The new ritual she shared with ChivalryAlive was fast becoming one of the sweetest parts of Lexi's day. In the evening, she would email him what she had written that day along with any notes and future ideas, sending it off like a message in a bottle across the pond. Morning brought his reply with suggestions, corrections and encouragement. Snippets of daily life caring for his wife accompanied his correspondence and Lexi quickly understood that she was not the only one benefiting from their daily exchange. He continued to tip for private messaging during her broadcasts, even though he could now theoretically email her any time for free. And although their relationship could hardly be called wholesome—he was still tuning in to see her in various stages of undress and arousal—Lexi was beginning to consider him a friend.

By the time Ethan and Lucas returned, Lexi had completed a rough draft and, desperate for a break, ordered an Uber to go and retrieve her car. She texted Jamie on the way to say that she would be in the neighbourhood and could pop by but received no reply. Once settled into the Mini, she leaned over to extract Travis' crumpled note from the glovebox, shaking her head at his almost illegible handwriting. Holding the note in her hands, she stared at it, trying to decide if she should text him. She rolled down the window to let fresh air into the stuffy interior and started the engine. As she flicked on the indicator, she noticed Travis striding out of the apartment building, looking at his phone. She laughed quietly, shaking her head. *Of course, he's here.* She called out to him, and he met her eye before shooting a quick glance back at the apartment building. He walked to her smiling, shaking his head.

'Need a ride?' she asked.

He raised his eyebrow at the perceived innuendo to which she laughed and rolled her eyes. 'Just get in,' she instructed.

He complied, contorting himself awkwardly to fit inside her car. 'Great timing, I was about to order an Uber,' he said, staring up at the building again.

'Worried she'll catch us?' Lexi said, leaning into him provocatively.

'What?'

'Ali. Are you worried she'll see us and think we set this up last night?'

He let out a breath and said, 'Yeah, I don't think she'd be too pleased about me hitting on her friends. Let's get out of here. Turn left at the next intersection.'

As Lexi pulled out onto the road, Travis shifted uncomfortably in his seat, taking up even more space in the cramped car. 'I think there's something...' he began.

Reaching a hand between his legs he pulled out Lexi's phone, and the scrap of paper bearing his phone number, out from under him. Realising what he was holding, he laughed. 'Pretty conclusive evidence right here, wouldn't you say?' he said, waving them in the air.

'Of what?' asked Lexi, shooting him a sideways glance.

'You've got the hots for me,' he said.

A surge of panic coursed through Lexi, surprising her. How much should she reveal? Channelling her camming persona, Jojo, she said, 'Look Travis, I do like you. There's something that feels so natural when I'm with you. But when I said it was complicated, I meant it. I'm not free to date you. That might change in the future, but for now we really need to be...'

'Mates,' he finished.

They drove in silence until Travis began giving directions. When they arrived at his door, she remained clutching the steering wheel and turned her head towards him. Travis held her phone up to her face, unlocking it. Startled, Lexi watched as he opened her messages and typed something quickly before dropping the phone on the dash with a *clunk*. Then, he grasped her neck and pulled her face towards his. She opened her mouth to protest as he planted a lingering kiss just shy of her lips. 'Thanks for the lift,' he said.

She sat there watching him walk away, touching the place where his lips had been. Coming to her senses, she took up her phone and checked her messages. From her phone to his he had written "Let's catch up for that drink soon, mate". A blinking ellipsis signified that he was on the other side of his front door replying. "That sounds great. I'm free next Saturday night. Pick me up at 8:00 p.m. I know a great little place not too far from here that we can walk to."

Lexi put her car into gear and sped away, shaking her head at his audacity. Next Saturday was her twenty-ninth birthday.

TWENTY-FIVE

BY Sunday night, Lexi had sent four short story drafts to Clive as well as a list of potential ideas. Although her story-a-day goal was self-imposed, it induced anxiety every time she thought about it. Now, she had a few stories up her sleeve in case life or a lack of inspiration got in her way.

She came downstairs to find Ethan sitting on the sofa watching an old British sketch show that Lexi had tried to love but suspected wasn't actually funny. When she sat, he tipped his body towards her to rest his head in her lap, his eyes never leaving the screen. She ran her fingers through his hair feeling the sting of regret. Here was a man who was good to his core and yet she couldn't seem to get close enough to know him. But then, what did he really know about her? And while the idea of packing her bags and saying goodbye to him and Lucas made her heart ache, wasn't that the outcome she was aiming for by camming?

He turned his gaze up at her and she held her breath, praying he couldn't make out the tears filling her eyes as the credits rolled on the television screen.

'I think I know what you're thinking,' he said.

She looked down at him, her body frozen.

'You're wondering when I'm going to bring up the subject of your birthday.'

She exhaled and smiled as he sat up.

'Now, I know you told me that you're not really into birthdays,' he said, palms splayed in a gesture of surrender. 'But what if we did something low-key here? I could do a seafood barbecue, get you one of those cakes that are too pretty to eat. We could get my brothers' families over and you can ask Linh and her crazy boyfriend and your new work friends from the café…'

Lexi's mind buzzed with static. How many lies upon lies would have to occur for Jamie, Ali and Cherry to walk through Ethan's front door? She paused, unsure of how she should respond.

Finally, she nodded and forced a smile. 'That sounds...' She continued to nod, searching for the right thing to say. She began again. 'Thank you for… for thinking about it. Can we say it'll be a lunch with your family? And then… Well, it's just that Xavier has a gig and I promised Linh we'd go along to see him. My anti-birthday has kind of been a tradition for us, for the last few years…'

As Lexi wove a story that would allow her to keep the date with Travis, her guilt renewed. She hadn't even spoken with Linh properly since their final shift at The Bean & Gone. What was more, almost every time she'd caught up with Jamie, Lexi had told Ethan she was hanging with Linh.

Ethan smiled and reached out a hand to stroke her cheek.

'I'm going to buy you a birthday cake so fucking wanky it has dry ice,' he said, grinning.

TWENTY-SIX

WHEN Lexi walked into the dressing room at Camnation, Cherry was peeling off a black, wet-look vinyl cat suit, her hair piled either side of her grinning face in space buns.

'You look amazing!' said Lexi, taking in a last glimpse of the ensemble before it was discarded on the floor where it lay like a moonlit puddle.

'Oh thanks, it was quite a show. Everyone was so… Oh, I don't know,' she said pulling out pins and shaking her hair loose.

'How was the rest of your weekend? Friday night was so fun!' said Lexi.

'Oh, I know! I was so excited when you walked in. I wasn't sure if you and Ali had met yet. So many of the women here are like ships in the night, you know?'

Lexi sat on the ottoman to unlace her sneakers. 'Ali's kind of great, isn't she?' said Lexi, thoughtfully.

'She's a hot mess.' Cherry laughed. 'But she's going places.'

Lexi laughed and stood to pull her jeans off. 'You two met through Jess?'

Cherry nodded. She stepped into a cream-coloured playsuit which made her look like a boiled egg and sat cross-legged on the floor.

'She was working two or three jobs, trying to scrape together enough money to start her label and I was making way more than her working about half the hours. She was cranky, and tired, and in the free time she did have, she couldn't find the energy to work on her business.'

Lexi nodded, considering whether she should ask her next question. 'And how does Jess feel about your camming?' Lexi asked, thinking of Ethan.

'She's cool with it. I mean, all the things that make me good at it are the things that Jess loves about me, you know? When we first met it was a really hard time in my life. I'd been camming for ages but hadn't told my family about it. And finally, I thought, fuck it, I don't have the energy to lead a double life anymore, you know? So, I told my mum and dad and brother, and they did not take it well. I mean, it was a nightmare. When I met Jess, I thought, you know what? Anyone who has a problem with what I do, isn't worth knowing. You've got to be yourself; you know?'

Lexi didn't respond. 'Do your chatroom guests know you're…' Lexi paused, trying to think of the right way to broach the subject of Cherry's sexuality. '… not into dudes.'

Cherry laughed good-naturedly. 'They know. Fuck! It's a selling point for most of the guys. The virginal pussy, untouched by human cock!' said Cherry, forming a heart shape with her forefingers and thumbs to encircle her crotch.

Lexi laughed.

'It's like you with your writing. It's who you are. Hiding it, even from your chatroom, would be impossible.'

Heat climbed up Lexi's neck. She'd spent her entire life hiding her writing. 'And all your friends know too? About the camming I mean.'

Cherry looked thoughtful.

'I lost some friends over it, but I've gained a lot more,' she said, indicating Lexi with an open palm. 'And Jess's mum is really cool about it too, which has been a blessing after my own family turned their backs on me.'

Lexi, suspecting she may cry, turned towards the nearest clothing rack and flicked through the hangers. She pulled out a skirt and held it up. It was a flouncy wrap which she unclipped from the hanger and threw around her waist. Pulling out a couple of nearby tops, she held them up to her chest and regarded herself in the full-length mirror.

'The black,' said Cherry.

As Lexi pulled it on, she said, 'It's my birthday this Saturday.'

'It is?'

'Yeah, I was thinking about maybe doing a small drinks thing. It's probably too last minute, you and Jess must have plans already,' she said, trying to backpedal.

'Nope. We don't. What are you thinking?'

Lexi thought of the invitation from Travis. If she could turn this into a group event, then maybe her guilt would diminish. The question was, would he go for it?

'I don't know yet,' she said sheepishly. 'Can I let you know later?'

'Save the date. Got it,' said Cherry, rising and stepping into her slides. 'Have a good one, you look beautiful. Try the suede sling backs with that.'

She hiked her bag onto her shoulder and walked out of the room.

Lexi pulled out her phone and clicked through to Travis's message exchange with himself. Her thumbs hovered over the keyboard. Finally, she typed, "Not that I'm agreeing to this. But… hypothetically speaking, which bar would we go to, if we did go out?"

Shoving the phone into her bag, she grabbed the heels Cherry had suggested and made for the bedroom where Veronica would be finishing up at any moment.

Lexi stood in the low-lit hallway trying to formulate a plan. Should she tell Travis that it was her birthday on Saturday? That she wanted to invite others along for drinks? Something in her gut told her that he'd shy away from the idea. She also worried that he'd think she was a freak for not already having plans with her *real* friends. But if it all happened around him, surely, he'd roll with it.

Veronica threw open the door and buzzed around the room.

'Hey, Jojo!' she said, collecting up her assortment of small sequined cushions from the bed. Peering over the glittering stack, she wiggled across the room, teetering precariously on platform stilettos.

Lexi narrowed her eyes at Veronica, wondering if she should include her in any potential birthday celebrations. This brief daily crossover was the only interaction they had, and it was hardly the basis of a long-lasting connection. Not only that, but Lexi always had the distinct feeling that Veronica was only skimming the top off their interactions. As Lexi watched, the elfin blonde lost her balance.

'Here, let me get that for you,' said Lexi.

She strode over to open the storage chest as Veronica lost her balance, dropping the furnishings unceremoniously onto the carpet and clutching at Lexi to avoid following them. Veronica giggled. 'These heels!' she exclaimed. 'I got my G-string snagged on them and almost broke my neck earlier!'

'Oh!' said Lexi, almost choking on the word.

Veronica walked cautiously to the bed, arms splayed like a tightrope walker, and sat down to undo the ankle straps. Once discarded, she gave them a dramatic little kick of good-riddance and looked at Lexi thoughtfully. 'You know what though? I think they like it.'

'Like what?'

'When I mess it all up. In the beginning I was embarrassed when things like that would go wrong, but then… I dunno. I guess I stopped worrying about that stuff.' She continued to sit there for a long moment, entranced. 'What am I doing? You need the room,' she blurted. She shook her head and continued flitting about the room putting her things away. 'Okay, well… bye!' she said, making for the door.

Lexi bent down to pick up Veronica's ridiculous shoes. 'You don't want to forget these?' she said, dangling them in the air.

After Lexi had dressed the room, she checked her phone one last time for a reply from Travis, before switching it to silent and placing it in her bag where it wouldn't distract her. She took a deep breath and arranged her face into something carefree before beginning her broadcast. Perched on the end of the bed, she regarded her image, tilting her head from side to side. She leaned into the webcam and lifted her chin upward to accentuate the fullness of her lips and then downward to draw attention to her heavily made-up eyes. As visitors arrived, she untied and retied her wrap skirt, drawing attention to her bare midriff and made angular shapes with her shoulders. Tips trickled in, and when someone asked her about her weekend, Lexi captivated the visitors with a made-up story about taking a scenic bike ride.

'I had to cross the river, but the bridge is made up of these timber slats. So, when you go over it, it kind of vibrates your… well. You can imagine,' she said chewing on her thumb, so her tongue was visible. 'I went over it, and it felt so good I turned around and went over it again. And again. And again.'

Tips poured in so she went on.

'It's my own fault really. I was wearing these shorts… if I'm honest they're probably a size too small so every time I move it feels like fingers pressing against me. So, with that and the bike seat feeling so hard between my legs… I forgot where I was going and kept going over and over that bridge.'

Comments and tips from excited users poured in. When TheCovertWolf tipped and told her he'd never wanted to be a bike seat more in his life, Lexi replied, 'Really Covert Wolf? You want me to sit on your face while I ride around town?'

After that Lexi asked her audience for countdown suggestions. Did they want to hear her latest story? Or perhaps she could take a bubble bath, get herself nice and sudsy. ChivalryAlive tried to advocate for the story he had already read and edited the night before, but in the end, the bubble bath option won out.

When the countdown target had almost been reached, Lexi killed some time by preparing the bath, pouring in copious amounts of marshmallow-scented body wash. She swept a hand through the water as the soap bubbled, rubbing the froth up and down her arms and describing how she longed to submerge her body in the warm water. Still talking, she retrieved her bikini and got changed slightly off camera, allowing brief flashes of her limbs to come into view. Then, wrapping a towel around herself, she perched on the edge of the tub as TheCovertWolf contributed the balance required to begin. Lexi made a show of taking off her towel, opening one side at a time, teasing. Once removed, she leaned into the webcam to adjust the straps on her bikini top, causing her breasts to bounce. TheCovertWolf told her not to bother, reminding her that it would soon be coming off. When Lexi stepped into the water, she pretended it was too hot, making *oohs* and *aahs* as she lowered her body down in increments. Once submerged, she languished for a moment, finding the experience genuinely pleasurable but knowing that the point of it wasn't for her own enjoyment. Moving onto her knees, she leaned over the rim to retrieve a bath puff and soaped herself slowly.

Comments and tips lit up the screen which Lexi acknowledged in turn.

She tugged at the saturated material of her bikini. 'If only you were here to help me get out of this thing,' she said to no one in particular.

"If I was there, you'd be getting more dirty than clean," TheCovertWolf commented.

'You're no help at all, Wolfie,' said Lexi, pulling the string at her nape. The bow slid undone, and she let the straps fall, revealing her slick breasts, to the approval of all. After untying the strap at the back and throwing the top onto the tiled floor with a *splat*, Lexi played a game in which she would lather her torso to the point of concealing it, only to dip into the water and spring up clean again. When her performance couldn't be stretched out any longer, Lexi stood and slid her bikini bottoms down, letting them linger at her knees. Recalling Veronica's misadventures, she placed a hand on the wall to steady herself before stepping cautiously out of them. She scooped up suds to cover her nudity, then waited as they slid downwards to reveal everything once more. Once these activities had exhausted themselves, she stepped from the tub to retrieve her towel, taking care to dry herself in a seductive and unhurried manner, all the while thanking her audience for a relaxing and pleasurable experience.

Back in the bedroom, Lexi sat on the edge of the bed, legs crossed, towelling off her hair.

'That was such a treat,' she said, 'Thank you. I feel so refreshed. So… what shall we do next? I still have a little time left with you. Does anyone have any ideas what we should aim for next?'

ChivalryAlive was quick to suggest a reading but once again TheCovertWolf dominated by purchasing body lotion off the menu. Lexi wagged her finger at the webcam, her face displaying a knowing look. 'You really know what a woman wants, Wolfie,' she said.

His reply was instant. "I know exactly what you need."

She raised an eyebrow at this as she reached for the lotion.

Lexi checked the time. Fifteen minutes until the end of her broadcast. She wondered if she could stretch this out until then. 'With all this moisturising, my skin has never felt so good,' she said, sweeping over and under her calf in a figure eight motion.

She looked over at her bag, wondering if Travis had replied to her message yet, all the while continuing to chatter about what she might do after they parted ways. Perhaps get a massage? Maybe meet a friend for cocktails? Go for another bike ride over that infamous bridge? In reality Lexi would be hitting the supermarket before collecting Lucas from childcare. Ethan was hosting an employee training session at the store. One of many tiresome affairs in which a pharmacy representative would promote the benefits of their brand to staff in exchange for a stale selection of iced buns and a convoluted incentive scheme. As Lexi set to work moisturising her other leg and answering a question regarding the merits of different types of underwear, she tried to think of what to cook for dinner that night.

When it came time to say goodbye, Lexi teased her audience for not fulfilling her desire to pleasure herself and encouraged them to make it up to her tomorrow. When she said this, TheCovertWolf commented that he knew exactly what she would be doing afterwards. She flashed a coy smile before waving goodbye and ending transmission.

Wrapping the towel around herself again, she retrieved her phone and was annoyed to find that there had been no reply from Travis in the hours since she'd messaged him. She clicked into the message thread to make sure she hadn't missed it and saw the flashing ellipses which signified he was typing a reply.

"The name of the bar is…"

She waited. What did he want? A drum roll? She watched the ellipses blink.

"The Covert Wolf."

Lexi's thoughts boomed in her mind, but her body remained stock-still. Hearing movement on the other side of the door, she sprang up, dressed and opened the door to reveal Sienna crouched down and rummaging through a giant tote.

'Hey,' said Lexi, still shaken.

Sienna stood and applied lipstick without a mirror as she walked in. 'Are you okay?' she asked, smacking her lips together before placing the lipstick back in her bag. 'You look kind of… flustered.'

Lexi forced a laugh.

'Oh, you know. It's just…' She made a twirling motion with her index finger to indicate the room and, although it meant nothing, it seemed to satisfy Sienna.

'Tell me about it,' she said, dumping her bag in the corner.

'I'll get out of your hair. I just need to give the tub a quick spray,' said Lexi, disappearing into the ensuite. As she cleaned, her mind raced. Travis had spent hours watching her. The idea of it was somehow shocking and exhilarating at the same time. When Lexi emerged, Sienna had already packed away her things and was redressing the room with her own.

'Oh, thanks,' said Lexi.

She bade Sienna farewell and, once the bundle of wet towels was discarded in the linen hamper, Lexi again pulled out her phone. In the five or so minutes since the text messages had come through from Travis, he had written to her three more times.

"Surprise!"

"I can't get up from my desk thanks to you."

"Come on, don't be mad. I loved watching you. You're like all my fantasies come to life."

Lexi combed her memories of the last few hours, trying to comprehend how Travis had been present the entire time. She couldn't believe his nerve but if he thought surprises were okay, then she had one of her own for him. Saturday night would be a birthday party. A surprise birthday party, at The Covert Wolf.

TWENTY-SEVEN

WATER sprayed up, misting Lexi's legs as she circumvented the pool.

'What did I say?' shrieked Kate, at the knot of children. 'Don't splash the mummies! I mean, *fuck…*' she swore under her breath. 'Don't splash the… ladies!'

'Thanks Kate, I don't mind,' said Lexi, peering over her sunglasses at Ethan's sister-in-law. Kate scowled alternately at her children and husband, her forehead glistening in the midday heat as she fanned herself with a well-thumbed copy of a trash mag. Sliding open the glass door, Lexi was roused by the cool interior and the smiling face of Marija muddling mint for the next batch of cocktails.

'Need a top up?' asked Marija, indicating Lexi's empty glass.

'Only if you do,' said Lexi.

Marija raised her thick eyebrows. 'What kind of friend would I be if I let you drink alone?' she said, deadpan.

Lexi smirked.

Pouring the last of the ingredients into the jug, Marija refreshed their drinks and clinked her glass against Lexi's.

Lexi took a sip. 'This batch is strong, no?'

Marija shrugged. 'I'm Croatian, we free-pour,' she said.

Lexi laughed. 'It smells amazing out there. Ethan's got crayfish tails. He's out there basting them with butter as we speak,' said Lexi. She looked around the kitchen at the partially constructed salads and asked, 'Can I help with this?'

'Just relax, birthday girl,' said Marija, her almost non-existent accent discernible on the word "birthday".

'Come on, let me help. I want to hang out with you in here and I need a plausible excuse,' said Lexi, throwing a deliberate look towards Kate who was busy bellowing at her children. Meanwhile, Lucas stood dripping on the side-lines, clearly terrified by the volume of his aunt's voice. Marija's eldest daughter Chloe put her arm around him and led him away from the shouting.

'Here,' said Marija, sliding a plastic packet over to her. 'You can toast the pine nuts.'

The pair worked in comfortable silence until Marija spoke. 'Ethan tells me you're going out after this? I can stick around and put Lucas to bed if you want to go together?'

Lexi turned from the cooktop to face Marija.

'That is so nice of you. But, um… me and my friend Linh have this tradition. It's from before either of us had boyfriends. We always spend our birthdays together, just the two of us.'

Lexi held her breath, waiting to see if her lie would be accepted.

Marija inhaled sharply. 'Are they burning?' she asked, indicating the smoking pan.

'Fuck,' spat Lexi. She grabbed for the handle with too much force, sending a shower of pine nuts over the stove.

Laughing, Marija came over and turned off the gas. 'Tell me again about how you want to help,' she said, relieving Lexi of the pan she held.

Lexi let out an exaggerated sob and slunk over to the other side of the island bench to sit down. Marija dumped the unsalvageable nuts into the rubbish bin.

'How are things going with you two anyway?' she asked, her eyes darting towards Ethan who stood at the barbecue with his brothers.

Lexi took a sip of her drink, wondering how she should answer. 'He's wonderful, I mean… you know. But sometimes I feel like he's holding back. Like he's worried that if he says too much, it'll be the wrong thing.'

Marija nodded slowly as she pulled fronds off a sprig of dill.

'Not that I'm perfect,' Lexi hastened to go on. 'I mean, I have been pretty preoccupied with my new job, plus there's Lucas to add to the equation.' Lexi sighed. 'Sometimes it feels… harder than it should be.'

They remained silent for a moment, listening to the whir of the air-conditioning and the distant squeals of the children.

Marija looked over at Ben, who was attempting to reapply sunscreen to their four reluctant children, and turned back to Lexi. 'Easy doesn't always mean fulfilling though, does it? Sometimes the things we work hardest for end up being sweetest.'

Lexi heard the door slide open and turned to see Ethan, cheeks pink from cooking. 'We're almost ready out here,' he said.

He deposited a sweaty kiss, wetting Lexi's cheek, and grabbed a large, lidded serving dish from the bench.

'Take these,' said Marija, thrusting a bowl of lemon wedges and chopped parsley at him.

'Oooooh, fancy,' he said, taking the bowl and all but colliding with Kate coming in.

'Need help bringing stuff out?' she asked.

'These two are ready,' said Marija indicating two brimming bowls. 'And this one needs pine nuts.' She flashed Lexi a teasing look.

'Give me another chance!' implored Lexi.

'Everybody deserves a second chance,' she said.

~

By the time the cake was brought out, the sun had lost some of its intensity. The children splashed in the pool as their parents looked on, enjoying a rare moment of peace. Having cleared away the plates and restored order to the kitchen, Ethan emerged holding a confection more sculptural than edible. Lexi returned his smile and her heart warmed.

'No dry ice available I'm afraid,' said Ethan, setting the plate down.

Lexi grinned.

'What did he say?' Kate asked, in a loud whisper.

'It's nothing to do with you,' snapped Michael.

'Shall we get the kids over?' Lexi asked.

'Nah, they're happy. Don't mess with it,' said Ben.

Marija leaned against Ben's shoulder, and he kissed her head.

'Are we singing?' said Ethan, lighting the candles.

'Nooooooo,' said Lexi.

As they all sang in loud operatic voices, Lexi covered her face with one hand and mimed a conductor's baton with the other. When it was over, she blew out the candles and plunged the knife into one of the glistening chocolate orbs adorning the cake before pressing down into alternating layers of sponge and mousse. 'Wowza,' she said.

'Did you make a wish?' asked Ethan.

'What could be sweeter than this?' she said, thinking of Marija's wisdom.

~

After everyone had left, Lexi headed upstairs to get ready. She longed to cancel drinks tonight and stay in with Ethan, to find the courage to share something of herself so that he might do the same. But she knew it was too late for that. Besides, it wasn't her friends that were the problem. After Travis' surprise visit to her chatroom earlier in the week, the thought of coming face to face with him made her feel sick with nerves. The more she considered it, the more she believed that he had violated her trust, although the parameters of the breach were sketchy. She consoled herself with the superficial promise they'd made to just be friends. Still, her guilt was peaking over the way she had been deceiving Ethan. In the beginning, the details of her new job seemed like a minor omission to a man she was planning on making a break from. But with her doubt in their relationship wavering, the situation was becoming increasingly complicated. She'd had no expectations of what camming would be like and it had surprised her, shaking her out of a rut and inspiring her to write again. But now she was living a double life with a whole new set of friends to go with it. And it wasn't like she could claim it as research for writing when Ethan knew nothing of that either. The more she tried to tease out a reasonable way forward, the more ensnared she became.

Lexi turned the water off and stood for a moment with her wet hair veiling her face, listening to the drips hit the tiles. From the other side of the wall, she could hear Ethan reading Lucas a bedtime story, his voice low and melodic.

When Ethan emerged from Lucas' room, Lexi was dressed in a grey boilersuit and was putting the finishing touches on her make-up. He stood in the doorway smiling at her mirrored reflection, looking sun kissed.

'Did you forget to reapply sunscreen?' she asked.

He stepped forward to inspect his face and Lexi caught the scent of barbecue smoke wafting off his clothes and hair. 'You worked so hard today. I don't think I've ever had a birthday that wasn't a total head fuck, so… thank you,' she said.

He smiled at her with eyes so adoring she had to look away.

'I'm going to jump in the shower if you're done making yourself beautiful. Well, more beautiful,' he said.

'I'm done, I should be heading off anyway,' said Lexi, stowing her make-up bag and making for the door.

'Say hi to Linh for me,' said Ethan.

'What?' asked Lexi, turning to look at him confused. 'Oh, yeah, of course.' She gave him a quick kiss and slipped out the door.

TWENTY-EIGHT

LEXI knocked on Travis' front door and waited, resisting the urge to adjust her outfit. The bar was a five-minute walk so if they left now, they would only arrive a littler earlier than the others.

'Coming!' Travis bellowed from within.

Lexi's phone chimed in her pocket with a message from Jamie. "Had pre-drinks at mine, lost track of time. We'll see you there in thirty minutes. Sorry!"

The door opened to reveal Travis, wearing a crisp white shirt. His face opened into a smile upon seeing her and he scooped her into a hug. His clean scent and the feeling of his shoulders beneath his cotton shirt made her involuntarily swoon.

'I wasn't sure if you'd come, Jojo,' he said, making way for her to enter. 'We'll have a drink here first?'

Lexi stepped forward and then hesitated with one foot either side of the threshold. Being alone in his house wasn't what she had agreed to but then, feeling silly, she complied. The others were probably more than half an hour away. She walked in and surveyed her surroundings. The space was devoid of personal style, like a furnished rental apartment. Still, she had to give him points for tidiness. She dropped her bag next to the sofa and followed him into the open-plan kitchen.

'Rum or vodka?' he said, holding up the bottles for her consideration.

'What mixers do you have?'

'Soda water, tonic. There're limes. I might have ginger beer?'

'I'll take a Dark and Stormy,' she said, entering the kitchen.

'Remind me?' he prompted.

'Dark rum, ginger beer and lime juice. Got any Tabasco? It's great with a dash of Tabasco,' she said.

He raised his eyebrows and tilted his head. 'In the fridge door, I think. Wanna check?'

He grabbed a lime from the fruit bowl, tossed it into the air and caught it before pulling down two tumblers from an overhead cupboard.

She rounded the bench, opened the fridge and located the Tabasco and ginger beer. 'It's alcoholic,' she said, reading the ginger beer label.

'Yeah, not very though,' he said, taking the bottles from her and placing them on the bench.

She took the glasses and filled them with ice from the dispenser.

'Not too much rum in mine please,' said Lexi, placing the glasses in front of him.

Although she had paced herself, and was by no means drunk, she couldn't ignore the fact that she had spent the afternoon drinking.

'Lightweight,' said Travis, flashing her a look.

Lexi stood next to him, leaning her body back against the bench where he worked, cutting the limes. Here, in the quiet of his kitchen, she was detached from reality and emboldened. Here, she was Jojo, and she was enjoying her anonymity.

'Will we be discussing your unexpected presence in my chatroom this week?' she asked, her tone serious.

He continued with his task, a smile barely visible at the corners of his eyes. 'Well, what can I say? I was… curious,' he said.

'And now?'

'Now I'm…' He laughed and handed her a glass.

She took a sip and was taken aback by its strength and unusual flavour. She was accustomed to a different brand of rum, spicy and complex. This had an underlying vanilla note that tasted artificial, almost saccharine and was at odds with the Tabasco. Travis sipped his drink, his eyes intense above the rim. Setting the glass down on the bench, he leaned in towards her mouth. Trying to appear unfazed, she turned her cheek and took another small sip of the unpleasant liquid. He dipped his head and laughed to himself, nodding. Turning away from her, he pulled his phone from his pocket and headed towards the sofa. She hung back for a moment, watching him as a nondescript beat permeated the house. Following him, Lexi placed her drink on the coffee table and kicked off her mules. She sat with her back against the arm of the sofa, her bent legs creating a barrier between them. They sat in silence, the clinking of his ice accompanying the background music. Lexi's eyes were trained on Travis' profile, staring straight ahead at their reflection in his television screen. He leaned forward to place his glass on the coffee table. Then, in one serpentine motion, he pressed his torso between her knees and approached her mouth once more. Lexi squeezed her thighs together, halting his trajectory. With their lips mere centimetres from one another's, she shook her head, feeling strangely powerful and self-assured.

'No?' he asked.

She hooked her ankles together at his lower back and squeezed his torso tighter. 'Nuh ah.'

'Oh? So, you're not going to let me?'

She felt the humidity of his breath as he spoke.

She released him and he made to retreat but then gripped her hips and pulled her towards him. She was shocked to find herself flat on her back, staring up at the ceiling. Shaken, she emitted a startled laugh before he flipped her over onto her stomach. The rough fabric of the sofa felt abrasive against her face and her pulse quickened. Before she could move, he scooped his right elbow under her chin, holding it in place with his left and compressing her neck.

'You really think you're the one in control of this situation?' he whispered into her ear.

All the air expelled from Lexi's lungs and a strained sound

escaped her lips. He squeezed harder. Devoid of breath, she tried to produce a laugh which might diffuse the situation, but no sound came, she was beginning to feel light-headed. And then he was off her, sitting back at the opposite side of the sofa, sipping that God-awful drink. Lexi got herself into a sitting position and tried to steady her breath, feeling as vulnerable as an injured animal. She needed to get out of here, but how? She reached for her drink, using all the will power she could muster to keep her hand steady, and took a sip.

'You're going to think this is so funny,' she said.

He turned his head towards her, his manner neutral, as though nothing unusual had happened.

'It's actually my birthday today.'

'Yeah? How old?'

'Twenty-nine.'

'And you're spending it with me?' he said, grinning at her.

'Well, at the last minute I invited some friends along too. They're meeting us at The Covert Wolf in about ten minutes.'

'What friends?'

'Oh, you know. Ali, Cherry and Jess and, have you met Jamie before? She lives in Ali's building.'

Travis was silent for a moment. 'I should have said something when you arrived. I don't have that much time tonight. I figured that if you came at all, it would be a one drink kind of deal,' he said, raking his fingers through his hair.

'Oh, sure, of course,' she said, standing and raising her glass. 'Well, I guess we've done that so I might head over there. Can't have birthday drinks without a birthday girl,' she said, replacing the drink on the table.

He hesitated as if considering something. 'It might be best not to mention you were here,' he said.

Lexi nodded. 'Of course.'

Lexi's phone chimed and she checked the text. Although it was an advertisement from her network provider, she said, 'That's them now, I better run.' She stepped into her shoes and grabbed her bag, slinging it over her shoulder. The movement felt laboured and mechanical due to her strained neck.

'I'll walk you out,' he said, standing.

Her gut lurched in the face of his dominant stature. Making for the door, her body braced for another choke hold. She kept her steps measured, opened the door and turned back towards him. 'Okay, well...' she said.

Just as he'd done the day she drove him home, he grabbed her neck and planted a kiss at the corner of her mouth.

She heard herself say, 'Thanks for the drink.' And then she was outside gulping down the night air.

TWENTY-NINE

LEXI groaned awake. The pain in her neck felt as though she were cast in concrete that was slowly contracting. As the memories of last night came back with sickening clarity, shame and disgust circled her, taunting. She had been dancing at the fire's edge and was now surprised to find she'd been burned.

Lexi had been the first to arrive at The Covert Wolf, had practically staggered in, feeling chilled to the bone despite the mild temperature. She made for the bathroom and sat in one of the stalls shivering and chastising herself for her naivety, tears streaking her face. When she emerged, the reflection of her mascara-smudged cheeks in the mirror made her start. She fished around in her bag and located a packet of wet wipes she carried for cleaning up Lucas' misadventures—the Salvador Dali moustache he sported after guzzling a babyccino, the greasy fingers that came after eating his favourite gozlemes from Preston Market. As she set to work cleaning her face, the scent of the wipes made her weep anew. How she longed to be at home with Ethan and Lucas. Home, where she was safe and loved. But how could she go home now? How elaborate a lie would she have to concoct in order to justify returning home just one hour after leaving? So, she cleaned herself up as best she could and took a seat at the bar to await her friends.

In any other circumstances, The Covert Wolf would have been a bar Lexi rated highly. The light was low and sepia-toned, sparkling down from low-hanging pendant lights. The music came courtesy of a turntable behind the bar. The tracks were selected by a lanky boy with a mullet who writhed ceaselessly to the beat, the occasional patron ordering drinks being the only thing standing between him and a perfect night. He dropped the needle on the next record and a melodic beat dripped slowly over Lexi. As a melancholic woman began to sing, Lexi dropped her head in her hands.

'What can I get you?' asked the bartender.

Lexi lifted her head to meet his gaze. 'What can you get me?' she repeated.

'She'll have a Negroni,' said Jamie, wrapping an elegant arm around Lexi's shoulders.

'Make that…' Ali wagged a finger in the air attempting to do a head count.

Jess laughed at her. 'Sit down before you hurt yourself. We'll take five, please.'

Lexi turned to look at Jamie who folded her into an embrace.

Holding her at arm's length, she said, 'I'm so sorry we're late! You haven't been waiting long, have you? You got my message?'

Lexi thought back. The text message from Jamie seemed like a lifetime ago.

'Are you okay?' Jamie asked, narrowing her gaze.

'Do you have any Nurofen?' asked Lexi, massaging the back of her neck. 'I…. ah, think I slept funny last night or something.'

She desperately wanted to tell Jamie about what Travis had done, but she could hardly do that in front of the others. Cherry, overhearing, undid the butterfly clasp on her wicker bucket-bag and produced a crumpled packet of Ibuprofen. She popped two capsules into Lexi's hand as the bartender lined up the drinks.

Jamie tapped her card to pay, and they each picked up a glass. 'Happy birthday, dear Jojo,' she sang.

'Happy birthday to you,' countered the others.

Lexi forced a smile and downed the pills with a slurp of her cocktail.

For the next couple of hours, Lexi performed a pantomime of enjoyment which was wholeheartedly accepted due to the inebriated state of her friends. Ali could barely stand, and Cherry and Jess seemed so preoccupied with one another that they wouldn't have noticed if everyone else ghosted them. Only Jamie searched Lexi's eyes for meaning.

'How about brunch tomorrow?' Lexi asked.

And Jamie, measuring the weight concealed in her friend's tone, muttered a solemn agreement.

~

Lexi lay in bed listening. The hand-held vacuum cleaner's drone marked the completion of breakfast. She pictured Ethan on his knees cleaning up crumbs from underneath Lucas' chair and longed for him to hold her. She looked over at last night's clothes thrown over the chair in the corner of the room and hated the woman who had worn them. How stupid she had been to think that Travis was a good guy, that she would be safe with him. But he had been so nice, was the brother of a friend, and was meant to be on the right side of the law. She dragged herself out of bed, located some Nurofen in the bathroom and downed it with water from the faucet as Ethan walked in chuckling. 'Sore head today?' he said, wrapping his arms around her waist and looking at her in the mirror. She turned and lay her head on his shoulder, held him tight without speaking.

'I'm surprised you're awake so early. Why don't you go back and sleep in a bit?'

Last night I was put into a choke hold by a federal cop I've been flirting with and the pain he inflicted upon my neck woke me, she imagined saying. Instead, she said, 'I wanted to hang out with you and Lucas before I meet Linh for brunch.'

'How was the band? Same old?' asked Ethan, pulling away from their embrace.

'Yeah,' said Lexi, 'same old.'

'Want me to make you a coffee while you have a shower?' asked

Ethan. 'I promise not to overheat the milk.'

Lexi smiled. 'That'd be lovely, thanks.'

Ethan turned to leave, and Lexi stopped him. 'Maybe I should cancel brunch. Stay with you guys.'

'Yeah, you can. But we're not going to be home. I promised Michael we'd go along to Harrison's basketball final.'

'Oh,' said Lexi.

'You're welcome to come. You can hang out with Kate,' he said.

'It's okay, I shouldn't cancel at the last minute anyway.'

'Okay, well. I'll go make you the world's most tolerable coffee.'

~

When Lexi arrived, Jamie was already seated at one of the tables lining the footpath, the thin vinyl of a café barrier the only thing separating her from cars parked along the roadside. Lexi detested sitting at the edge of the road and couldn't help imagining dust coating her food right before she ingested it. And then there were the pigeons. Winged disease carriers foraging for discarded morsels as they bobbed and weaved amongst designer shoes and handbags. She shuddered and made her way over.

Jamie sat, gazing out into the traffic, most of her face concealed by a large pair of black sunglasses. As Lexi approached, she turned and offered up her cheek up for a kiss. When Lexi was seated, Jamie dipped her sunglasses to reveal dark circles.

'Oh dear,' said Lexi.

'I do not remember the last time I got that wasted. Does this place do Bloody Marys?' asked Jamie, picking up the menu and turning it over.

A text message came through from Travis. "How's the hangover, birthday girl?"

Lexi stared at the screen in disbelief, considering if she should bother responding at all, when a waiter appeared.

'I'll have a Bloody Mary please. Do you want one, Lex?' said Jamie.

Lexi shook her head. 'I'll have a short mac please.'

'Sure. I'll come back to get your food order in a tic,' she said.

'Sorry,' said Lexi, inwardly seething at Travis' audacity, 'I have to reply to this real quick,' she said, indicating her phone. "No hangover, I paced myself. But you should know that move you pulled on me last night really hurt, I'm still in pain."

'Sorry, done,' said Lexi, setting her phone down on the table. She leaned forward and squinted at Jamie. 'Is that a hickey?' she asked.

Jamie reflexively placed a hand up to her neck and tugged up her collar. 'I may have had a booty call last night,' she said.

They both giggled.

'Actually, the guy I've been seeing lives right around the corner from the bar we went to last night.'

The waiter appeared and listed the food specials. Jamie ordered and Lexi, having heard none of the exchange, said, 'I'll have the same.'

When the waiter was gone, she asked tentatively, 'It's going well then, with this guy?'

Jamie tried to suppress a grin. 'It really is, but it's a little complicated.'

'Oh?'

Jamie hesitated. 'I'll tell you, but you can't tell anyone. Especially not Ali.'

Lexi swallowed. 'Why not Ali?' she asked.

'It's her brother and she'd be so mad. We're keeping it on the down-low for now.'

Lexi took a deep breath as her brain screamed.

Jamie, mistaking her silence for judgment, hastened to go on.

'I know, I know. But he's so nice and totally accepting of me and… I guess I haven't been that lucky in love and… I will tell Ali, eventually. But it's so fresh and I don't want to rock the boat, you know?'

Lexi forced a weak smile and nodded, dreading what she would have to do next. She uncrossed her legs as if to steady herself and placed her foot down on something sickeningly soft. A yelp escaped her lips as a pigeon flapped frantically out from under the table and into the path of the approaching waiter. The Bloody Mary, tall and elaborately garnished, toppled from her tray crashing onto their table, causing a cascade of tomato juice, glass and ice to fall into Lexi's lap. She gasped and stood as Jamie tried to evacuate their belongings.

'Oh my God, I'm so sorry,' said the waiter. 'Let me get some napkins.'

'It's okay. Is there a hand dryer in the bathroom?' Lexi asked.

'Yes, it's just past the kitchen and around to the left.'

As Lexi removed and rinsed her dress in the sink, she thought of how she would broach the subject of Travis. Although Jamie would see that none of it was Lexi's fault—that Travis was nothing but a player and a misogynist—she wasn't looking forward to being the bearer of bad news. From the little that Jamie had confessed to Lexi, she really thought their relationship had some kind of future and this revelation might put an end to that. Lexi continued to rinse her dress with warm soapy water before wringing out the fabric and holding it under the hand dryer. She emerged damp and creased and took her seat opposite Jamie.

'I bet this means brunch is on the house,' said Lexi.

Jamie looked up from her phone, her face steely.

Foreboding washed over Lexi. She took in the scene again, noticing for the first time that the phone Jamie was holding was hers.

Lexi opened her mouth to speak, but no words came.

'You fucked him!' Jamie spat, the shadow of her father's face crossing briefly over her fine features.

Lexi, unaccustomed to Jamie swearing, recoiled as if she'd been slapped. 'What? No! Why would you even…'

'"That move you pulled on me last night really hurt, I'm still in pain",' recited Jamie, in a grotesque impersonation of Lexi.

'Uh, yeah. That's what I was about to tell you before this shit happened,' said Lexi, indicating her ruined dress. 'Last night, I went over there, and I don't know why it happened… One minute we were having a drink and the next minute…'

'You were fucking my boyfriend!' Jamie opened Lexi's messages and shoved the phone across the table. '"Poor baby, I'll go easier on you next time",' quoted Jamie bitterly.

Lexi looked down at the screen, taking in Travis' reply.

'His name flashed up while I was wiping tomato juice off it,' said Jamie, shaking her head. 'So original having your birthday as your passcode.'

'Jamie, look. We need to press pause here. I need to tell you what really happened. I did not have sex with Travis.'

'I wonder how Ethan will feel about this,' asked Jamie, twisting her mouth scornfully.

Lexi felt as though she'd been plunged underwater as Jamie collected her belongings.

'You can't leave. We need to sort this out,' blurted Lexi. 'I went over there for a drink, yes, but… well, he kind of tricked me into it…'

Jamie rolled her eyes.

'And then while I was there, he was hitting on me and I guess I rejected him, so he overpowered me into some fucking police hold, and…'

Lexi could hear how crazy she sounded, but what else could she say?

'And…' She searched her mind frantically. 'And I didn't know he was your boyfriend!'

Jamie placed her palms down on the table and stood. She leaned close. 'Well, I know who your boyfriend is,' she said and strode away.

Lexi sat frozen, replaying the last couple of minutes over on a sickening loop. After weeks of justifying her secrecy and lies to Ethan, it was all about to come crashing down for something she didn't do. What would Jamie do? She could be headed to Ethan's house now. When Lexi's phone started ringing, she was so deep in thought that she didn't register it belonging to her. It was nothing but a persistent noise in the periphery. When she noticed the woman at the next table glaring at her, she snapped back into reality. It was Linh calling.

'Hey, Linh.'

'Hey? Hey? Lexi, what the fuck?' demanded Linh.

'What?'

'I went over to your house with flowers to surprise you, and Ethan told me you were out for brunch, with me!'

Lexi's mouth fell open and the word, 'fuck,' fell out.

'Yeah, fuck. *What* the fuck?'

'What did you say?'

'I said I must have stuffed up. That I thought I was meant to pick you up for brunch,' said Linh.

Lexi exhaled. 'Did he buy it?'

'He started laughing. Said we must have been smashed last night when we made our plans.'

Lexi covered her face with her hand.

'What the fuck is going on? Why are you using me as an alibi? Where are you? Where were you last night?'

Lexi remained silent, unable to decipher her life. She scrunched her eyes tighter as each second passed.

'That's what I thought,' said Linh and hung up.

The waiter approached with two waffle-laden plates and set them down.

'My friend had to leave, can I please get the bill?' said Lexi.

'Look, I'm really sorry. It's only my second day here and…'

Lexi held up a hand. 'It's fine.'

The woman fell silent but remained standing there.

'The bill?' prompted Lexi.

'Oh! No, I mean, you don't have to…'

Lexi stood and strode away muttering a thanks before the waiter could finish.

As she walked, her heart fought its containment in her ribcage. Her insides twisted, pushing everything up to a bottleneck at her throat. In the driver's seat, she fumbled the keys and scrambled to retrieve them with shaking hands. She sat upright, took a deep breath and willed herself to get it together before successfully guiding the key into the ignition and starting the engine.

When she pulled up in front of Ethan's house, she scanned the street for Jamie's car. Maybe she had been and gone? Once inside the house, she listened.

'Ethan? Lucas?' she called into the silence.

Then she remembered, they were out watching one of the cousins play basketball. She walked to the kitchen and sat at the bench, clutching her phone as if it somehow held all the answers. Had Jamie made it here before Ethan had left? Surely, he wouldn't have kept the plans with his brother if an irate stranger had turned up telling tales of infidelity? She had to assume that Jamie's threats were empty. An overreaction to a colossal misunderstanding that she could sort out. Once Jamie had cooled down, she would see reason.

She thought about Linh. Imagined her standing on the doorstep holding flowers. Lexi had been so preoccupied with herself that she'd neglected her best friend. And yet, even when faced with Lexi's lies, Linh's first instinct had been to cover for her. But how could she explain the situation without outing herself completely? Without going back to the very beginning and trying to justify every ill-conceived decision she'd made?

The ticking of the kitchen clock seemed deafening in the quiet of the empty house. Lexi set down her phone and rested her face in her hands. After last night's encounter with Travis her first instinct had been to run home to Ethan. To the man who had shown her nothing but kindness since the moment they'd met. In the beginning, she had justified her lies by reasoning that camming was providing the financial means for her to leave him. To extract herself from a life that she was unprepared for. It was as if she had walked into a prefabricated marriage complete with a child, having desired neither. Like she was being pressed into a Justine-shaped space that she couldn't fill. Lexi looked up at the clock, it would be ages until Ethan and Lucas returned. She had never felt so alone and needed desperately to offload to someone.

Lexi made herself a coffee in lieu of eating and headed upstairs to change out of her damp dress. The last thing she had eaten was her birthday cake, in a previous life it seemed. Seated at the small desk in the bedroom, she opened her laptop and composed an email to Clive. He was the only person she could think to share her troubles with. In a way, he wasn't even real to her. Just a name on a screen, in an alternate reality. It was because of this disconnection that she was able to share the truth with him.

She told him of her fast-tracked relationship with Ethan, of her increasing suspicion that he was still in love with his wife. About the loss of her job at the café and the humiliating and fruitless job-hunt that followed. Then, how she had been dazzled by the glamour and excitement of camming at a time when she'd felt stagnant. She even surprised herself by realising that her need to tap into her own sexuality had come at a time when the world was projecting on her a role of wife and mother. Camming had been a rebellion. A means of proving to herself that there was more to her than met the eye.

And then along came Travis. Young and handsome and unencumbered. One-dimensional and predictable, sure, but at the time it hardly seemed to matter. Travis held up a mirror and reflected only the most exciting parts of her. The parts that were fading into the background in her life with Ethan. She told Clive about her weak attempts at propriety, all while craving Travis to lead her astray. How she had felt bold and self-assured until he had come to her chatroom uninvited. She explained how shocked she'd been when he overpowered her, seemingly to prove a point. Reminding her that even if she was unwilling to give herself, that he could simply take what he wanted from her, not that he would. Because, of course, he was a nice guy. A good man. A cop.

Silent tears streaked Lexi's face as her fingers feverishly

deciphered the mess in her head. As Lexi pressed send, the solution to everything came floating up to the surface. She could see now that she had to try to build a deeper connection with Ethan, that she had been immature and unappreciative of him. Distant and guarded while resenting the same characteristics in him. All she needed to do to turn things around was to stop camming, stop lying and be present in her reality. To open herself to Ethan and hope that he followed suit.

She would concoct a story to mend things with Linh and cut Jamie and the others loose. She could pretend that none of it had happened and slip back into her life with the newfound perspective that relationships required work.

Lexi picked up her phone and texted Margot, telling her that she'd had a change of heart and would no longer be camming. She thanked her for the opportunity and wished her well before switching off her phone for the first time since she'd gotten it. Leaning back in her chair, Lexi felt lighter. She heard the front door click and walked to the top of the stairs to see Ethan removing Lucas' sandals in the entry hall below. Standing there a moment, she appreciated the quiet beauty of him, the way the strength of his body was juxtaposed by every gentle movement, the soft kindness of his face as he muttered something inaudible to his son. She bounded down the stairs and he turned to look up at her. Skipping the last step, Lexi leapt into his arms, all but bowling him over in the process.

'Again!' Lucas squealed.

'What a welcome,' said Ethan, setting her down.

'I missed you,' said Lexi. She crouched down to Lucas. 'How was the basketball game, mate?' she asked.

'I ate popcorn,' said Lucas.

Lexi laughed and stood but remained clutching Lucas' hand.

'How was brunch? Did you find each other?' asked Ethan.

Lexi tilted her head, confused. 'Oh! Yes, Linh called, we found each other. So silly,' she said, slapping her forehead.

'Want me to make you a cino mate?' she asked Lucas.

He nodded. 'Yes peas.'

'Where are your flowers?' asked Ethan, following them to the kitchen.

'Flowers?'

'From Linh. Huge, spiky, native monstrosities,' Ethan prompted, emptying his pockets out onto the bench.

It took Lexi a second to think. 'Fuck,' she mouthed over Lucas' head.

'What?'

'I put them on the roof of the car so I could open the door. They must have slid off when I drove away.'

Ethan laughed. 'Oh, you,' he said, shaking his head.

'Oh me,' she repeated, turning away from him.

THIRTY

LEXI'S skin felt hot to the touch. Although she was fastidious about sunscreen, it had slipped her mind while at the beach with Ethan and Lucas and she had gone all afternoon without reapplication. After her nightmarish encounter with Jamie and the debacle with Linh, Lexi had been content to dive headfirst into the surety of her place with Ethan and had lost herself in a way she hadn't been able to in years. Now, she sat on the sofa next to Ethan, wearing a camisole and pyjama shorts, rubbing argan oil into her stinging skin and feeling a profound sense of calm.

Noticing he was looking over at her, she placed the bottle of oil onto the coffee table and said, 'Look at this!' and lifted her shorts to reveal a blatant tan line across her hip.

Ethan traced the line with his finger before leaning down to follow the path with his tongue. The gesture made goosebumps bloom down the length of her body, and she shuddered pleasurably.

'Sorry,' he said, sitting upright and positioning himself a little further away.

'No. Don't apologise,' she said, her eyes flicking towards the blissfully silent baby monitor. 'I liked it.'

He smiled into his drink and took a sip. As he leaned in closer to her, condensation from his glass dripped on her leg. His mouth was cold and wet as it traced a path from her lips to her neck and down to her collarbone. Brushing the strap off her shoulder to expose one breast, Ethan paused to take another sip of his drink. His eyes sparkled mischievously as he rolled an ice cube around on his tongue. Lexi braced. Having melted the ice, he leaned down and took her nipple in his mouth. She gasped. He sought out her eyes for confirmation of her enjoyment and, having received it, brushed the other strap off so that her camisole fell to her waist. He took another sip of his drink, captured an ice block with his tongue and again, rolled it around. Raising an eyebrow, he placed down his glass and dropped the ice block into his hand. Lexi's eyes widened. He took her left nipple into his freezing mouth but this time he replicated the sensation by sliding the ice block in a circular motion around her right; his free hand snaked around the small of her back.

He pulled back. 'Your skin is radiating heat,' he said.

'That's what I've been trying to tell you,' she said, her voice breathless.

'Let me help you,' he said, adjusting some cushions, and repositioned her so she was lying down.

Lexi was unaccustomed to being commanded. She wanted to take over, wanted to pull him into her but she was so curious about this new dynamic that she resisted the urge and complied. Ethan leaned over to cup his glass as one might do to a mug of hot chocolate in the cold. Once satisfied, he placed a hand either side of her still tender neck and ran his hands over her breasts, her ribcage and down to her waist. Here, he paused before removing her camisole and shorts in one fluid motion. She lay there, her nakedness a stark contrast to his fully clothed form. She waited, unsure of what he would do next, her body pulsing with the wonder of it. He picked up the bottle of oil from the coffee table and squeezed a generous measure into his palm. Setting it down, he rubbed his hands together and took up her wrist, massaging oil down the length of her arm, his strokes long and fluid. Pausing to take each of her nipples in his mouth in turn, he blew on them while massaging the other arm. Lexi sucked in a breath as the cold air hit her wet skin, her back involuntarily arching. He let out a low knowing laugh and Lexi was surprised by the nervous anticipation that possessed her. Bypassing her breasts, he circled her pink-blushed stomach before setting to work on her legs, beginning with her calves and then moving up to her thighs. Each firm flourish of his fingers ventured higher and higher until they fleetingly brushed the growing slick between her legs.

Lexi's desire was urgent, but she was so astonished by what was taking place that she remained silent, fascinated by what he might do next. Taking up the bottle once more, Ethan poured oil over her breasts in a slow drip, the excess running off in rivulets in alternating directions. As he inched closer to her, Lexi could see the unmistakable outline of his desire. She balled her hands into fists, stopping herself from reaching for him as he circled her breasts, occasionally breaking rhythm to pull gently on her nipples. Over and over, her back arched, the jolt surprising her each time. Next, he dripped a line from her throat, along her sternum to her stomach and pubic bone. Lexi looked down to see oil pooling in her belly button and laughed. He traced the drips with his hand, pausing with a flat palm on her stomach before swirling his hand in a half circle to change the direction of his fingers. He scooped between her legs, massaging firmly with the heel of his palm before running his fingers up and down. This motion progressed to include an occasional open and close of rigid fingers which captured her swelling flesh.

Lexi eyes were rolling back in her head and she could not dissuade them.

'Okay?' Ethan asked.

All she could do was nod.

Without stopping, Ethan leaned over, grabbed his drink and took a sip. Brandishing an ice cube between his teeth, he lowered himself down.

'No,' said Lexi.

'No?' he said, halting. The ice cube bulged in his cheek.

Lexi let out an indecisive groan. 'Yes, actually, yes.'

He smiled and continued his descent.

The moment the ice met her body, Lexi was struck by the sharpness of it. She wasn't sure if it was pleasurable or painful, just startling. He moaned softly, as if tasting something decadent and forbidden and then his fingers were inside her, rhythmically beckoning. His free hand moved up to her waist and as his fingers penetrated her with growing force, he mirrored the beat by pressing down slightly on her hip bone. Lexi was cast adrift, as if she'd lost the thread of a conversation she had no interest in. Her hands found her breasts, and she mimicked the tugging motion Ethan had used on her nipples earlier. Lexi's body twitched with spasmodic jolts and she heard a low humming note that she didn't have the presence of mind to attribute to her own vocal cords. As her body was consumed by the sheer force of her orgasm, she thrust her ribcage upwards and was surprised to find in the aftermath that her entire torso was lifted like a bridge, anchored only by her shoulders and tail bone. Ethan's hands, still in position, guided her down slowly to rest once more on the sofa. His fingers slid out of her. After a moment, Lexi opened her eyes and blinked into awareness of her surroundings. Everything seemed vivid and her body pulsed warmly. She made to sit up, but he placed his hand on her chest and whispered, 'Stay.'

He stood to remove his clothes before kneeling between her legs. Picking up one glistening leg, he scooped it up onto his shoulder and nudged the other off the sofa, grounding her foot. She reached for a cushion which he placed underneath her lifted hips. Running his hand over her slick stomach to coat his fingers in residual oil, he took himself in hand, his gaze unwavering. 'You are the most...' he began.

'So are you,' she said, urgently.

He gently nudged himself into her, the contraction of her recent orgasm causing a bittersweet resistance. Pausing, he asked, 'Is this okay? Are you comfortable?'

'Better than okay,' she said, placing a hand on his hip to coax him in.

He dropped his head and let out a husky breath, pressing himself into her.

At first the pace was glacial. Ethan turned his cheek against Lexi's calf, kissing and gently biting it as he moved. Her fingers instinctively migrated towards augmenting her own pleasure, but Ethan placed his hand over hers and asked, 'May I?'

'You may,' she laughed, mimicking his formality, and watched as he licked his thumb and index finger before positioning them and gently pinching.

She tittered and he stopped.

'No good?'

'So good. Don't stop,' she said.

He gave a sly half-smile and settled into the movement.

Lexi rolled her shoulders back, making herself more comfortable and let coherent thought wash away like grains of sand in a tide. The sensation of relinquishing control of her pleasure felt exhilarating and reckless. Ethan once again turned and pressed his face into her leg, his sideways glance locked on her. As the intensity and pace increased, his hot breath was on her, his jaw locked in a restrained bite which looked like a stifled scream. Lexi threw her head back, enraptured.

'Hey,' said Ethan, his voice a throaty whisper.

Lexi opened her eyes.

'Are you close?' he asked.

She nodded.

'Resist it,' he said.

Lexi's eyes grew wide. 'I don't think—'

'Resist.'

He slowed his pace but increased the pressure of his fingers on her clit, all the while shaking his head "no".

Lexi was on the edge of a precipice, teetering precariously, trying in vain to delay an inevitable fall. Her chest rose and fell though no breath passed through her body.

'Don't come, Lexi. Don't you come,' he said, forcefully.

He let go of her leg, pressing into her deeper as he reached forward to encapsulate both breasts in his large hand. Lexi's body was turning back onto itself in an ecstatic loop. She had ceased to exist in a reality where her mind could be counted on for anything and so succumbed to the unrelenting current of pleasure pulling her under. Lexi could just register a primeval growl rising from Ethan's throat as they came in unison.

When Lexi looked back on this moment, a few minutes would always remain unaccounted for. The next thing she knew, Ethan was slumped on top of her, his skin goosebumped and clammy, his chest heaving from his exertions. Lexi's mouth remained open in partial disbelief. They lay there for a time in the quiet of the house, the distant whir of the dishwasher and the low chorus of cicadas outside accompanying their breathing.

As the ache in her neck returned, Lexi shifted her position, inadvertently rousing Ethan from the entrancement of the moment. He lifted his head from her shoulder to look at her.

'What was that?' she asked, awestruck.

He cast his eyes downward as he brought himself up into a seated position and rummaged around the knot of their discarded clothing to find his trunks. 'I, ah. I'm sorry, I guess I...'

She placed a steadying hand on his thigh, surprised at the about-face of his demeanour.

'It was *amazing*,' she said, putting extra emphasis on the last word.

His shoulders relaxed and although his face remained dipped, Lexi saw a smile creep across his lips.

'What I mean is, where did it come from?' she went on.

Ethan played with a loose thread in the hem of his underwear but remained silent.

'It's just that, you've never...' Lexi searched for the right words but came up short.

Ethan reached for his glass and downed the remainder of its contents. 'There's something I haven't told you,' he began.

Lexi, feeling inappropriately naked, scooped her pyjamas from the floor and stood to climb into them. The leather sofa gleamed greasily in the low light. Taking in Ethan's grave expression, Lexi worried that whatever he had to confess wasn't something she wanted to know.

'Oh my God, look at the sofa!' she exclaimed.

She disappeared into the kitchen and returned with a cleaning cloth and spray. 'Get up, I just have to…'

Ethan laughed and the tension of the moment dissolved. He stood and smiled down as she cleaned away the evidence of their slippery tryst.

Setting the cloth and spray on the coffee table, she sat, relieved to see that Ethan's pained expression had been replaced by something lighter. He smiled at her for a moment before leaning in to deposit a kiss on her forehead. 'It's about Justine,' he began slowly.

Lexi looked down at her pink thighs.

'We weren't in a good place when she died. Our relationship, I mean. It was, threadbare, I don't know, shaky, precarious.'

Lexi fought to keep her brow smooth as she tried to make sense of his words.

'But after the car accident… the police, they gave me a bag with her belongings in it, and… but wait, I need to go back a step.' He swept a hand roughly over his face. 'It's embarrassing,' he added quietly.

Lexi placed an encouraging hand on Ethan's shoulder.

'I guess Justine and I were not what you would call sexually compatible. She wasn't all that interested and when we did occasionally do it, she would preface it by saying things like "Be quick" or "Make sure you don't take too long".'

'Ethan, that's awful.'

He let out a sad laugh. 'I guess I always felt like I was some kind of inconvenience. Another chore on a very long list, you know?'

Lexi nodded.

'She made me feel like some kind of pervert. She even called me that once when I tried to go down on her.'

Ethan's voice had become so quiet that Lexi had to lean in closer to hear him.

'That's hardly a fetish, Ethan,' she said.

'Well…' he said, giving a resigned shrug.

'And even if you did have a fetish, surely you should be able to tell your fucking wife about it,' said Lexi.

Ethan met her eyes for the first time and gave her a half-smile.

'But what does all this have to do with the accident?' she prompted.

'After the funeral, I went through her phone and found out she was planning to leave. There were all these texts between her and her best friend. She described me…' He shook his head at the memory.

'Go on, it's okay,' said Lexi.

'I don't really want to repeat exactly what was said, but… she made out like I was some kind of sex pest. Like I never stopped hounding her. Which wasn't true, by the way.' He threw his hands up for emphasis. 'To be honest, I stopped initiating because the rejection was getting harder and harder to deal with and then one day, she was… gone.'

They sat in silence for a long while. The finality of Justine's departure from life hung in the air like an unanswered question.

Finally, Ethan spoke. 'And then you came along, and it was such a surprise. And you were so… that first night you came over. I got more head that night than I'd had in the last five years.'

Lexi, whose eyes had begun to well, let out a choked laugh.

Ethan smiled broadly but it faded fast. 'I'm so fucking terrified of doing the wrong thing that sometimes, I do nothing,' he blurted. 'I'm so afraid that you'll get fed up and want to leave too. So, I wait, doing nothing, hoping you won't find me as tiresome as she did. And I don't know… since you moved in, things have felt different. It's like you're somewhere else sometimes and I worry that all you see now is Lucas' dad and not the guy that you used to make coffees for. And when I look at you…'

Lexi, whose gaze had fallen to her lap again, lifted her head to face him.

'I feel wild. You've got this energy about you that I want to be close to. Want to be… inside of.'

Lexi's eyes widened. If anything, she had felt increasingly invisible to him. Could it be that what she had perceived as indifference was actually his self-censored desire?

'Let me get this straight. Your wife shattered your confidence so thoroughly that you feel like your sexual needs are a burden to any woman?'

Ethan flinched but remained silent.

'Look. I'm going to shut this shit down here. I do not want to speak ill of the dead, or whatever, but if Justine didn't appreciate you then that was her loss. Those moves you just pulled were… that was the hottest fucking shit I've ever experienced. And if you come at me with that every damn day, it will not be too much.'

Ethan blinked rapidly. 'You didn't feel like I was experimenting on you for my own gratification?' he asked, cautiously.

'Yeah, that's exactly what it felt like,' she said.

Ethan's expression turned grave.

'And that's what I fucking loved about it.'

THIRTY-ONE

WHEN Lexi looked back on this moment, she would realise her error. In her post-coital stupor, she switched on her phone in order to switch off her morning alarm, not realising that it wouldn't have disturbed her anyway. When she did this, her phone lit up with text messages from a life that she had fooled herself was over.

From Travis she received a predictable, "What the fuck did you tell Jamie?" which made her do little more than roll her eyes.

It was the reply from Margot however that turned her skin cold and made her curse her naivety. It simply said, "I understand if you wish to move on but if you refer to your contract, it clearly states that a notice period of two weeks is required. If you wish to leave without notice, we are entitled to two weeks of projected earnings based on your average revenue."

Lexi knew that the figure in question would be in the tens of thousands and was money that, after paying off her credit card and the remainder of her car loan, she simply didn't have. She had no other choice but to see out the next two weeks before beginning her life on the straight and narrow. She knew she could do with the cash, especially if she had a stint of unemployment ahead of her, but the idea of clicking that broadcast button and feigning enjoyment for an audience when her heart wasn't in it was almost too much to bear.

She glanced over at the sleeping silhouette of Ethan and her heart panged. There was no other way.

~

The next morning, perhaps sensing the shift in Lexi's mood, Ethan tentatively orbited her as they went about their morning routine.

'Is everything okay? Last night, I mean. Are we okay?' he asked, haltingly.

Lexi, who had been so thoroughly lost in her own thoughts, took a moment to register the implication of his anxiety. Her face softened. 'Oh, of course. Better than okay. It's just work. I'm not looking forward to it.'

'Oh,' he said, relieved and simultaneously surprised. 'I thought you were really enjoying it over there.'

'I guess there's some staff bullshit that I didn't realise was there,' she said. 'I'm thinking I might not stick around. I might see what else is out there.'

'Oh, okay, sure. Well, anywhere would be lucky to have you.'

Lucas appeared by his side brandishing Vegemite fingers. 'Grubby, Dadda,' he said.

Lexi, closest to the drawers, took out a cloth and wet it under the faucet. She made to hand it to Ethan, but Lucas extended his chubby hands towards her and stuck out his smudged chin. Lexi laughed and squatted down to his level.

'I had so much fun at the beach yesterday,' she said, wiping off each finger in turn.

Lucas nodded but then his expression became worried. 'Where are my shells?'

'I washed them for you, they're drying in the laundry,' said Lexi. 'You know, I was thinking. We could decorate them, if you want. With paint and glitter? I used to decorate rocks when I was a kid,' said Lexi.

'Together?' asked Lucas.

'Yeah, together,' she said, feeling her heart swell unexpectedly. 'If Daddy doesn't mind, maybe I can pick you up early from childcare this afternoon and we can do it before dinner?'

Lucas looked up at Ethan with imploring eyes.

'Of course,' he said.

Ethan smiled down at them for a long while until Lexi made a face at him and stood.

'We'd better get going, mate,' said Ethan.

Ethan leaned in to plant a lingering kiss on Lexi's cheek. 'I love you,' he whispered into her ear.

She pulled back to seek out his eyes and then four jewel-like words tumbled from her mouth. 'I love you too.'

After they'd left, Lexi floated upstairs to her laptop. Everything would work out fine if she could get through the next two weeks. She logged into her email to find a reply from Clive. Resisting the urge to read over the reams of her emotion-fuelled confession to Clive, Lexi instead focused on the succinct response.

"Jojo, you have been assaulted by this man and it must be reported."

Lexi read and reread the email as if trying to solve a word jumble. She wasn't sure how long she sat there like that, unblinking, but the next thing she knew, she was running late. During her drive to work one word thrummed in her head. *Assaulted.*

~

When she arrived at Camnation, Lexi felt like a teenager creeping into the house after curfew. The last thing she wanted was to be confronted by Margot. After receiving her text message the night before, Lexi had replied to say that she'd comply with the required notice period and would report for duty in the morning. Although Margot had been nothing but professional in her response, Lexi couldn't help transposing some of her own self-doubt onto her boss and she worried that she was being perceived as feeble.

Lexi crossed the kitchen and living area, keeping her eyes trained on the stairs as she moved swiftly through. As she placed her foot on the first step, Margot appeared, framed by her office door.

'We'll be sorry to see you go,' she said, and her tone was kinder than Lexi had expected it would be.

Lexi stepped down to face her and gave a sad smile. 'I feel like

I'm leading a double life,' she admitted, quietly.

Margot nodded. 'In my experience, living your truth and risking losing a few friends over it is the only sustainable option,' she said.

Lexi considered this. 'That's why I'm leaving. So, I can align myself with the version of the truth I've been telling.'

Margot looked sceptical but remained silent as Lexi climbed the stairs.

Having arrived later than normal, the dressing room was unoccupied by Cherry this morning. Lexi was relieved to be spared from their encounter. She wondered what Jamie might have told her and shame lapped at her, eroding her resolve. As Lexi quickly dressed in an outfit she had worn before, she turned over Clive's email in her mind. *You have been assaulted and it must be reported.* From the moment Lexi had read Clive's words, a persistent thought had plagued her. Like most women, she had a laundry list of inappropriate actions perpetrated against her by various jerks, starting from her early teens. With the arrival of Clive's summation, Lexi knew that with no consequences, Travis would be free to harm others in the same way he had harmed her. Others perhaps who possessed a less robust resilience than she had cultivated over the years. But what hope did Lexi have of officially reporting something that would be impossible to prove? Against someone who was a federal police officer, no less. She felt sick over it but had no time to slip into the self-pity that beckoned. She had a show to put on.

With just a few minutes until broadcast, Lexi sat and recalled the advice Veronica had bestowed on her first day. *Just be yourself as you are on your best, happiest day.* Lexi supposed it was a happy day. She and Ethan had exchanged 'I love you' for the first time, and with Lexi's fears over Justine's claim on Ethan's heart mollified, she was enjoying a profound sense of certainty regarding their relationship. Still, when she logged into the Camnation user interface, her mirrored reflection looked grave. She arranged her face into a sarcastic smile, mocking herself, before dialling it back several shades and clicking the broadcast button.

As Lexi waited for guests to arrive in her chatroom, she marvelled at how little time had passed since her last broadcast, though it seemed like a lifetime. A few regulars popped up and she was heartened by their presence, but it was the advent of ChivalryAlive that comforted her most. She paused to send Clive a private message but was so choked with gratitude she could only manage emojis to convey her sentiments.

Although she tried to get into the character of Jojo Cortado, Lexi was a cheap imitation rather than a convincing knock off. She tried her best to remain focused, reminding herself of the bigger picture. When today was done, she would be one day closer to beginning her life beside Ethan. But when TheCovertWolf popped up as a guest in her room, Lexi's bravado drained. Travis was prowling at the perimeter of her tolerance, and she was unnerved. As her fingers hovered above the touchpad, poised to block him, he tipped for the most expensive item on her menu, making herself orgasm. Afterwards, Lexi would commend herself for one thing only, her impassive reaction. Without acknowledging him individually, she addressed the group saying, '*Someone* has very generously tipped for an orgasm. But you know, I've always felt like this system is all a bit backwards. I'm the one having such a good time. Surely, it's me who should be tipping you?'

She looked down, running a finger underneath the neckline of her dress in a show of bashfulness, all the while panicking over whether she could legitimately perform the act. What if she was unable to bring herself to climax? Would she have to fake it? Would they even believe that? She imagined her audience turning against her, the thought of it augmenting her panic.

Bypassing the KY Jelly and reaching for the argan oil, Lexi extracted herself from reality and was transplanted into the memory of last night's revelatory experience with Ethan. As her fingers set to work, she smiled into the thought that she was replicating Ethan's movements. The open palmed pressure, the long sweeping strokes, the gentle compression of flesh between rigid fingers. At some point, Lexi was able to relinquish her anxiety and slip into the pleasure of it. For several moments afterwards she breathed heavily, enjoying the release. As her awareness returned in increments, she was able to pull down her hem, lean towards the keyboard and block TheCovertWolf.

She smiled into the webcam, thanking guests for their tips and replying to their questions and comments, all the while trying to decide how to fill in the time. Coming to her aid, ChivalryAlive proposed she begin a countdown which would culminate in the reading of not only her latest story but the entirety of her back catalogue of stories. He suggested that perhaps not everyone had been with her since the beginning and would be interested in learning the origin story and subsequent adventures of her protagonist. Putting it to the group, Lexi was surprised to find that many guests were in favour of the idea. And although she did notice an unusual number of guests departing her chatroom and even received one crass comment from someone who hadn't tipped at all, she did her best to shut out the negativity and focus on remaining in character. As the broadcast progressed Lexi slipped into her old familiar enjoyment of the experience. Here in the sanctuary of these four walls, with her motley assortment of broken souls, she was at ease.

When they reached the countdown target, Lexi settled in to read the collection of stories she'd written in the two weeks she'd been camming. Before she began, she opened her mouth to rattle off an assortment of disclaimers as to the quality of her work and the limited time in which she had to compose it but stopped herself. Instead, in a slow, measured voice, she read. By the time Lexi reached her tenth instalment she had realised two things. 1. Together, her stories read like the chapters of a novel; and 2. Her protagonist needed a villain to overcome.

After thanking her guests and ending her broadcast, she sent a private message to ChivalryAlive. It read, "Clive, I think my stories could become a novel." His reply was almost instant, "Glad you've finally realised."

Back in the dressing room, Lexi smiled at a couple of cam models who were chatting but didn't engage with them. She pulled out her phone to text Linh but instead was confronted by a message from Travis. "Can't believe you blocked me today. If you're mad about Jamie, don't be. I managed to smooth things over and it's not like you're not with someone too. If you won't tell, I won't. When can I see you again?"

Lexi stared at the message, incredulous. Was there no end to this man's arrogance? She seethed. Replying, she tapped her phone with such force that the two women in the dressing room paused their conversation to exchange raised eyebrows. "I'm going to make this very clear because I realise you're not very bright. I have no interest in seeing you, ever. And I am considering reporting you to the police after what you pulled on me at your house the other night."

She pressed send and, enjoying the feeling of assertiveness, added. "You assaulted me, and I have the injuries to prove it."

His reply came back instant and venomous. "Don't get pissed off because I put an end to your cock-teasing. I didn't even hurt you. The police? They'd laugh in your face."

Indignation and outrage hammered in Lexi's skull as she changed her clothes, and she tried to calm her breathing. As she walked out to her car, she typed out a message to Linh. "I can explain everything. Please don't be mad. Can we please catch up?"

Lexi wasn't sure how she would explain anything, but she had no intention of losing Linh's friendship so she had to do something. But what about Jamie? Lexi's initial reaction had been to walk away from Jamie, just like Jamie had walked away from her in Hamilton. Because even if Jamie did believe her side of the Travis story, where did her friend fit into her new life with Ethan? Lexi would be forced to keep her hidden from him or else convince her to corroborate a fabricated backstory, which was at odds with her decision to end her duplicity. The more Lexi turned the problem over in her mind, the more ensnared she became.

~

Lexi and Lucas were sitting at the kitchen table when Ethan returned home. The surface, covered in layers of newsprint, displayed their work in progress of decorated shells. Having painted them, they were now engrossed in a collaborative effort which involved Lexi coating the shells with glue and Lucas dumping fists full of glitter on top. The effect was gaudy and grotesque and Lucas could not have appeared more thrilled with the results. As Ethan walked in, Lucas picked up his closest creation and waved it proudly in the air, sending a flurry of sparkles into the air.

'It's like Studio 54 in here,' said Ethan, waving a hand through the air.

'Blame it on the boogie?' said Lexi.

Ethan laughed heartily.

'You're home early,' she said, brushing a thin layer of glue onto an abalone shell.

'Not really,' he replied.

Lexi looked up at the clock and shrieked. 'Oh no! I meant to start dinner. I guess we got caught up,' she said, indicating the mess.

Ethan leaned down to kiss her and Lucas in turn.

'Oh no, you're covered now,' said Lexi, rubbing at Ethan's glittery cheek and making it worse.

'You guys finish up; I'll get dinner started. Great artists must not be disturbed,' he said, tickling Lucas' neck.

'Okay, thanks. We're nearly done here anyway,' said Lexi. She turned to Lucas. 'Shall we count how many we have left?'

He nodded but looked nervous.

'Together? One, two, three, four,' they sang.

THIRTY-TWO

LEXI'S chest heaved as she blinked awake. The warm, solid outline of Ethan breathed evenly in the darkness. Since Lexi had been reunited with Jamie, the nightmares which had plagued her for the last decade had vanished. But tonight, she had been plunged into a monstrous funhouse in which Jamie morphed and melded, spinning in front of her as she tried desperately to bring the dizzying blur to a stop. She grabbed at the figure, dislodging great glittery chunks that crumbled and blew out of her hands until there was nothing left but a terrifying quiet which screamed into her ears.

Next to her, Ethan sighed in his sleep and turned away from her. Lexi, laying on her back staring up at the ceiling, waited for the last threads of terror to dissipate. She wondered what the dream meant and then chastised herself, recalling how eager her mother had been to interpret her dreams when she was a child. It was before Monique had married Darrin, and the little kids had come along, and were some of the only times Lexi had felt her mother's attention fixed upon her. Lexi had revelled in it. So much so that on mornings when she had nothing to report, she would lay in bed trying to concoct something to tell her. It usually backfired—Monique could sniff out a lie like a bloodhound—but Lexi, always desperate to hold her mother's interest, would try anyway. Perhaps it was here that Lexi's propensity for storytelling had been born.

Lexi fingered the scar tissue on her forearm then turned to spoon Ethan. She ran a hand up and down the smooth warmth of his muscular back, his familiar scent comforting her. She wanted to be closer to him, to feel her bare skin against his. Careful not to wake him, she slipped out of her pyjamas and pressed herself up against him. Relief washed over her. Resting her cheek against his shoulder, she exhaled and closed her eyes, ready for sleep to take her again. He stirred and shifted slightly, his movement brushing her nipples. Lexi emitted a small and involuntary moan, rousing him. Ethan placed his hand over hers where it rested on his stomach, her fingers brushing the soft hair below his belly button. Her hand felt small and delicate compared to his as he guided it beneath the waistband of his shorts. She took him in hand, marvelling at how instantaneously his body responded. He manoeuvred her hand up and down, setting a slow and deliberate pace and Lexi had a sudden pleasurable vision of him conducting this practiced movement alone. Releasing his shadow grip, he threaded his hand backwards to explore between her legs, coating his fingers in her arousal. Then, he stopped with his fingers rigid and crooked slightly, their tips pressed static against her clit. For a moment Lexi wondered if he had fallen back asleep. Her hand stopped moving but remained encircled as if awaiting instruction. He pressed himself up into it and she understood. She writhed against his fingers in a slow circular motion. They fell into rhythm and when Lexi tilted her hips forward and up so that his fingers were enveloped, Ethan thrust deep into her strengthening grip. She moved to once again writhe against the tips, her breath in Ethan's ear growing increasingly husky. There was something so alluring about being positioned behind him, something converse to their usual dynamic, that Lexi felt as though she was inhabiting Ethan's body rather than her own. She felt powerful, and he fragile, as her movements evolved from fluid to jarring. The urgency of their stifled moans echoed around the quiet room as Lexi's frenzy peaked. Ethan, feeling her body convulsing down the length of him, shuddered into his own orgasm and then all was quiet save for their diminishing pants and the drumming of their hearts.

That morning, Lexi padded into the kitchen to find Ethan making breakfast for Lucas. She pressed her face into his nape and inhaled the fresh, soap-scent of him.

'I had the most amazing dream last night,' he said.

She could hear the smile in his voice.

'Mmm,' she agreed.

'What did you dream, Dadda?' asked Lucas.

They turned to smile at Lucas where he sat at the kitchen table, his top lip displaying a milk moustache.

Lexi grinned at Ethan. 'I'm going to get ready,' she said, walking out of the room.

As Lexi made her way upstairs, she reflected on her nocturnal interlude with Ethan. Having been conducted in the anonymity of darkness and with the absence of words, the entire experience had possessed a dream-like quality. A restorative remedy to the nightmare that preceded it. In the clarity of daytime, Lexi wondered if the extraction of Jamie from her waking life would result in a reprise of her nightmares. Until last night, the memory of them had faded, the distress they brought, how she was plagued and prayed upon by them. How they lurked.

Before stepping into the shower, Lexi composed a message on her phone to Jamie. She stared at the screen; the last message received from her was the one that came through while standing on Travis' doorstep. If only her friends hadn't been running late to meet her that night. Lexi typed, deleted and typed again, settling on the phrase. "I don't want to lose you again, please can we work this out?"

When Lexi emerged into the steam-filled bathroom, it was a reply from Linh and not Jamie which awaited her.

"Want to come over tonight so we can talk? Mum's going out."

~

When Ethan sprang into the bathroom to say goodbye, Lexi was posing in her lingerie, taking a photo of herself in the mirror for her Snapchat account. She jumped at the sight of him behind her and almost dropped the phone.

'Am I interrupting something?' he said, narrowing his eyes.

Lexi's cheeks pinked.

'I, ah… I was just… I was going to send a pic to you, while you're at work,' she heard herself saying.

Ethan's face opened into a look of fascination.

'Now it won't be a surprise anymore,' she muttered.

'I still want it. I'll forget I ever saw a thing, I promise,' he said. He stepped forward and pulled her gently towards him by the waistband of her underwear. He glanced down and looked as though he might pounce. 'I have to go,' he said, shaking his head to rouse himself. Giving her a quick kiss, he left, closing the door behind him. Lexi's heart laboured. *Too close.*

~

'Hey, I missed you yesterday,' said Cherry. 'Everything okay?'

'Yeah, fine. I was running a little late,' said Lexi, walking into the dressing room and putting down her bag.

'I thought you might have called in sick after your birthday weekend. I don't know about you, but as I'm getting older the hangovers are lasting two days. You should have seen me yesterday, I looked like a puffer fish, I had to put false eyelashes on to detract from it,' said Cherry, chuckling.

Lexi felt relieved. Jamie's scorn seemed, for now, to be contained. 'I wasn't too bad actually, I paced myself. How was the rest of your weekend?' she asked.

Cherry blew out her cheeks to mime vomiting and they both laughed. 'Anyway, I'd better run. Have a good show,' she said, giving Lexi an affectionate punch on the arm before walking out the door.

As Lexi zipped herself into a black wiggle dress, she felt a twinge of regret. When all this was over, she would never see Cherry or the others again. Making friends had never come easily to Lexi and the little circle she now found herself in was an unexpected gift. But how did this incongruous group of social misfits fit into her reality?

Grabbing a pair of slingbacks, Lexi made for the door and collided with Veronica. The woman teetered on her heels and burst into tears.

'Whoa, sorry. Are you okay? Am I running late?' said Lexi, confused at Veronica's presence in the dressing room.

'No, I finished my broadcast early,' said Veronica, slumping down onto the ottoman.

'Is everything okay, did something happen?' said Lexi, crouching down in front of her.

'It's so stupid,' sniffed Veronica. 'It's my own fault for checking my phone while I was live.'

She took a deep breath and leaned down to unfasten the buckle on her shoes. 'I've been seeing this guy. It's casual, just a bit of fun, I guess. But I like him. And my mum and her boyfriend are coming down from Brisbane, so I thought maybe…' She removed her shoe and made a circular swishing motion with it. Lexi nodded. 'Anyway, he told me that I was getting too serious, making him feel suffocated.'

'What a prick,' hissed Lexi.

Veronica nodded, her bottom lip beginning to quiver again. 'He broke up with me.'

'Over text message?'

Veronica nodded.

'Prick,' said Lexi again. 'Is it too early to say you're probably better off?'

Veronica smiled sadly. 'Oh my God, I'm going to make you late. And the room. It's a mess!'

Veronica jumped up, forgetting she only had on one shoe and lost her balance. She fell back down onto the ottoman with a comical squeal.

'It's okay,' said Lexi. 'I'll put all your things away.'

'Thanks, Jojo,' Veronica called out as Lexi hurried out the door.

~

Towards the end of Lexi's broadcast, she remembered the photo she had promised to send to Ethan and surreptitiously reached for her phone, just off camera. She sent it off with a quip about Ethan dispensing Viagra in the pharmacy with a hard on and continued with her show. When she saw the flash of his reply, she clicked to open the message. "You're spectacular, you do know that right? So dead here today. I'm coming to visit. Make me a coffee?"

Lexi's head was going to burst. Ethan was on his way to Poste-Haste Espresso. Trying desperately to hold focus on her viewers, she typed a reply saying that it was a terrible day to visit the café as they were short staffed, and she wouldn't be able to hang out. As she awaited his reply, eyes darting towards her phone every few seconds, B16_B00B5 tipped for a boob flash. Lexi wanted to scream. Halfway through her partial strip tease, Lexi saw a reply come through but couldn't interrupt her routine to read it.

Once the flash was complete and Lexi was redressed, she read his reply. He was going to meet her at the end of her shift. But Lexi was 20 minutes away from the café and would be ending her broadcast at Camnation when Ethan arrived there. She needed to head off before he had the chance to ask after her. Could she just walk out early, or should she make some excuse to Margot? Lexi thought of Veronica signing off early and wondered if Margot even noticed such things. Although, in Veronica's case it had only been five minutes, not the half hour that Lexi required. As the clock ticked, Lexi became cagey and distracted and it must have shown. When ChivalryAlive sent a private message asking if everything was alright, Lexi had no time to respond, choosing instead to announce her early departure. She apologised profusely, thankful that she didn't have a countdown in progress. The last thing she needed was a disgruntled mob ganging up on her at a time like this. When a few of her regulars expressed their disappointment, she promised to think up something special for them the following day. Once the transmission had ended, Lexi tore around the room gathering up her belongings and shoved them so hastily into the storage chest that it wouldn't close. She strode to the dressing room to discard her borrowed attire and climb back into her own clothes before creeping down the stairs and passed Margot's closed office door.

As she checked her rear vision mirror before reversing, Lexi saw the unmistakable figure of Travis Nolan climbing out of his car and striding towards her. She swore under her breath. As she turned the Mini around and made to leave, he called, 'Don't do anything stupid, Lexi!'

THIRTY-THREE

THE sound of teaspoons against ceramic was jarring to Lexi's ears as she slunk into Post-Haste Espresso to scan the crowded space, looking for Ethan. Confident she had beaten him, she took a moment to regain her breath as her heart hammered. What the hell was Travis doing turning up at Camnation to ambush her like that? The way he had used her real name chilled her. She peered out the front window of the café but there was no sign of Ethan. Feeling parched, she looked over at the self-serve water station on the far side of the bar and then back out the window. There was time. She hurried over and poured herself half a glass of water, threw it down her throat and then turned to see Ethan walking in. She stepped around to the service side of the bar, took up a nearby cloth and wiped the bench in front of her. From the corner of her eye, she saw the café's sleazy owner approaching. Waving at Ethan, she threw down the cloth and walked out from behind the bar as the owner exclaimed, 'Hey, what are you…?'

Lexi turned back towards him and waved. 'See you tomorrow!' she said brightly, before hurrying over to Ethan and hustling him back out onto the street.

Once outside the café Lexi turned to survey Ethan.

'Hello, you,' he said. 'It's nice in there. You didn't tell me about the big, fuck-off brassy number.'

In Lexi's current state of agitation, it took her a moment to register that he was referring to the espresso machine. 'Oh, yeah,' she said, trying to regain her composure. 'It's a Berezza Classic. It's a dream to use.'

'I was kinda hoping you'd make me a coffee. Things that bad?' Ethan asked solemnly. 'You seemed to be in a big hurry to get out of there.'

You have no idea. 'Yeah, I'll give it another week or so, but after that…' She trailed off, linking her arm in his and leading him into a saunter down the street. She smiled and nodded to passers-by whom she had never laid eyes on, trying to act the part of local barista and woman about town, all the while hating herself and yearning for a time in the not-too-distant future that all this self-created bullshit would be behind her.

'You know,' Ethan began cautiously. 'If you need to take some time before jumping into a new job. I mean… you don't have to worry about… about the financial side of things.'

Lexi stopped walking and turned to face him.

'Like, if you wanted to wait for some place you're going to really love working at. Or if there was something you thought you might like to study.' Ethan clasped the back of his neck, searching for the right words. 'Look, I know you've always had to fend for yourself and that can't have been easy. I guess I want you to know that you're not alone anymore. You can take some time to decide what's really going to make you happy.'

Lexi opened her mouth to speak. This was the moment she would tell Ethan about her writing. About how her mind played in a parallel fantasy world of her own creation. How she had sometimes felt ashamed of working behind a coffee machine all day, making drinks for people who didn't even register her existence. That when she wrote, she could do anything, be anyone, be more than what people saw.

'I…' she began.

Ethan's phone buzzed and he pulled it out of his back pocket to look at the screen. 'Lex, I'm sorry. It's Lucas' childcare. Just let me… Hello? Ethan Thomas speaking,' he said, turning and walking away.

Lexi's phone vibrated in her pocket. She pulled it out and her heart sank when she saw that a text had come through from Margot. "What you did today was again a breach of your contract. I will let it slide this time but just know, this is the last time I will be so understanding."

Lexi bit her bottom lip as Ethan strode back towards her.

'I'm sorry, Lex, I have to go and get him. He's been stung by a bee for Christ's sake. I could hear him howling in the background,' said Ethan, scrunching his brow and walking back towards his car.

'Oh no! Poor little guy,' said Lexi, falling into step with him. 'Do you want me to go? I've got hours until I need to meet up with Linh, and...'

Ethan stopped and his brow smoothed. 'You wouldn't mind? I've got a bunch of reps coming in this afternoon, and...'

'Of course. I want to.'

~

When the elevator doors opened, Lexi saw Lucas seated with one of the carers in front of the fish tank. His face was blotchy and tear-streaked, and he cradled his left hand in his right with the delicacy one might show to an injured bird. He turned towards the sound of the doors opening, stood and thrust his hands skyward to coax her down into a hug.

'What happened, buddy?' she asked, folding him into her.

The carer stood, and drawled, 'We had a bit of an accident. Didn't we, Lucas?'

'We had a bit of an accident,' parroted Lucas. 'I was watering the garden.'

The carer nodded, pursing her lips. She went on, 'He was watering the garden and he put his hand down on the edge of the planter.' She turned to Lucas. 'Isn't that right, Lucas? You didn't see the bee and you put your hand down on the planter?'

Lexi, fearing she may put her hand down on this woman's face, hastened to leave. 'Well thanks for calling us. I'd better be getting him home.'

'Alright, Lucas,' droned the woman, 'you go on home with your mummy, and we'll see you tomorrow, mkay?'

Lucas glanced up at Lexi, looking worried.

'Come on, buddy, let's go home. I'll make you a babyccino with sprinkles.'

'With sprinkles?' he asked, eyes widening as if he could not quite believe that something so wondrous could exist in the same cruel world in which bees attack.

Lexi nodded. 'Come on.'

She scooped him up onto her hip and he buried his face into her neck, the intimacy of the gesture taking her slightly aback.

~

When Ethan returned home, Lexi and Lucas were putting the finishing touches on macaroni and cheese. Or at least Lexi was, while Lucas sat up on a bar stool, eating fistfuls of grated cheese with his good hand.

'Where's my brave boy?' said Ethan, striding over.

Lucas removed the ice pack from his swollen hand and held it up for Ethan's inspection. Taking it gingerly and turning it this way and that, Ethan emitted a succession of low, *mmm* sounds before kissing it gently and replacing the ice pack. Satisfied, Lucas recommenced eating.

Ethan rounded the bench to plant a kiss on Lexi's neck. 'I thought you were going out with Linh tonight?' he said, taking in the dinner prep.

'Yeah, I am. But I wanted to make you guys something before I go.'

'Roni and cheese is like a hug for your tummy,' Lucas informed Ethan.

'Oh, it is?' asked Ethan, grinning at Lexi.

'It's a scientific fact,' she said, picking up the dish and turning towards the oven.

'May I?' asked Ethan, stepping to open the oven door for her.

Lexi jolted unexpectedly as she recalled their passionate post-beach encounter on the sofa.

'You may,' she said, her eyes fixed on his.

The slight curl of his lip confirmed their shared memory.

~

Lexi had hoped that by the time she met Linh, she would have some semblance of an explanation formulated. But since they'd made plans, the day had unfolded to reveal one catastrophe after another. Now, she climbed the stairs to Linh's apartment, foreboding mounting with each step. Reaching Linh's front door, Lexi paused for a moment, hoping for clarity to strike. Instead, she was struck by the compact figure of Linh's mother hurtling out the door.

'Ah, Lexi, I'm so late!' she exclaimed, trying to smooth her clothes back into place.

'Out on the town tonight, Vien?' Lexi asked, grinning.

'Out on the town, painting it red!' said Vien, proudly. 'Not like my daughter, waiting for boys. I don't need.' She shook her head, indignant. 'That skinny boy,' she said, with disdain. 'I call him Mick Jagger. He break her heart.' Vien clicked her tongue disapprovingly. 'When I saw that skinny boy, first time, I said to Linh, "That skinny boy only cause you problem."' Vien sighed heavily and said, more to herself, 'That skinny boy can't get no satisfaction.'

With that, she pulled Lexi down by the shoulders, planted a noisy kiss too close to her ear and hurried down the stairs. 'Come back soon and make sure you eat, okay?' she called over her shoulder.

Lexi walked through the open door, calling, 'Hello?'

Linh appeared in the living room, scrubbed of make-up and looking tired.

'Tough day at the office?' Lexi asked.

Linh gave a resigned shrug and led the way to the kitchen. 'I'm going to Uber something in, wanna join?'

'Sure,' said Lexi, feeling heartened. Surely this was a good sign.

'How about those burrito bowls? From that place that used to be the bakery?'

'Yum,' said Lexi, nodding her head. 'I'll transfer you some money.'

'You don't have to—' protested Linh.

'Shut it,' Lexi interjected.

Linh and Lexi each sat and tapped at their phones before proclaiming, 'Done,' in unison.

They giggled and then fell silent.

'I've missed you,' Lexi began.

'Please tell me you're not using me to cheat on Ethan,' blurted Linh.

'I'm not using you to cheat on Ethan,' said Lexi.

Linh's shoulders relaxed. 'Okay, so what the fuck?'

Lexi tried to think of a version of the truth which would explain her appalling behaviour. 'It has to do with my new work crew I guess,' she began. 'But maybe I need to go back a step.'

'Want a beer?' asked Linh.

Lexi let out a relieved laugh. 'Yes.'

Linh retrieved two cans from the fridge and sat.

They popped the tabs and Lexi took a sip. 'I've been in two minds about Ethan, as you know,' she said.

Linh rolled her eyes and opened her mouth to speak, but Lexi put up a hand to stop her. 'I'm not anymore. But I was. So, when my birthday came around, I wanted to hang out with my new work crew and there was a guy. The brother of one of the women I work with. So, I made up some birthday tradition between you and I so that Ethan wouldn't want to tag along on our night out.'

'Okay,' said Linh, trying to follow along. 'But what about the next day? When I came to your house, Ethan said you were meeting me for brunch. Did you meet up with that guy?'

'No, nothing like that. Actually, I met up with one of my work friends, to tell her about something kind of awful that happened with that guy. He turned out to be a total fucking psycho, by the way.'

Linh shook her head slowly. 'But why did you have to lie about seeing your work friend?'

Lexi buried her face in her hands. 'I don't know. I actually don't fucking know anymore.'

When Lexi lifted her head, she saw that Linh had tears in her eyes. 'Are you okay?' she asked.

'Xavier and I broke up,' said Linh, roughly wiping her eyes.

'Oh, Linh,' said Lexi.

'Anyway, it doesn't matter about that. Whatever weird fucking crisis you're going through. It's not fair for you to be lying to Ethan like he's an idiot.'

Lexi dipped her head, like a school kid being reprimanded.

They sat in silence for a while until Lexi asked in a soft voice, 'What happened with Xavier?'

Linh sighed. 'He went and fell in love with one of the "thirds",' she said, making sarcastic air quotes either side of her head.

'The thirds?'

'A guy we had a threesome with,' Linh said, tersely.

Lexi remained silent, unsure how to respond.

'I should have known,' Linh said, shaking her head. 'I was like a third wheel with those two. They were so into each other. But then when I'd ask him about it, he'd say I was imagining it. That I was being paranoid.'

'Oh, Linh,' Lexi said again.

Linh looked up at the ceiling and blinked. 'He kept telling me he was busy with rehearsals and sound checks and all this band-related bullshit. So, one Saturday I ran into Tommy on Brunswick Street, and I was like, "Why aren't you at the rehearsal?" and he goes…' Linh opened her mouth and made her eyes dart around dumbly. 'I went straight to his place and found them in bed together. Everyone in the share house had been covering for him.'

Linh shook her head bitterly at the memory.

Lexi felt ashamed. She nodded slowly, looking into her lap.

~

The air was a velvet cloak as Lexi made her way up the path to Ethan's front door, the crimson horizon foretelling a scorcher tomorrow. She eased the door open quietly, knowing that Lucas would be asleep upstairs, and walked into the lamp-lit glow of the house. She found Ethan sitting on the sofa, with the television playing, looking at his phone. Hearing her come in, he looked up to smile at her. She kicked off her slides and slunk down next to him, contorting her body to fit against his. 'Hi,' she said into his chest.

His slight movement told her he was smiling but he didn't respond. Their breathing synchronised and Lexi's stresses fizzed and flickered away.

Ethan turned his face into the coconut scent of Lexi's hair and spoke in a low voice. 'Do you know I haven't had a holiday in over three years?' he said.

'Oh?' said Lexi, drowsily. She was succumbing to her fatigue.

'Yep, it's true. Justine and I went on a babymoon before Lucas was born.'

Lexi sat up. 'I'm sorry? A babymoon?' she said, laughing.

'It was a babymoon,' said Ethan laughing along. 'I didn't make up the term,' he protested. 'It's a thing. Anyway, you're focusing on the wrong thing.'

Lexi continued to laugh.

'What I'm saying is I need a holiday. *We* need a holiday.'

'Well, it'll have to be camping or something,' said Lexi. 'Because I. Am. Broke.'

Ethan smiled and kissed her forehead.

'*We* are not broke,' he said, putting deliberate emphasis on the word. 'And we should go on a holiday.'

Lexi shifted uncomfortably. 'I don't know, Ethan.'

Ethan used his thumb to smooth the crease between Lexi's eyebrows and her face softened.

'I know,' he said.

Lexi emitted a *mmm* sound and they resumed their slumped embrace. As sleep began to take Lexi, she remembered the promise she'd made earlier in the day when she ran out early on her broadcast. But what special activity could she possibly come up with now?

'Are you okay?' Ethan asked.

'Yeah, sorry. I was dropping off. It might be time for bed,' she said.

'Me too.'

He turned off the television, stood and took her hand.

'I'm going to get a glass of water, do you want one?' said Lexi.

'I'm okay, thanks.'

She made to drop his hand, but he held on, pulling her close to him. His breath was humid as he kissed her neck, sending a fine trail of goosebumps down her right side.

'Night,' he muttered before ascending the stairs.

Once in the kitchen, Lexi pulled out her phone and googled, "cam model games". She clicked into a blog and scrolled through the suggestions before creeping to Lucas' craft supply cupboard and retrieving balloons, confetti, markers and coloured paper. She slipped these into the internal pocket of her bag, poured herself a glass of water and went upstairs to bed.

That night, Lexi dreamt of Jamie, but this time she was joined by another. This much larger beast writhed ceaselessly as a tornedo of confetti twisted above a quaking ground. The monstrous figure grew and shrunk with the fluidity of an ocean swell. Lexi tried to steady herself, to get a better look at the creature but there was nothing to hold on to. Squinting and holding her arms thrust outward, she made out the sinister scowl of Bruce Holloway, Jamie's father. As Lexi reeled back, the creature shapeshifted into Travis Nolan and then back to Bruce. All the while Jamie gazed up at it, transfixed.

THIRTY-FOUR

'BUM spank? Really ManYouKnighted?' said Lexi, raising an eyebrow. 'Okay, let's do a few of those. One spank, five spanks, ten spanks?'

Lexi wrote each phrase down on a small square of coloured paper before folding them several times and adding them to the growing pile on the floor beside her. 'Who else has got one?' she asked.

She looked at the screen and scrunched up her face. 'I am not doing that Bisous69. Get your mind out of the gutter.' Lexi's tone was playful as she teased the perpetually cheeky regular. She looked up towards the ceiling and chewed the end of her pen with exaggerated ponderance. 'How about a private show?' she wondered out loud.

When a new visitor asked for clarification, Lexi explained, 'It's a little like seven minutes in heaven. You and I alone in a room together and we… see what happens.' Her newsfeed lit up in agreement, so Lexi wrote "Private Show" on a pink square of paper and folded it.

'Now, you know…' she said, her eyebrow cocked, 'This wouldn't be a game of chance if you didn't stand to lose. So, I'm thinking we add a few that say, "You Get Nothing".'

Good natured riling and protests followed, and Lexi scolded, 'Come on now, if you don't play fair, I won't play with you at all.'

Lexi wrote out the phrase several times and added the knots of paper to the pile, swishing them with her fingertips. Next, she pulled out a balloon and inserted one of the notes into the neck, added a pinch of confetti and blew it up. Once securely tied, she smacked it into the air. 'Now it's a party,' she said.

This continued until she was surrounded by balloons.

'Okay, so who's going to buy the first balloon?'

Bisous69 tipped the required number of tokens and commented, "Give me the green one by your hand!"

Lexi picked it up and jiggled it, sending the confetti dancing around inside.

'Pin or bum, Bisous?' she asked, knowing what his answer would be. 'Okay then,' she said, getting up onto her knees so she could position the balloon under her bottom. She grimaced as she lowered herself timidly down. The balloon popped and Lexi fell to the ground with a yelp, her feet thrust skyward. She laughed raucously, surprised by how much fun she was having.

"What did I win?" Bisou69 prompted.

'Oh yeah,' laughed Lexi. She unfolded the slip of paper, holding it close to her face as if protecting a winning poker hand and peered over the top. 'Feeling lucky?' she asked.

"Always lucky when I'm with you, *cherie*," he wrote.

Lexi read the note and laughed. 'It's a handstand,' she said, covering her face with her hand. 'Well, I'm not going to lie to you, it's been a while since I've done a handstand. Let me adjust…' Lexi moved the laptop to allow for her full height and said, 'Okay, here goes nothing.'

She flung herself downward, hands spread, her feet gingerly hitting the wall with a soft thud. Her dress flopped down to cover her face and expose her lace Brazilian bikini pants. She stayed in position for as long as she could until her giggles sent her toppling back over. The newsfeed came alive in response and Lexi had trouble keeping up with the comments and tips which poured in.

ManYouKnighted was next to pay for a balloon.

'Please tell me I don't have to sit on this one,' Lexi said, holding up the balloon.

"Sit on it, darling," came the response.

She perched once more, pointing out that she was like a broody hen before releasing her weight, bursting the balloon and falling backwards.

"Gimme them bum spanks, Jojo!" pleaded ManYouKnighted as Lexi fished around in the mess of confetti, looking for the folded paper.

Locating it, she opened it and smirked. 'No bum spunks,' she said, shaking her head. She paused for effect before turning the paper around and holding it up to the webcam.

"Undies off, twirl," it read.

As Lexi wiggled out of her underwear, she received a tip for private messaging. She clicked into the message from a user named StonedMason. It read, "Lexi, is that you?"

Time stopped.

It wasn't until several guests commented asking what happened that Lexi realised, she was frozen on the spot. She forced a laugh, made some self-deprecating joke about zoning out and twirled. Her skirt whirled up like a dervish as her thoughts spun frantically. Coming to a stop, she forced her face into a bright smile and asked, 'Anyone else want to choose a balloon?' Then she typed her reply. "Who is this?"

Lexi tried to mask her terror by continuing to banter with her audience, but she knew it was a farce. The reply, which took mere seconds to arrive, seemed to take forever. "Lexi, it's your brother. It's Mason."

THIRTY-FIVE

THE last time Lexi had seen her half-siblings was a rain-streaked Sunday morning. Creeping in through the back door after an all-nighter, Lexi was stunned to find her mother serving breakfast to Mason and Mia. Lexi was diligent about arriving home before the household awoke but, on this morning, in her hazy state, Lexi had miscalculated her departure from the party. Thinking back now, she couldn't even recall the evening which preceded this life-altering event. She was sleepy, drunk, and a little high, ready to fall into bed fully clothed.

Instead, her mother released a venomous tirade in a clenched teeth attempt at restraint in front of her wide-eyed children. Monique's husband, Darrin, had left early for his shift at the supermarket so was not present to *shoo* them away from one another when things ventured into dangerous territory.

Lexi, startled by her family's presence in the kitchen, was caught off-guard when her mother released the flood gates on what seemed like a lifetime of resentment. Although she had guessed at Monique's animosity, it was then Lexi realised that she had held onto a naive hope that deep down her mother loved her. That morning, she was having all her deepest suspicions confirmed as Monique spat allegations of Lexi's selfishness and deplorable behaviour. In Lexi's compromised state, these accusations punctured her like machine-gun fire—too quick for her to individually defend or deflect. Lexi did not bring up the many ways in which she assisted in the smooth running of the household, her financial contributions or the incalculable hours spent babysitting. Instead, she remained silent, unaware that she was flinching with every growled jibe.

Monique paused to regard her daughter, hip thrust askew. 'I keep looking at you and wondering how much longer I have to put up with this.' She turned her back in disgust and spooned coffee into her mug. 'Why can't you leave me in peace to raise my children?' she muttered.

This was enough to rouse Lexi from her stupor and she moved into a slow nod, looking over at Mason and Mia who had stopped eating their Weet-bix to stare at the exchange. She forced a smile and a wink for their benefit before wordlessly walking out of the room to pack. That day she moved out of the house and out of town, for good.

~

As Lexi crawled around the room on all-fours, manoeuvring the handheld vacuum cleaner, she cursed herself for using so much confetti. She took her finger off the trigger to brush some off the valance and heard Sienna knocking.

'Coming,' she shouted, hoisting herself up from the floor.

She flung open the door to reveal Veronica. 'Hey Jojo,' she said.

Lexi cocked her head in confusion. 'Hey. What are you...?' she asked, making way for her to enter.

Veronica walked in ruffling her long hair, leaving a faint apple scent in her wake. 'Margot called me to cover Sienna's slot,' she said.

'Oh, is she sick or something?' Lexi asked.

Veronica closed the door and leaned in, her eyes like saucers. 'She got fired,' she whispered.

Although they were alone, Lexi matched Veronica's hushed tone. 'Why?'

Veronica shrugged and sat on the bed. 'She was meeting up with some of her chatroom visitors. Had a whole side hustle going.'

Lexi's eyes widened. 'You mean she was...?'

Veronica nodded.

'Fuck,' said Lexi.

'Did you have a party in here or something?' asked Veronica, taking in the fallout from Lexi's balloon game.

'Shit! Yeah, something like that,' said Lexi, coming to her senses. She crouched to resume brushing confetti off the bed before vacuuming it up. Veronica sat perched on the bed, her feet lifted like a child making way for its parent, chattering about the guy she'd been seeing. Lexi, engrossed in thoughts of her brother's emergence, emitted noises of interest.

The condition of the floor finally restored, Lexi docked the vacuum into its charger and gathered her belongings. She needed to get out of there and call Mason.

'Travis admitted he was overreacting. He said sorry and everything. He said as long as we keep it casual, we can keep seeing each other,' Veronica went on.

Lexi straightened. 'I'm sorry, did you say Travis?'

Veronica clapped a hand over her mouth. 'You're friends with Ali, aren't you?' she said, the words muffled through her fingers.

'Your boyfriend is Travis Nolan?' asked Lexi slowly.

Veronica raised a hand. 'Not boyfriend. Just casual. But don't tell Ali, she'd be mad if—'

'She found out her brother was hitting on her friends?' finished Lexi.

'Yeah,' said Veronica, sounding delighted.

~

Lexi held her breath and listened to the ringtone, waiting for her brother to answer. The midday heat had baked the interior of her car and she sat gingerly on the driver's seat with her legs extended out the open door. She thought of the air conditioning inside the Camnation house and experienced an almost lustful desire to re-enter. But this was personal, and she didn't want to risk Margot or any of the other cam models overhearing the conversation. She was about to hang up and try again later when the line was picked up and her brother coughed out a 'Hello?'

'Um, hi. Mason? It's Lexi.'

Lexi tried to block out the knowledge that her little brother had seen her twirling about sans-underpants.

'Yeah, hi. Just gimme a…'

She waited, listening to a nondescript shuffling and the lighting of a cigarette.

'Okay, sorry,' he said.

'How'd you know it was me?' she asked, cutting to the chase.

'You look the same,' he said, simply.

'Yeah, but you were five when I left. How do you even remember me?'

'I have photos. After you left, I dunno. I guess I didn't take it so well and Mum didn't want to talk about it. Dad snuck an envelope of photos into my room and told me not to tell her.'

Lexi heard him take a long drag of his cigarette and tried to imagine what it must have been like in the aftermath of her departure.

'Anyway, I wasn't sure it was you.'

She could almost hear him shrug.

'What were you doing on a cam site?' she asked.

'What were *you* doing on a cam site?' he countered.

She grinned, impressed by his brass. 'I'm twenty-nine, you're fifteen,' she said, aware of how weak an argument it was. 'And my site's meant to block users from Victoria. Are you guys not in Hamilton anymore?'

'We're here. Same shit house. Same shit car,' he said, the smile audible in his voice. 'I set up a VPN so I can stream US Netflix for the old man.'

Lexi shook her head, dumbfounded, trying to reconcile this almost-man with the image of the smear-faced little brother she remembered.

'How is Darrin?' she asked.

'Still slogging it out waiting for Henderson to retire so he can be king of the castle.'

'He's still at the supermarket?' said Lexi, unable to fully suppress a laugh which he echoed gruffly. They fell silent.

'And Mia?' Lexi said.

'She's like a mini-Mum.'

Lexi laughed, trying to imagine it. She rubbed the scar tissue on her wrist.

'How is Mum?' Lexi asked, hoping to sound casual.

His silence lasted for so long that Lexi asked, 'Mason?'

'She's been better,' he said.

Lexi waited for him to elaborate.

'She passed, Lex.'

The words echoed around her head, but they didn't make sense. Passed what? She realised Mason was still talking and tried to focus on what he was saying.

'...long battle. In the end, I guess, it kind of came as a relief.'

Lexi shook her head. 'But, when?'

'About six months ago. It was pretty rough for a while. Mia took it the hardest. Is *still* taking it the hardest.'

'But why didn't anyone try to contact me? Didn't she want me…?'

Lexi heard a distant knock and Mason exhaled forcefully and coughed. She heard a dull thudding, presumably the butting out of his cigarette.

'Look, I gotta go, but I'll buzz you soon,' he said.

Lexi opened her mouth and emitted a series of vowels before the line went dead.

Lexi dropped her phone onto the passenger seat and tucked her legs inside the car, despite the heat within. Gripping the steering wheel seared her hands and she focused on the pain. When the temperature made her feel light-headed, Lexi started the car. Once she was moving, the air billowing through the open windows brought little relief from the scorching heat but she was no longer being slow roasted. She thought over the conversation and tried to focus only on Mason. On how grown up he sounded. When Lexi quit Hamilton, her singular motivation had been to remove herself from the toxic, passive aggression of her mother. Leaving her siblings had hurt but she had dealt with it by pushing down the memory of them. Having Lucas sprout up in her life had reawakened some long-forgotten part of her, a muscle memory of how she had been with them. The tones of voice used exclusively for addressing children, the way your embrace could become a sanctuary against any hardship, any disappointment from grazed knees to torn pages. When Lexi recalled her siblings, they were frozen in time. Two little faces staring up over their breakfast bowls. But those children didn't exist anymore, and for the first time Lexi considered the teenagers they'd grown into. Fully fledged humans with opinions and pastimes and social circles. Individuals, no longer tethered to their mother.

Their mother. Lexi realised that the image of her mother was also frozen in time. Her set mouth, the deep crease that formed between her eyebrows when regarding her. The long, disappointed glances and exasperated exhalations. Somewhere, in the depths of Lexi's soul, she had believed that she and her mother would one day reconcile. That enough time apart might smooth down her mother's sharp edges. But that dream had been snatched from her and replaced with the knowledge that even in her final days, being farewelled by the people she loved, Monique had not felt Lexi's absence. Had craved neither absolution nor closure from her eldest daughter. Lexi's suspicion that her presence in the world was the unfortunate by-product of one of Monique's botched schemes, had just been confirmed in one startlingly grotesque moment.

Fresh out of high school and with no prospects in her hometown of Ballarat, Lexi's mother, Monique, had set her sights on Dimitri Karras, the son of one of the most established and affluent families in town. Dimitri's fifth-great-grandfather had arrived at the tail-end of the Victorian gold rush with a wave of Greek migrants seeking to make their fortunes. When his young bride joined him and witnessed the gruelling and largely fruitless work of her husband, she set out to subsidise their income by providing simple home-cooked meals to the throngs of hungry men working the fields. And so the Karrases struck it rich, establishing themselves as restaurateurs.

The details of Monique and Dimitri's love affair were sketchy to Lexi, who only pieced together what she knew from her grandmother's disapproving jibes. Whatever the story, young Monique found herself pregnant and convinced she was on the brink of life-changing nuptials. Instead, Dimitri got a one-way plane ticket to Greece and Monique got a baby and a modest cheque, which came with the proviso that she leave Ballarat for good. Lexi's memories of her early childhood were of being shunted from neighbour to neighbour while her mother tried to recapture her lost youth. Her second chance came in the form of Darrin, the assistant manager at the Richie's supermarket and Monique's junior by four years. At twelve years of age, wearing an ill-fitting lilac taffeta dress, Lexi looked on as Monique Ryan became Monique Sutcliffe, just two weeks shy of her thirtieth birthday.

Lexi had hoped her mother's new-found happiness would be the catalyst that brought them closer together. Instead, it heralded the birth of her two half-siblings and, as Lexi bore witness to the formation of this new nuclear family, she surmised that she was a blight on her mother's otherwise perfect image. The only Karras in a sea of Sutcliffes, as it were. A constant, glaring reminder of a past that Monique could never run from. The burn of her suspicion being confirmed came courtesy of a literal burn, while at work at the barbequed chicken shop.

It wasn't Lexi's negligence that caused it, although her mind had been elsewhere. There were any number of ways to burn yourself on the industrial rotisserie—her co-workers' forearms bore the evidence of that—but Lexi was always careful. During this shift, though, as she was painting oil onto the glistening, rotating birds, thinking of Geoff and castigating herself for driving him away, the taut golden skin of a chicken leg exploded, showering her wrist with a scalding burst of oil.

The searing shock of it broke her reverie and she dropped the basting brush onto the coals where it charred and smoked before igniting. Lexi spat curses and clutched her wrist to her chest.

'Bloody hell, love,' said her boss, Ros, rushing over.

She pried Lexi's hand away from her body to reveal a Saudi Arabia-shaped burn on the inside of her wrist. A thin layer of sticky skin remained stuck to Lexi's branded polo shirt. Lexi's eyes widened and she swayed a little. Ros, still holding Lexi's fingers, placed her other hand on her elbow and all but dragged her over to the sink. As the cold water made contact with the raw flesh, Lexi let out a howl and struggled to break free.

'You have to, love,' said Ros, using her whole body to hold Lexi in place. 'Barry!' Ros yelled over her shoulder. 'Barry! Lexi's burned herself! Come out here!'

The blaring of the television ceased, and Barry emerged through the grimy PVC strip door. 'What are you yelling about now, woman?' he grumbled.

'Lexi's got burned, you lazy prick. I need to take her to the hospital,' she said, still straining to keep Lexi's arm under the stream of water.

Barry came to life at this. 'Shit! Shit! Sorry! Jesus!'

He stepped lightly on the spot, turning this way and that like a cartoon character.

'Get me a clean tea towel,' hissed Ros.

He did as instructed and Ros ran the towel under the water and wrapped it around Lexi's wrist.

'Keys!' yelled Ros, and Barry scurried to retrieve these too.

On the drive to the hospital, Lexi tried calling her mother. It rang through to voicemail and although she tried to keep her words measured to avoid Monique's unnecessary worry, her voice came out thick with the suppression of tears.

In the emergency waiting room, Ros chattered beside Lexi.

'It's a good thing this happened early in your shift. It'll be hours before all the drunken mishaps come through the door. Saturday night's the busiest night here I reckon,' said Ros.

Lexi checked her phone for any response from her mother and found none.

Seeing Lexi's deep exhalation, Ros rubbed her back and said quietly, 'She's left her phone on silent or something, darl. Probably busy getting dinner ready for the littlies.'

Lexi nodded.

After the wound had been treated, Ros drove Lexi home.

'You get some rest, love,' said Ros, pulling up in front of Lexi's house.

Lexi nodded and muttered her thanks.

She scuffed up the driveway, recoiling slightly as the harsh sensor light turned its attention on her. Approaching the front door, she heard animated conversation from within. She knocked.

The door opened to reveal Monique's painted face. Her smile dropped to her stilettos upon seeing Lexi.

'What are you doing home?' she hissed.

Lexi held up her bandaged wrist. 'I had an accident at work,' she said quietly.

Monique's jaw clenched as she searched for answers over Lexi's shoulder.

'Who is it, Mon?' Darrin called out.

Monique opened her mouth, but no words came.

'It's just me, Darrin,' said Lexi, stepping past her mother and making her way down the hallway.

Monique shut the door hurriedly and click clacked after Lexi. 'Wait,' she hissed as Lexi arrived in the living area to find the furniture pushed back to accommodate a clothed table. Darrin, halfway to standing, wore an ill-fitting suit, Mason was pulling at a bow tie, trying to loosen it, while Mia seemed to be suspended in a froth of pink tulle.

'Hi?' said Lexi.

An older couple that Lexi didn't recognise sat cattycorner to

Darrin, their faces open and kind, awaiting an introduction.

Lexi suddenly became very aware of the dishevelled state of her appearance. Her greasy black hair was piled haphazardly into a top knot and her teal Hot Chicks Chicken polo still bore the remnants of her seared skin, and the oil which had caused it.

Monique and Darrin locked eyes and, as the moment stretched uncomfortably, Mason won his battle with the bow tie and threw it to the ground.

'This is, ahhhh,' began Monique.

'This is my stepdaughter, Lexi,' said Darrin. 'Lexi, this is Mr. and Mrs. Henderson. Mr. Henderson owns the supermarket where I work,' he added.

Lexi's shoulders dropped and she looked at her stained Volleys. 'Nice to meet you.'

Lexi stole a glance at Monique standing with a hand on her hip like a gameshow model.

'Stepdaughter!' exclaimed Mr. Henderson. 'How old are you, Alex? My, my, my Monique, someone was a naughty girl, wasn't she! You barely look older than she does!' He leaned back in his chair and chuckled.

Monique's smile was plastic and her eyes seared Lexi more painfully than the oil had.

Darrin forced a laugh and sat.

'Will you join us, dear?' asked Mrs. Henderson, indicating the table although there were no spare chairs.

'Oh, I don't think…' began Monique.

Lexi forced her chin up as fragments of her heart broke off and were swallowed by her body.

'Thank you but no. I have a lot of homework to do. It was very nice meeting you though, Mr. and Mrs. Henderson.' She completed the act with something she hoped resembled a smile and turned to retrace her steps down the hallway.

As Lexi closed her bedroom door behind her, she heard her

mother say brightly, 'Sorry for the disturbance, everyone. Who's ready for sweets?'

~

Now, as Lexi pulled up at a red light, a text came through and she gathered up her phone, desperate for further communication from Mason. Instead, it was from Jamie. "I don't want to lose you again either," it said.

Lexi sighed heavily, thinking of Travis and Veronica. She could hardly mend her friendship with Jamie by revealing her boyfriend to be a philandering love rat. In situations like this it was always the messenger getting shot. And coming from Lexi it would sound more like an "I told you so" than an "I'm looking out for you."

Travis had made this mess. It was time he cleaned up. Although she had vowed never again to speak to Travis Nolan, Lexi typed out a message to him. "I know about you messing around behind Jamie's back with Veronica. Come clean to them both or I'll come clean for you. You have until the end of the week."

'OKAY, mate. Take your shoes off and wash your hands, please.'

Since learning of her mother's death, Lexi had thrown herself into reworking her short stories into a narrative. Hearing Ethan's arrival home, her eyes flicked to the laptop's clock. Hours had passed without her noticing.

She whipped around to stare at the bedroom door, listening to the sound of Ethan plodding upstairs.

'Hi honey, I'm home,' he sang.

She turned back around to face her computer screen, the cursor poised to hide her work. What was the point of it all if people could up and die at any moment?

The door opened and Ethan leaned against the door jamb, smiling at her.

'Hey,' he said, the word like a private joke.

She forced a forlorn smile and felt an overwhelming desire to be held by him.

'Hey. Are you okay?' he asked, striding towards her, his brow knitted.

Lexi opened her mouth to tell him about her mother and stopped. 'I'm okay, a little tired, I guess. I've been writing all afternoon,' she said instead.

'Yeah?' he said, leaning down to squint at the screen.

Regret rose in her chest, but she breathed it away and continued, worried that the alternative was for her to break down and confess everything about the last few weeks.

'Yeah. I've written a few short stories and I'm going to see if I can turn them into…' Lexi faltered, unsure if she would be able to say "a novel" without feeling like a wanker. '…something longer,' she finished.

'No shit,' Ethan said. 'How long have you been writing for?'

'About fifteen years.'

Ethan's eyebrows shot up and he misplaced his voice for a moment. He lowered himself down to sit on the edge of the desk, looking sideways at her. 'Why didn't you tell me about it?'

Lexi thought for a moment. 'It's not just you. I've never told anyone before.'

He nodded. 'Sometimes it's easier to say nothing than to risk an unkind reaction.'

He lifted her chin with a crooked index finger and kissed her. When he pulled back, his eyes were locked on hers. 'I see you. And I love you. You can tell me anything,' he said.

Lexi's cheeks grew warm, and she looked towards the doorway where Lucas had appeared holding something in his outstretched hands.

'What's this?' she asked, thankful for the pivot in focus.

'I made it for you,' he said, in a small voice.

He walked over to Lexi and placed in her lap a plastic juice bottle trailing pieces of wool and loopy braid. She held it up, turning it this way and that as if it were a precious artifact.

'This is for me? Are you sure?' asked Lexi.

Lucas nodded, puffing out his chest a little.

'Do you want to tell Lexi what it is, mate?' Ethan prompted.

'It's a jellyfish,' said Lexi.

'It's a jellyfish,' echoed Lucas, grinning.

'Ha!' said Ethan, looking between the two.

Lucas shuffled closer to Lexi and leaned his body towards her. She wrapped an arm around him and planted a kiss atop his head, still clutching the prized possession in her other hand. He smelled like sunscreen and watermelon.

'I love it, buddy. Thank you,' she whispered into his ear.

He wriggled free of her embrace, and she stood.

'I thought we could make those little pasta bowls for dinner. And the sauce you liked with the pumpkin and pine nuts,' she said, taking Lucas' hand.

'And boat cheese,' he said, nodding.

Lexi smiled down at him. 'Yep, the goat cheese is yummy,' she agreed.

Ethan placed a hand on her shoulder before she could walk out the door. He looked at her intently. 'I'd love to read your work sometime. When you're ready,' he said.

She turned away smiling and led Lucas downstairs.

Later that evening, after putting Lucas to bed, Ethan returned to find Lexi in the kitchen, wiping down the countertops. He stacked a few remaining plates into the dishwasher, inserted a tablet and started the cycle.

'Drink?' he asked.

'Wine, maybe?'

He walked to the wine rack and twisted a few bottles until he located a pinot noir and held it up for Lexi's consideration. She gave a neutral, conceding shrug and he poured two generous measures into stemless wine glasses.

As they made their way to the sofa, Ethan emitted an elongated, 'Soooooooooo.'

'Yes?' she said, throwing herself back into the sofa and sloshing wine onto her black denim A-line. She agitated the patch until it disappeared into the fabric and turned her attention back to Ethan as he lowered himself down beside her.

'I was doing some research today,' Ethan began.

Lexi sipped her wine.

'…so, I know Fiji isn't the most exotic destination, but it's only a five-hour flight and there's this resort with a kid's club and a babysitting service.'

Lexi shifted her weight to lean against him, losing herself in the sound of his low voice. He described days spent fossicking at the beach with Lucas and evenings spent alone, sipping cocktails and listening to waves lap against the shoreline. After a long pause he said, 'You'd have time to write, if you wanted to.'

Lexi smiled against his chest but said nothing.

'With you finishing up at the café soon, and the store is usually dead after Christmas, it's perfect timing and I don't know when we'll get another opportunity like this.'

Ethan paused for her to respond. When she didn't, he went on. 'But I don't want to go ahead and book anything unless you're in and you seemed, well, less than enthused when I brought it up last time.'

'It's not that I'm not *enthused*,' she said, putting emphasis on his word as she repositioned herself against the arm of the sofa. 'Who wouldn't be enthused about being whisked away to paradise by you?'

She fixed an adoring gaze on him, and he looked away, bashful in the face of her compliment.

'Look, by the time I finish up at the café, I should have some savings. If I can contribute, I'm all in. In fact, I can't imagine anything better than hitting the beach with my two favourite guys.'

Ethan's face opened into a radiant smile before he dialled it back to something more playful. 'I tell you what,' he said. 'I'll let you pay for airport parking.'

THIRTY-SEVEN

'YOUR phone is lighting up like a Christmas tree in there,' said Ethan, indicating the bedroom door.

'Oh, really?' said Lexi, reflexively touching her back pocket.

She wondered if she had somehow enabled Twitter notifications without meaning to, and her neck grew hot. This was why she never left her phone lying around. Appearing nonplussed, Lexi stayed where she was, finished applying her mascara and glossed her lips, all the while trying not to look at Ethan as he styled his hair next to her. Once finished, she stowed her make-up bag and walked into the bedroom where she sat on the bed and retrieved her phone from the side table. As she did, it came alive displaying a string of text messages from an unknown number. She thought of Mason, whose number she hadn't yet saved in her phone.

Clicking in, she was confronted with image after image of herself in various stages of undress. Terror shuddered through her, and her brain became too big for her skull.

'Is everything okay?' asked Ethan, exiting the ensuite.

Lexi could barely focus on him for the throbbing in her head.

'Yeah, sorry,' she stammered. 'My brother… my brother Mason, from Hamilton, found me on Facebook. It surprised me, that's all.'

'Yeah, right,' said Ethan, threading a belt through his trouser loops, wide-eyed. 'You haven't seen him since you moved out, right?'

'Ten years,' said Lexi, nodding.

Her phone, face down on her leg, was vibrating silently.

'That's huge. How do you feel about…?'

The sound of something hitting the kitchen floor, followed by Lucas exclaiming, 'Uh oh!' broke their exchange.

'Coming, mate!' Ethan yelled. He turned to Lexi. 'I'm sorry, I should…'

'Go, of course. We can talk about it later,' said Lexi.

'I can call you from the car, if you want?'

'No, no. Tonight will be fine,' she said.

She waited until she heard him arrive in the kitchen, then turned her phone over and scrolled through the mounting number of pictures. She recognised herself but couldn't help feeling removed from the woman depicted. In some, her facial expression was garishly effervescent. In others, where she was shown pleasuring herself, her expression looked twisted and pained, almost grotesque. Lexi, fearing she may vomit, placed a hand over her mouth. As she did, a video came through. In it, Lexi lifted the hem of her skirt, pushed her underwear aside and brought herself to orgasm. Immediately afterwards, a message appeared on screen advising that the user had been blocked from the chatroom. The video ended.

A blinking ellipsis foretold of more to come. Lexi instinctively braced herself as a quick succession of messages burst onto her screen.

"In what universe do you think YOU can give ultimatums to ME?"

"Keep your fucking mouth shut, Lexi, or I will broadcast all your dirty secrets."

"How will Ethan react when he finds out he's sharing his bed with a dirty little whore?"

"What will they say at Lucas' childcare?"

"I'm sure they'd love to know that Lucas' new step mummy is a fucking dirty slut."

As Lexi read the vitriolic words, white-hot panic screamed into her ears and she felt as though she were falling. She had believed that what she was doing was harmless, a frivolous rebellion against a life that had felt too grown up for her, an egocentric lark. She had dipped a toe into the exotic waters of camming and was now surprised to find herself submerged, soaked and gasping for air. How would Ethan react if he found out that he had opened his life up to a duplicitous fraud? Someone claiming to be upstanding and true when in fact she was a morally bereft deviant. What kind of person would perform sexual acts on demand for the entertainment of eager voyeurs? What kind of person would enjoy it? She had been so smug, had compartmentalised her life so neatly, believing that Lexi and Jojo could reside in separate worlds that would never intersect. She scrolled through the photos again and again, feeding her sickening shame. She didn't deserve to be with a man like Ethan. Her mother was right. She was a toxic weed whose presence could threaten an entire ecosystem.

Lexi rubbed the scar tissue on her wrist and the blinking ellipses returned like a bad omen.

"We used to get along so well, Jojo. Surely we can kiss and make up."

"All this can go away if you want it to. I'll even delete all my favourite pictures of you."

"But you'll need to think of a way to make it up to me."

"You're a clever girl, I'm sure you'll have no problem thinking of something."

"So, I guess it's me who is giving you till the end of the week."

"And don't bother blabbing to anyone about this. You can't trace it back to me."

THIRTY-EIGHT

LEXI exited the Mini on shaky legs and made for the front door to scan in. The thought of smiling for the camera today, of peeling off her clothing on demand, made her feel wretched and cheap. Sickened as she was by Travis' proposal, she wondered if it was so far removed from what she had already been doing. She could be one blowjob away from leaving this chapter of her life behind. But the thought of complying repulsed her so thoroughly that she could scarcely even think about it. And who was to say what Travis would demand of her? What he could continue to demand from her. He could hardly be trusted to keep his word and delete the pictures. She imagined him like a virus lying in wait, flaring up whenever he was feeling bored. How could she continue her life with Ethan if Travis was their constant shadow?

Lexi ascended the stairs, clutching the banister for support. Her stomach turned inside out. She arrived at the dressing room to find Cherry shoving things into her bag, looking flustered. Looking up at Lexi's face, blotchy from weeping, she exclaimed, 'Oh my God! Allergies? Me too! It's been so bad lately, hasn't it?'

Lexi opened her mouth to respond but was cut off.

'I'm late!' Cherry exclaimed, slinging the overflowing bag over her shoulder. 'Jess and I have a meeting at the bank this morning. We're buying a house. At least, we want to buy a house. Oh, who the fuck knows? I'll see you tomorrow, okay? I hope you feel better.'

Lexi stood staring at the doorway in Cherry's wake. Catching her reflection in the mirror, she turned to regard herself. Her expression was confused, battle weary. Her shoulders slumped and she looked dejected and pitiful. How could she alchemise this into Jojo Cortado? She gazed around the room as if seeing it for the first time and flinched as two cam models came in chatting. They acknowledged her without breaking conversation.

'You do what?' exclaimed the tall brunette, sitting on the ottoman to remove her pumps.

Her friend, a round-faced, chubby blonde, giggled. 'I slap the bag,' she said.

'For tips?'

'Yes, for tips!'

'But why?'

'I don't know, they like it. Look.'

The blonde fished around in her bag and pulled out a silver bladder of wine. She held it up to her suggestively open mouth and slapped the bag, making it slosh and ripple as her friend laughed.

'What the hell made you put that on your menu in the first place.'

The blonde, cradling the bag of wine like a newborn, cast her eyes up to the ceiling. 'I think I did it once, during a drinking game and then they kept asking me to do it again and again. So… yeah, I just added it. It's not expensive or anything, obvs. But they love it.'

The brunette continued to laugh and shake her head as she changed her outfit.

Lexi stepped forward.

'Is that real wine in there?' she asked.

~

By the time Lexi was ready to hit the broadcast button a short time later, she had already consumed a third of the wine she'd paid her fellow cam model one hundred dollars for. Once inside the bedroom, as Veronica chattered, Lexi had slipped into the ensuite, emptied the contents of her water bottle into the sink and then filled it with wine. What remained, she downed in one. Wincing at the acidic tang of it, she ran her tongue across her front teeth. It was not quite 8:00 am, and with nothing in her stomach but coffee, she felt an overwhelming urge to vomit.

Lexi squinted into the webcam, willing it to remain still as she bobbed like a dinghy in a swell. She hit the broadcast button.

Catching her image on screen, she saw that one eye was scrunched tight, giving her a disfigured quality. She laughed, softening her expression and, in a voice an octave lower than usual said, 'Hello, boys,' to the few guests present.

'Do you ever try to do the right thing, but no matter how hard you try you just seem to fuck everything up?'

Comments appeared in her newsfeed but focusing on them made Lexi feel nauseous, so she looked away. She unscrewed the cap from her water bottle and took a gulp of wine. She slumped and nodded woefully, barely noticing users leaving her chatroom.

Receiving a private message, she exclaimed, 'ping!' and laughed as she attempted to open it. It was from ChivalryAlive asking if she was alright. Lexi swayed, laid back on the bed and closed her eyes to the spinning room.

~

Lexi woke to pain in her neck and flinched, thinking of Travis. As she straightened, leather groaned around her.

'Water and Panadol,' said Margot, raising her eyebrows to indicate the items on a side table next to the sofa. She resumed typing and Lexi sat up, wiping drool discreetly from the side of her mouth. A corresponding wet patch glistened on the sofa. *Fuck.* As Lexi reached for the water, she flipped the cushion and snuck a look at Margot who remained oblivious. She gulped down the capsules and ran her tongue over her furry teeth.

'Mind telling me what that was about this morning?' asked Margot.

Lexi's head throbbed. She looked up at the wall clock. Almost 2:00 pm. Casting her eyes downward, she winced at the wastepaper bin placed next to the sofa.

Lexi took a long draft of water. 'Margot, I'm sorry.'

Margot closed her laptop, removed her glasses and leaned back in her chair.

'I'm going through some… personal stuff, and… I tried to quit, as you know, but you reminded me about the notice period, and I guess I'm having a hard time getting through it.'

Margot nodded slowly and was silent for a long moment.

'I run a reputable business here, Lexi. I recruit the best talent and provide a safe work environment in a luxurious setting. What sets us apart from every other Dolly with a two-dollar webcam is class. What you did today—being intoxicated during a broadcast—is not acceptable. Now I could boot you out for breach of contract and sue for damages right now…'

Lexi sat up straighter.

'… but I'm not going to. At the same time, I cannot have you compromising a reputation which has taken me years to build. I can see that you are grappling with some demons, and I am not about to add to your troubles.'

Lexi held her breath as Margot slid a sheet of paper across her desk.

Lexi stood on shaky legs to take the page.

'This absolves you of your contract with Camnation. You will be paid up until yesterday.'

'Margot, I…' Lexi began in a thick voice.

'I know,' Margot said. She indicated the door with her eyes. 'Go.'

In the blazing sun, Lexi felt dishevelled and dirty, her body excreting cheap wine. With Camnation in the rear-view mirror, she considered Travis' ultimatum. If she did nothing, he would expose her. Lexi's head throbbed as she gripped the steering wheel, weaving through traffic with the extreme caution of the possibly drunk.

Pulling up in front of Ethan's gleaming home, Lexi felt there was only one thing she could do. Run.

THIRTY-NINE

ALTHOUGH her eyes were closed to the afternoon sun, Lexi wasn't sleeping. She lay in the shady corner of the garden, her hair still wrapped in a bath towel, listening to the whir of the pool's filtration system and a winged insect struggling for survival somewhere on the water's surface. If she remained still, she could keep the nausea at bay and if she kept her eyes closed, she could pretend that she wasn't staring down the barrel of leaving behind the only man she'd ever loved.

Lexi heard the sliding door open, and Lucas arrived, nuzzling himself into her embrace.

'You smell like treasure fruit,' he said into her neck, and it took her a moment to register that he meant the pomegranate body wash she had shared with him when he was unwell.

She pulled him into her, tighter.

'This looks cosy,' said Ethan, walking over.

Lexi could hear the smile in his voice and kept her eyes closed.

She felt his weight on the daybed and then his arms were around her, with Lucas nestled between them.

Please universe, kill me now. Her heart broke over and over until every cell in her body hummed with the pain of it. *I'm a ghost now. I have ceased to exist in this world.* And there was solace in that.

But her thoughts were interrupted by Ethan muttering, 'I kinda wish I didn't invite my brothers over now.'

An hour later the doorbell announced the arrival of Ethan's two brothers, their wives and their combined six children. They shuffled over the threshold in a cluster, disturbing the peaceful interior of the house with their reverberating commotion. As Lexi accepted offerings of wine and desserts, Lucas clung to her leg, bashful in the face of their ruckus. He flinched as Kate screeched at Michael. 'How is it that Ethan knows how to cook, and you don't even know how to boil an egg?'

She shouldered her husband roughly as she moved past him, and he scowled at the back of her head.

When Marija appeared, she wordlessly planted a kiss on either side of Lexi's face before pulling her into an embrace. Then, she crouched down to Lucas, smoothed his hair, and whispered something Lexi couldn't hear. She watched as the boy's face lit up and he allowed himself to be lifted onto her hip.

'How was the rest of your birthday?' asked Marija.

'It is a distant memory,' said Lexi.

'We'll have to start planning next year. Thirty, right?'

A lump formed in Lexi's throat. What would Marija think of her when she left without a trace? Misunderstanding Lexi's forlorn expression, Marija said, 'Don't worry, thirty is just a number.'

Kate's shrill voice cut above the din, saving Lexi from further exchange, 'For eff's sake, Harrison, get your disgusting shoes off the couch!'

Marija and Lexi exchanged a look.

'Come on,' said Marija, 'let's open a bottle of something.'

She turned to Lucas on her hip and said, 'Why don't you find Anouk? She brought her unicorn; you can brush its mane and everything.'

Lucas turned his mouth into an O and wriggled to be put down.

Marija linked Lexi's arm, scooped a bottle of wine off the bench and ventured further into the kitchen in search of glasses.

Ethan, grinding pink salt onto thick slabs of steak, looked up as they approached.

'You two look like you're planning trouble,' he said.

'Who, us?' asked Marija, wide-eyed.

Lexi saw her life from the other side of a lens. If she were another type of woman—the right kind of woman—she could spend a lifetime living happily like this. As Marija and Ethan exchanged banter, Lexi tried to imagine the person who would replace her—someone more like Marija. Marija exuded goodness, wit and intelligence. Lexi felt like the stupidest woman on the planet. How else could one explain how thoroughly she had fucked up her one chance at happiness?

Lexi retrieved six wine glasses and filled them, thankful for the distraction. Once she was finished, she lifted the first glass with the intention of passing it to Marija, but Kate swooped in to claim it before she could complete the gesture.

'God give me strength,' she said, downing most of the contents in a single gulp.

'I'm driving then,' observed Michael, shuffling over. 'Hi, Lex,' he said, claiming a glass and turning on his heel to take up residence on the sofa.

Marija picked up two glasses and made for Ben out on the lawn, where he was lifting each child upside down, making them squeal.

Ethan gathered the steaks onto a plate.

'I love you,' said Lexi.

Her voice sounded choked and foreign to her ears.

Pulling the tea towel from his shoulder, he wiped his hands and threw it on the bench. Then he was wrapping his strong arms around her, and she was liquefying, her face pressed into his neck as he held her.

'What?' said Kate, appearing by their side to refill her glass. 'You two haven't seen each other for fifteen seconds?'

She turned on her heel, taking the bottle with her and Lexi looked up at Ethan who was stifling a laugh.

'I'd better get these on,' he said, releasing her and collecting the plate of meat. He took a few steps then turned. 'I love you too,' he said.

Lexi placed her hands on the bench to steady herself. Noticing, Marija approached. 'Are you okay?' she said.

'I got woozy for a second, I'm fine.'

Lexi unwrapped packets of deli goods and arranged them on a meandering series of wooden boards across the vast island bench. Marija opened boxes of crackers and nestled them like fallen dominos amongst the antipasti. She stopped to take a sip of her wine, her eyes on Lexi's untouched glass.

'You're not pregnant, are you?' she whispered.

It took Lexi a moment to understand Marija's logic.

'Oh my God, no!' she said, picking up the glass and taking a miniscule sip for show.

'So, then…?'

'I quit my job today. I guess I'm feeling like I don't know what I'm supposed to do now. Where I'm supposed to go…' she said, trailing off.

Marija's brow softened. 'I'll let you in on a little secret,' she said. 'As long as you have chosen the right people to spend your life with, everything else is just details.'

Lexi closed her eyes. Her phone rang, rousing her and she snapped open her eyes.

'Get it,' said Marija, tapping her on the arm before resuming her task.

Lexi walked slowly towards the stairs and pulled her phone out of her back pocket.

'Hi, Linh,' she answered, feeling weary.

'I've got the day off work tomorrow,' said Linh. 'Want to skip work and go to the beach?'

Lexi smiled into the phone. 'Yes. Yes, I do.'

FORTY

THE ocean's surface reflected a billion tiny, frenzied suns as Lexi descended the precarious steps towards the sand. Shielding her eyes with a raised hand, she scanned the shore for Linh amongst the mothers with young children and high-school kids bunking off. Spotting her face between gargantuan headphones, Lexi made her way through sand that felt as though it may swallow her.

'Hey,' said Lexi.

Linh's eyes remained closed as she writhed to the music.

'Hey,' she said again, nudging her friend's thigh with her bare foot.

Linh's eyes opened and she smiled. 'Hey!' she exclaimed, thrusting her arms skyward, beckoning a hug.

Lexi dumped her tote and kneeled on her friend's towel, allowing herself to be pulled down into a giggling heap. When their laughter subsided, Lexi lay next to Linh, regaining her breath. She wondered what life would be like without Linh once she left this life behind and tears fell beneath her sunglasses.

At first, Linh didn't seem to notice, but the more Lexi tried to rein in her emotions, the more they conspired to unravel her. Finally, Linh propped herself up onto one elbow and asked in a gentle voice, 'Lex? What is it?'

After that, a landslide of words came tumbling out of Lexi's mouth. She told Linh about how suffocated she felt after moving in with Ethan, how the essence of herself had diminished with every passing day. She told the story of her best friend, Geoff, who disappeared a decade earlier and re-entered her life, unfathomably transformed. Of the exotic world in which Jamie resided. A world which Lexi longed to join. And finally, with her eyes locked tight against the all-consuming shame, she told her of her attraction to Travis Nolan and the disastrous chain of events that followed. Afterwards, she lay there spent and tear-streaked, heaving.

Linh, who had sat up cross-legged, remained still and silent for a time trying to process what she had heard.

Finally, she spoke. 'You've been doing... sex work?'

Lexi smarted at the phrase "sex work" but begrudgingly nodded. Now was not the time to clarify how she believed camming was in a category all its own. She feared she may throw up.

'And some misogynistic prick is blackmailing you, so you're going to walk away without a fight?'

'What fight, Linh?'

Linh was making it sound as though Lexi had some other option and she began to regret her confession. Feeling exposed and foolish, Lexi sat up.

'Look,' she said, shifting slightly away. 'The way I see it, there aren't a helluva lot of options. He's a fucking cop for Christ's sake. What the fuck am I meant to do?'

Linh thought for a while.

'You say this guy's a wolf?' she said. 'Maybe it's time we set a trap?'

FORTY-ONE

LEXI held her breath as she waited for the door to be answered, fidgeting with the hemline of Linh's top, which she now wore as a dress. Her whole body screamed at her to run, but instead she stood rooted to the doorstep she had vowed never to set foot on again. The deadlock clicked from the other side and she arranged her face into a coy expression.

'You sure do know how to get a girl's attention,' she said, stepping over the threshold and kissing either side of Travis Nolan's face before slipping past him into the house. She placed her handbag down on the coffee table and resisted the urge to look at the small hole Linh had cut into its side.

Travis, still standing at the front door, fixed his gaze on her.

'Aren't you going to offer me a drink?' she asked, seating herself and crossing her legs.

Why had she worn this absurd outfit? He would see right through this obvious ploy and probably kill her.

He crossed the room to tower over her and she leaned back into the sofa in a show of complete ease.

'You're not mad?' he asked, eyes narrowing.

She laughed and took his hand, pulling him down to sit beside her. She hoped they would be perfectly framed by the phone, gaffer taped to the inside of her handbag, but she dared not look.

When Linh had suggested this hare-brained scheme on the beach, Lexi had baulked at the idea. This was not some B-grade spy movie.

But that night, lying awake listening to Ethan breathing beside her, she had conceded that this could be her only chance of remaining with him. The next morning Lexi had called Linh to tell her she'd do it.

'Where do we start?' she asked.

'Fuck, I don't know. I guess first we google, like, recording devices or something?' said Linh.

Lexi's heart sank. She had spent half the night awake, psyching herself up for a plan she had believed was at least partially thought out.

Feeling desperate but trying to sound light, Lexi asked, 'Aren't you meant to be some burgeoning IT whizz now that your uncle is sending you to TAFE?'

'Well, yeah. If you want to build a website for this fuckstick then I'm your girl. But this is a little outside my skill set.'

That's when Lexi remembered Mason. When Lexi phoned him, he had cancelled the call and texted her saying he'd call her back. She wondered if he was in class and prepared herself for a long wait, but he called a few minutes later. His voice bore a tell-tale echo which Lexi assumed was from the toilet block at school. When she told him the nature of her conundrum, she heard the click of his lighter, followed by a lip-smacked inhalation. A succession of low grunts was her only indication that he was following what she was saying. As she neared the close of her story, Lexi felt foolish and ashamed, bracing herself for his dismissal, even his mockery. But neither of those things came. Instead, he said, 'Zoom recording'.

'Excuse me?' she said, sure that she had missed something.

'Zoom. It's a video conferencing tool. Let's you record meetings. It means someone can keep an eye on you. Instead of just using your phone to film.'

Lexi's sluggish comprehension left her silent.

'I'm guessing you know how to video conference,' he prompted and took another deep drag of his cigarette.

She was about to contradict him when she realised, he was referring to her experience with camming. A further explanation about the Camnation interface had him chuckling at her technological ineptitude but something in the tone of her pleading made him stop abruptly and provide her with all the information she needed.

Now, both he and Linh were dialled into a Zoom conference being hosted on her phone, taped to the inside of her bag. Mason sat in his bedroom in Hamilton, recording the stream while Linh sat parked two doors down, in Travis' street. Lexi fought hard to remain focused. She was playing a part and could not afford to let her mind wander.

'Of course, I was mad. Women get mad after they get jealous,' she said, as though it pained her to admit it.

Travis' lips curled into a smile and he visibly relaxed.

She went on.

'It was kind of hot, you know,' she said, fiddling with her bra strap.

'Hot?' he asked, running his eyes over her cleavage.

He leaned back into the sofa. Spreading his legs wide, he rested a knee against hers and ran his index finger under her hemline, brushing against her thigh. Lexi fought the impulse to slap his hand away, instead gently pressing her leg into his hand.

'You taking all those screenshots of my Camnation broadcasts.'

Lexi made certain she was leaving nothing unsaid.

Travis looked down into his lap and laughed huskily.

'It's okay,' she teased. 'So you put me in the spank bank.'

He leaned over and slapped her thigh. 'You're the one that needs a spank,' he said.

Lexi, feeling repulsed, took a breath to centre herself. 'Would you have done it?' she asked.

Her ears seemed to whistle with the certainty that she was venturing too far.

'Done it?' he asked, with unsophisticated innuendo.

'Sent the photos to Ethan, to his kid's childcare,' said Lexi, unable to say Lucas' name.

'Well, I guess we'll never know.'

Lexi wondered frantically if this was enough of an admission. Had the wolf been trapped? Or was he still prowling, just out of reach?

Travis made to stand but Lexi placed a hand on his knee to stop him, worried that if they moved, she would not be able to relocate her bag without arousing suspicion.

'Is that your new phone number? Should I delete the old one?' she asked, trying to sound casual.

Travis laughed scornfully. 'I texted you from a burner.'

Lexi's heartbeat quickened.

'A burner? You mean a phone that can't be traced back to you?'

Travis' eyes narrowed and it took all of Lexi's willpower to keep her features impassive.

Don't look at the handbag, don't look at the handbag.

'Well, what kind of muppet would blackmail someone from his own phone?'

His gaze bore into her for an excruciating beat before his face cracked into an arrogant arrangement that she longed to punch.

I've got him.

'You're so bad!' she squealed, shoving him playfully.

'Drink?' he asked, standing.

'Finally! I'm parched.'

She stood with him and muttered to herself, 'While you're doing that, I might just…' As he retrieved glasses she rummaged around in her handbag, pulling things out and making a show of having misplaced something.

'Everything okay over there?' Travis called out from the kitchen, a measure of sarcasm detectible beneath his words.

Lexi sighed loudly, keeping her head down as she replaced all but her sunglasses into the bag. From her bent position, she looked up at him and said, 'It's kind of embarrassing.'

'What is?'

'I think my diaphragm case fell out of my bag. It must be sitting in the front seat,' she said.

Lexi had never heard of any woman using a piece of birth-control paraphernalia so antiquated, but she was banking on Travis being too clueless to know that they were all but decommissioned.

'Don't worry about it,' he said, making his way over with the drinks he'd prepared. 'I've got dingers. Or maybe…' he said, handing her the drink, 'I can pull out.'

He handed her a drink, which she accepted. With eyes fixed on his, she took a long sip.

'I hate the feel of condoms and I'm in the middle of my fertile week.'

She placed her drink down on the coffee table.

'I mean, maybe we could chance it…' she said, thoughtfully.

'Go get it. You said it's in the car?'

'Just in the car,' she repeated.

She rose onto her toes, making for his mouth as if to kiss him and then snapped her teeth together in a biting motion just shy of his lips.

Lexi's blood coursed hot and severe through her body as she turned from him and made for the front door. The fear that he would demand to know why she was taking her handbag with her for a quick trip out to the car screamed in her ears. As she placed her hand on the deadlock which kept her from freedom he spoke. 'Hey,' he said, sharply.

Lexi cocked her head, but her body remained in position, ready to bolt.

'Don't take too long,' he said, 'Or I'll be forced to start without you.'

She turned to see him unzip his jeans and take himself in hand, brandishing his erection with pride.

'You're so bad,' she said again. And then she was out the door, striding towards the Mini, the hunched figure of Linh barely visible in the driver's seat.

Lexi flashed a look at Jamie, whose car was parked a block down.

Seeing Lexi, she gave a single nod and started her engine.

'Drive,' instructed Lexi as she climbed into the car next to Linh.

She turned around in her seat to see Jamie park in Travis' driveway and walk to the front door carrying a bottle of wine and a brown paper grocery bag.

Lexi struggled to untape her phone from the inside of her bag and send a text to Travis.

"Fuck, just saw Jamie arrive so I bailed."

Lexi turned to Linh, her face a desperate question mark.

'We got him,' she said.

After downloading Zoom as Mason had suggested, Lexi and Linh had sat in Ethan's kitchen fleshing out details of the plan.

'The question is,' Linh mused, 'how are we going to get you out of there without arousing suspicion? I mean, if you make some excuse to go out to your car and then don't come back…'

'There's nothing to stop him from sending all those screenshots to Ethan and Lucas' childcare on the spot,' Lexi said, nodding.

Linh clicked her fingers and shot out her index finger.

'Unless…,' said Lexi.

'There was a *reason* you couldn't come back inside,' said Linh, finishing the thought.

As Lexi listened to the ringtone, waiting for Jamie to answer, she thought about the last time they had seen each other. The venomous words Jamie had spat at her. The way her fine features had twisted with contempt. With no answer and feeling deflated, Lexi removed the phone from her ear to end the call and heard Jamie say, 'Hi, Lexi,' in a small voice.

Fearful that she would not be able to explain the situation before Jamie hung up on her, she opened with, 'Jamie, I need your help. Can you come over, please?'

An hour later, the three women were seated at the island bench, a platter of fruit sweating between them for no other reason than to affect normalcy.

Something about Linh's presence in the room made Lexi feel supported enough to succinctly tell the entire history of her and Travis to Jamie. Still, Lexi was unable to meet anyone's eyes. She stated the facts mechanically, folding her unused paper napkin over and over until it would fold no more, only to smooth it out and resume the sequence again. When the sordid story ended, she looked up with the trepidation one might use to peek through latticed fingers in the aftermath of a horrific film scene. Her gaze flitted to Linh who gave her a reassuring nod and then landed on Jamie, whose head was bowed inspecting her kempt cuticles. Lexi held her breath.

'You know I don't want it to be true, right?' said Jamie.

Lexi nodded solemnly.

'Because if it's true, I'm an idiot.'

'You're not an idiot,' said Lexi and Linh in unison.

Jamie laughed, a raspy and pitiful sound which Lexi recognised from when they were kids. It was resigned and melancholic. It was the sound which had concluded pained confessions in Lexi's childhood bedroom.

Lexi placed a hand on Jamie's leg, and she covered it with her own.

'I'm sorry, Lex,' she whispered.

Tears prickled the corners of Lexi's eyes and she blinked them back.

'I was so caught up in who I hoped Travis would be that I was blind to who he actually is,' said Jamie.

The three sat in silence until Jamie spoke again. 'What do you need me to do?'

After that, Lexi and Linh shared the emerging elements of the plan. When they came to the part where Lexi would make an excuse to return to her car and Jamie would appear for an impromptu visit at Travis' house, Jamie wrinkled her nose.

'I'm not really cool with being the bait in this scenario. I mean, now that I know about him all I want to do is text him that we're over, you know? It's not like I want to turn up with wine and cheese and get sexy with him.'

'Of course. You're right, I'm sorry,' Lexi said, feeling embarrassed by her oversight.

Meanwhile, Linh cradled her chin, thinking. 'Okay,' she said, 'when Lexi goes in there she asks for a drink, so when you turn up you see two glasses in there, maybe one with lipstick on the rim.'

Lexi perked up at this and nodded eagerly. 'And I could leave something behind, a jacket or something,' she said.

'In this heat?' asked Jamie.

'Sunglasses, whatever,' said Lexi.

'I walk in, see that he has company and break up with him on the spot,' said Jamie.

'You can even throw the cheese in his face,' quipped Lexi.

'I better make it a Gorgonzola then,' said Jamie, laughing.

Lexi echoed the sound before turning sombre.

Picking up the change, Linh spoke. 'You're only going to be in there for a few minutes. And I'll be right outside, watching you from my phone. If anything goes wrong, I'll call the cops and I'll break a fucking window to get you out of there.'

Lexi, who could easily imagine Linh breaking a window to get to her, gave a sad laugh.

'And your little brother will be making a recording?' asked Jamie.

Lexi thought of what little she knew of Mason. His Camnation username, StonedMason, was a huge red flag but, even though he seemed to be a school-skipping pothead, she could tell that this outward persona masked a highly intelligent and thoughtful young man. Still, the entire plan hinged on his participation and there was a part of Lexi that saw this as a major weakness.

'He'll record it and then we'll take the video to Linh's uncle,' she said.

'He's a criminal lawyer,' Linh added proudly.

FORTY-TWO

LEXI checked her phone for the hundredth time but there was still no response from Mason. Once Lexi had received confirmation that Jamie had successfully ended her relationship with Travis and fled, she had placed a call to her brother. When it rang through to his voicemail—which opened with the unmistakable gurgle of a bong being pulled, followed by the coughed laughter of several voices and a choked "Leave a message. Or don't"—her heart sank. Turning to meet Linh's expectant gaze, she forced a smile and said, 'It went to voicemail, I'll text him.'

Now, hours had passed, and she was distractedly preparing dinner with Ethan and Lucas. She had stolen away to the downstairs powder room so many times that Ethan had sidled up to her as she was chopping capsicum and asked, 'Tummy bug?'

Taking a moment to understand the implication, she said, 'Oh. Yeah, maybe I ate something a bit dodgy today.'

Carefully removing the knife from her grasp Ethan placed a guiding hand in the centre of her back and said, 'Why don't you go upstairs and have a little lie down? We've got this, haven't we, mate?'

Lucas nodded.

'Thanks, guys,' said Lexi, feeling guilty in the face of their concern for her.

~

Now, Lexi lay on the bed holding her phone, attempting to conjure a response from Mason. When her phone lit up with an incoming text from Travis, she all but jumped.

"Sorry our party was cut short today. Want to come over now? That fucking bitch broke up with me, I need cheering up."

Lexi's heartbeat quickened and she glanced at the door. The distant chatter of Ethan and Lucas rising from the kitchen confirmed her continued solitude upstairs.

She sat up and chewed her thumbnail. She needed to keep the tone light.

"Poor baby! I wish I could. Stuck here in Snoozeville tonight."

His reply was almost instantaneous.

"You better hope I don't get bored tonight. Might be forced to send out those screenshots early. Tick tock, Lexi."

Lexi realised she'd been hoping that Travis would forget the whole thing now that she was onside again. Somewhere deep down she had thought that if she could stall him and placate him that he would tire of his game and simply fade from her life.

Even if Mason did come through with the recording and she was able to get it to Linh's uncle, what then? It wasn't like she could hide an entire criminal case, with court appearances, from Ethan. All the optimism she had mustered was bleeding from her, leaving a hollow dread in its place. Letting the phone rest in her lap, she covered her face with her hands and exhaled, awaiting the flood of tears she knew was about to descend. But instead, her breath caught in her throat when her phone lit up with Mason's call.

Fumbling to answer, her phone hit the floor with a thud just as Ethan appeared in the doorway.

'Feeling any better?' he asked, coming to sit beside her.

'Not so much,' she said, truthfully, her eyes darting towards her phone, face down on the floor.

Ethan, following her eyes, looked at the phone. As Lexi bent forward to retrieve it, Ethan placed a hand on her leg and reached for it himself.

He placed it in her hand without looking at it and brushed a stray hair from Lexi's forehead. 'You rest,' he said, kissing her on the cheek and standing.

Lexi snuck a glance at her phone, which displayed a notification of the missed call, and turned it face-down on her thigh as Ethan turned back to look at her.

'Can I get you some water? With some Hydralyte, maybe?'

Lexi shook her head too quickly and Ethan, misunderstanding the gesture, looked towards the ensuite door and said hastily, 'I'll leave you to it.'

Once the sound of Ethan's footsteps had petered out, Lexi turned over her phone.

Since she'd failed to answer his call, Mason had sent a text.

"Sorry I've been MIA, Dad caught me wagging school and took my phone. Just emailed you the vid. That pig is a fucking prick."

Lexi crept to the ensuite and closed the door behind her. She sat down on the toilet lid and clicked into the email address she had set up as Jojo Cortado. Underneath the email from Mason was one from Clive, and Lexi realised that she hadn't been in contact with him since that last Camnation broadcast in which she had gloriously written herself off with cask wine. *He must be worried sick.*

She opened the email from Mason and steeled herself before clicking into the video link.

It opened with her knocking on Travis' door, and she could hear herself greeting him as the door opened to reveal a view of his torso only. Her voice sounded foreign and strange, the flirting inflection made her feel sick. When the bag was placed down on the coffee table, the video showed a brief flash of Lexi's underpants under Linh's top, before she seated herself on the sofa and looked up at Travis. Lexi thought of this video being shown to countless people and wondered what they would think of her, how they would judge not only this but all the events preceding it. Even if they didn't say it, they would all see her as a manipulative whore who deserved what Travis was doing; that women like her were fair game. Nice girls didn't get themselves in situations like this. Good girls don't use their sexuality as currency and then complain when things don't go their way.

Lexi had expected to feel victorious in this moment but all she felt was shameful and stupid. Despite the balminess of the evening, Lexi's skin bloomed with goosebumps. She set her phone down on the floor, kneeled beside it and lifted the lid of the toilet to vomit.

When Lexi had cleaned herself up and crawled into bed, a single memory rose to the surface of her turbulent thoughts. Paige, her former boss at The Bean & Gone Café, promising to hire her again if she ever found herself in Perth. Perth was the furthest Australian city from Melbourne, which made it even more attractive to Lexi in this calamitous and hopeless moment. She reached for her phone and texted Paige with a lightness that contradicted the contents of her heart.

"Thinking of a move out to the wild, wild west. Need some help kicking off your next venture?"

Lexi pulled the covers up over her head and begged for sleep to take her.

FORTY-THREE

AS Lexi shifted on the leather upholstered chair, she could hear her skin peeling from the material with a *tchurp*. She looked at Linh sitting behind a reception desk, her hair pulled back to accommodate a headset which buzzed incessantly, alerting her to inquiries that Lexi imagined were far more important than her own.

Although Lexi had decided in her fitful slumber the night before not to see this thing through, she owed it to Linh to meet with her Uncle Hung, the criminal lawyer, and to hear out what he had to say. How else would she be able to torment herself with "what-ifs" from Perth if she didn't have a clear picture of exactly what all her options had been in the eye of this storm? Lexi knew damn well that she didn't have the courage to subject herself to the level of public scrutiny required to press charges against Travis Nolan, but she did feel an obligation to make a show of it for Linh. Her friend had shown up for her, and she couldn't yet reveal her cowardice in the face of such loyalty. No, Lexi would hear what Hung had to say and appear to deliberate over it before boarding a flight to Perth in a few days' time. Once there, she would throw herself into helping Paige set up a new café. She was going to fall back into her old habit of running away from her problems and kid herself that she was better off alone, and the knowledge of this felt so familiar that it was almost a comfort. She was a fuckup who, for a brief shining moment, had believed she could be otherwise. Shaking her head imperceptibly, she reached for a magazine and thumbed through it, unseeing. She gripped it tighter to steady her trembling hands, riding the familiar waves of self-disgust and disappointment that engulfed her. *Don't fucking cry*, she cautioned herself. *Don't you dare fucking cry.*

A door opened and she looked up to see a handsome middle-aged man cross the reception area towards her. Linh removed her headset to follow him as he extended his hand. Lexi rose to meet him.

'This is my good friend, Lexi Karras,' said Linh, gesturing towards her with an open palm.

'Lex, this is my uncle, Hung Nguyen,' she said, giving Lexi an encouraging smile.

'Nice to finally meet you, Lexi, Linh has told me a lot about you.'

'Nice to meet you, Mr. Nguyen,' said Lexi, taking his hand.

'Please, call me Hung.'

He released her hand and gestured towards the door he had emerged from. 'Shall we?'

Lexi looked towards Linh who, to her horror, was reseating herself behind the reception desk.

'Aren't you going to come with us?' she asked, tipping her head towards the open door.

'Oh, I have to…' said Linh, indicating the blinking switchboard as she donned her headset and sat. 'Roberts and Nguyen Criminal Lawyers, Linh speaking,' she said, positioning her fingers on the keyboard in front of her.

Lexi turned towards Hung, framed in the door, forced a weak smile and followed him through.

Once seated, Lexi's eyes swept over Hung's various certificates and awards, emanating like an aura on the white wall behind him. Sensing his face opening into a smile, Lexi snapped her gaze towards him, wondering if he expected her to begin.

'Linh tells me you two worked at the café together,' said Hung.

Lexi released the breath she was holding.

'Yeah. Yes. We did,' she replied.

'And that when you two lost your jobs, that's when you found yourself in a bit of trouble?'

Lexi nodded and looked down at her lap. 'She's told you the story,' she said, relieved that she wouldn't have to recount all the embarrassing details.

'No, all she said was that you're in a situation that I may be able to assist you with.'

Lexi's heart sank.

Sensing her discomfort, Hung leaned forward to rest on his forearms and said, 'Just start at the beginning.'

Lexi smoothed down the hem of her dress and nodded slowly. 'After I lost my job at the café…' she began.

FORTY-FOUR

THUD, *thud, thud.* Lexi's head connected with the steering wheel over and over, sending bursts of pain through her skull. She continued this action until her attention was caught by a slack-jawed elderly woman, pushing a plaid shopping trolley alongside her car. Lexi jammed her keys into the ignition and started the engine and, ignoring her buzzing phone, pulled out onto the road. She dragged a fist across her eyes, leaving thick black smudges on the back of her hand.

When it had all turned to shit in Linh's uncle's office, Lexi had been surprised by the soul-crushing disappointment that engulfed her. For all her self-assurances that the plan was to cut and run, somewhere deep-down Lexi had been harbouring a hope that the video of Travis admitting to blackmail would somehow guarantee her passage into a quiet life with Ethan.

When Lexi came to the end of the story and removed her phone in order to play Hung the video, he let out a long exhalation, his eyes falling briefly on his closed office door.

'It's just that…' he began.

Lexi could tell by his tone that he was about to reveal something regretful and so replaced the phone in her bag.

'I should preface this by saying that this area of the law is very, shall we say, murky. Up until quite recently the only laws surrounding the gathering of evidence via recording devices centred on telecommunications hardware, infrastructure, the interception of calls, that kind of thing. They don't consider that almost everyone carries a recording device on their person every single day,' he said, picking up his phone and giving it a decisive shake.

Lexi nodded slowly.

'What you're describing—recording someone without their consent—is illegal in most Australian states.'

Lexi looked down at her clasped hands and swallowed.

'And even if you have someone confessing to a crime…'

Hung paused and Lexi lifted her head to meet his gaze.

'It may not be admissible as evidence.'

Lexi smoothed her hair and nodded. 'Of course, I get it.'

When Linh had suggested this audacious plan, Lexi had naively believed that, legally, it would hold water. She had put herself and Jamie in danger and it had all amounted to nothing. Now it seemed that the plan had more likely come from one of Linh's late-night Netflix binge sessions rather than from her experience at the legal firm. Lexi hadn't even bothered to google if this type of evidence had any legal standing and the oversight stung like a barb.

'It's just that, with the absence of any other evidence…' Hung let his words trail off as Lexi gathered up her belongings.

'Of course,' said Lexi again.

She wished her body could dissolve into the carpet so she wouldn't have to smile and shake hands with this sophisticated man. She was embarrassed; she felt like her very presence in this stylish, white cube of an office was somehow an affront to him.

As she was led back out to reception, Lexi tried not to look at Linh. Instead, she turned towards Hung, took his outstretched hand, and said, 'Thank you for seeing me, I'm sorry to have wasted your time.'

'Not at all.'

He placed his free hand atop their clasped hands and gave a reassuring squeeze.

When Lexi turned around, Linh's expression was grave. She

opened her mouth to speak but Lexi silenced her with a brief shake of her head.

Then she was out in the bright morning sunshine, striding towards her car and away from her last shred of hope.

~

Lexi's cheeks were hot and wet as she dragged the desk chair over to the wardrobe. She climbed atop it and reached for the suitcase she had arrived at Ethan's house with just months before. Placing it down on the floor, she unzipped the case and extracted a photo of her family from the internal compartment. She looked at her mother, radiantly beautiful and more petite than Lexi, even back then. Monique stood, hip thrust out to support a chubby Mia, her hand resting on Mason, wrapped around her leg. Darrin stood beside their huddle, the four of them creating a singular blob. To Darrin's left Lexi stood—her hair still dark back then—head inclined pitifully towards their blonde ones. Lexi had stared at this photo so many times over the years that the memory of the day it was taken had faded along with its colour. She couldn't even remember who had taken it. Instead of a captured memory, the photo had become a symbol of Lexi's solitude, of her being the piece that never quite fit. She rubbed at the scar on her wrist.

As Lexi packed, she considered her next course of action. The easy option was to leave without a trace. Pack her bag and leave before Ethan returned home with Lucas. She could get a hotel room at the airport and be on the first flight to Perth in the morning. Travis would send Ethan the photos and video of her camming which would serve as a grotesque explanation for her disappearance. All she would have to do was move forward, without looking back. But she loved Ethan and the idea that she would have no opportunity to even try to explain her side of the story sickened her. The surety of his heartbreak felt crippling. How could she disappear without a trace, knowing that Ethan would need to push aside his own tempest of feelings in order to concoct a reasonable way to explain things to Lucas? To stare into the child's soulful eyes—as he'd done after the sudden death of his mother—and tell him that Lexi too was gone without warning or the opportunity for goodbyes. No, she would look Ethan in the eye and tell him the humiliating truth, she owed him that much.

Lexi's phone rang again. She stared at Linh's name on the screen and, taking a deep breath, swiped to answer. 'Hi.'

'Lex, I'm so sorry. I thought… I was stupid. I should have checked. I guess I—' blurted Linh.

'It's okay, Linh,' Lexi interjected.

She closed her eyes as if to shut out Linh's feelings of responsibility and regret. 'You've got nothing to be sorry about. You were trying to help,' said Lexi.

Linh sighed. 'I feel like going over there with a baseball bat, you know?' she said.

Lexi let out a weary laugh. She didn't know. At this point she didn't have the energy to even lift a bat, let alone beat Travis into submission with one.

'What are you going to do now?' Linh asked, hesitantly.

'I'm packing, I'm going to tell him tonight.' Lexi swallowed the lump in her throat before going on. 'I got in contact with Paige. She's been bored shitless stuck at home with her sister and the kids. She's started looking for spaces for a new café. Says the coffee around Watermans Bay is like dishwater.'

Linh laughed. 'Classic Paige.'

They fell silent.

'He might understand, you know. Maybe you won't have to leave at all. You could work it out. Try counselling or something. I'm sure people have worked through worse shit than this,' said Linh.

An unexpected flicker of hope burst within Lexi which she immediately scolded herself for.

They fell silent again.

'I was wondering if you could look after my car, maybe help me sell it?'

'Let's see what happens tonight, okay?' said Linh.

Lexi sighed. 'Anyway, I should go. I want to have all this taken care of by the time Ethan gets home.'

'Yeah, okay. You'll call me after?'

'I'll call you.'

As Lexi resumed packing, she experienced her surroundings in hyper-awareness. The way the plush carpet felt beneath her bare feet, the subtle hum of the air conditioner, the view of the swimming pool glittering in patches of afternoon sun through the bordering foliage. It was as if she were taking stock of each miniscule detail, willing herself to never forget this, the backdrop of her fleeting happiness. The sight of the half-empty wardrobe with its swinging clatter of hangers stung as she slid the door closed. Picking up the juice-bottle jellyfish Lucas had made, she smoothed a piece of masking tape beginning to curl at the edges and tucked it into her suitcase. She zipped it closed, then unzipped a small section, roughly shoving in one of Ethan's discarded t-shirts which had fallen short of the laundry hamper that morning. The premonition of burying her face into his familiar scent each night rose like a taunt. Lexi stood the case upright, labouring under its weight, and manoeuvred it downstairs. Reaching the foot of the stairs, she took a moment to catch her breath before wheeling it into the downstairs powder room and out of sight.

~

Although Lexi had run before, she had never left anywhere or anyone she wasn't desperate to be shot of. As she sat by the pool sipping a coffee, she was struck by how physical her inclination to stay felt. How much she wished to bury herself into the very bedrock of her life here so that nothing could pry her from it. It felt as if her body was rejecting what her mind was about to do and it hurt. She thought of the expanse of time following Ethan and Lucas' arrival home. The familiar routine of dinner, bath, bed which would need to take place before she could be alone with Ethan. Before she was able to sit opposite him and tell him that she was not the person he thought he was in love with.

Next to her hand, Lexi's phone buzzed with a text from Jamie.

"How did it go with the lawyer today? I thought you were going to call me after?"

Lexi shook her head, disbelieving that her appointment with Hung had been just a few hours ago. Her fingers hovered over the keyboard before she typed, "The lawyer was nice, but he said that even with the video, I have no case. Time to come clean, I guess."

Lexi stared at her phone screen for evidence of an impending reply, but none came. Jamie would be kicking off her broadcast now. Lexi wondered if she should tell her about her move to Perth but decided that if Jamie checked her phone during her show, the news might unnerve her.

Downing the last sip of cold coffee, Lexi closed her eyes, wishing she could fast forward to the moment when she and Ethan were alone. Now that she knew what needed to be done, it was the waiting that was slowly killing her.

Looking at her phone again, she remembered the unanswered email from Clive. At least she wasn't going to lose him in all this. And because their friendship was a virtual one it was the one thing that could remain constant. She brought up his email and began her long, pained reply. When she was done, Lexi returned to the kitchen with her empty cup and was surprised to find Lucas bounding towards her, holding up a piece of crinkled paper. Experiencing a nausea-inducing jolt of adrenaline, Lexi's eyes darted around for Ethan.

'You're home early,' she said, cupping the boy's soft cheek.

The boy ignored her, instead shaking the sheet of paper to indicate she should take it. Lexi took in the crayon scribbles that were washed with blue watercolour.

'For you,' he said proudly. 'You know what it is?'

Lexi crouched down so they could look at it together. 'Is it the fish tank at childcare?' she said, her voice an unrecognisable knot.

He smiled his confirmation.

She opened her arms to envelop him, pushing her face into the softness of his hair and when she looked up Ethan was standing in the doorway, holding her suitcase.

'What's this?' he asked, his face an arrangement of concerned confusion.

The wind had been knocked out of Lexi. She turned her face back into Lucas' neck and whispered, 'I love it. I love you and I will keep this with me forever.'

As she stood, she felt Ethan's eyes on her. 'You guys are home early,' she said.

It wasn't meant to happen this way.

Ethan's eyes narrowed into a pained expression and then fluttered briefly to Lucas whose gaze bounced between them. 'Ben called to see if we want to have an early dinner over there tonight,' he said.

Lexi thought for a moment.

'Maybe Lucas can go and have a play with his cousins so we can… talk,' she said, faltering on the implied gravity of the last word.

Ethan's face remained outwardly unchanged, but his eyes welled. He sucked in his bottom lip, biting it in a slow release which drained all the colour from it. He turned and walked away, rolling the suitcase behind him.

Lexi looked down at Lucas, who was still clutching her hand. 'What do you reckon? Want to have a visit to Uncle Ben and Aunty Marija's house tonight? Maybe Chloe will share her glitter pens with you this time.'

'I want you to come, Daddy,' he said, as Ethan arrived back in the kitchen.

Ethan crouched to address Lucas. 'What do you say, mate? We'll go upstairs and get you changed? Your t-shirt is covered in paint,' said Ethan, rubbing at a smear of blue on the boy's chest. 'Didn't you have an art smock on?'

'Too hot,' Lucas admitted.

Lexi's heart panged as Ethan rose and stared at her. 'Okay,' he said, in a resigned voice before leading Lucas out of the room.

~

When Ethan returned thirty minutes later Lexi was seated on the sofa. He looked weary, as if he'd endured a week of sleepless nights. Lexi imagined the moment his depression would turn to rage and the anticipation of the sting felt like penance. He walked over, his eyes cast down and dropped to his knees in front of her, laying his head in her lap. The unexpected gesture rendered Lexi mute. She leaned forward, running her hands across his broad shoulders, knowing it was for the last time. She wondered how she could ever have considered leaving this man. How she could ever have seen him as anything other than kindling for her soul.

'Don't do this,' he said, his voice muffled in her lap.

Before Lexi could fully suppress them, a few rebellious tears fell atop Ethan's head and he straightened to look at her.

'Don't do this,' he repeated. 'I love you. Whatever it is, we can work it out.'

Lexi shook her head, despite her suppressed desire that it could be true.

'I love you,' he insisted.

'You're only in love with the me that you see,' she said, still shaking her head.

Ethan furrowed his brow, sifting for meaning in her words. 'What does that even mean?' he asked, shifting to sit beside her.

'It means that once you hear what I have to say, you might not love me anymore.'

Colour drained from his face, and he fell silent, waiting for her to elaborate.

Lexi, sensing this may be her last chance to touch him, drew closer to him so that their legs were pressed together. She smoothed his hair, and he pressed his cheek into her palm, closing his eyes. The infantile gesture caused Lexi's heart to lurch. She wanted to gather him in her arms, to wrap herself protectively around him so that nothing would ever hurt him again. But instead, it was she who was about to hurt him. It was she who was about to sever his lifeline to her and cast him adrift into a familiar grief. His eyes remained closed as she leaned in, placing her lips on his and she wondered how a pain so physical could be the product of feelings alone.

As she pulled back, he opened his eyes.

'For the last few weeks,' she began, 'I haven't been working in a café.'

Ethan's face, so fragile just moments before, twisted into an expression which leaned towards the comical. 'Of course you have, I visited you there.'

Lexi, momentarily thrown off, shook her head. 'I was worried you'd catch me out in the lie, so I met you there,' she said.

Ethan opened his mouth to contradict her, so she hastened to go on.

'I've been working as a cam model. I've been camming,' she said, trying to make the confession as plain as possible to avoid further delay.

'Camming? You don't mean like porn camming, do you?' he asked, slowly recoiling.

'I don't really consider it—' Lexi began.

'With the webcam and the creeps paying you to do shit?' he interjected.

Lexi's head swam with how quickly she had lost control of the conversation. 'Well, they're not all creeps, but…'

'But what?' he demanded.

Lexi opened her mouth, but words failed her.

'But what?' he repeated.

His hands shot up to his face and Lexi started from the sharpness of the gesture. He ran his fingers up and down his hairline with such ferocity that the skin on his forehead turned white under the pressure. When she tried to place a reassuring hand on his shoulder, he shucked it off, so she clasped her hands together and wedged them between her knees.

Finally, he looked up, looking dishevelled and affected.

'All those stories you came home with, about customers and work mates, they were all lies?'

'Well, not exactly.'

'Oh! They were really your Johns?'

In any other situation, the high pitch of Ethan's voice and his use of the outdated term "John" would have been comical to Lexi. But there was nothing amusing about it now.

'I'm not a prostitute,' she said quietly.

She tugged at the hem of her skirt, wishing it was longer.

Ethan, meanwhile, seemed to be conducting an internal conversation which she wasn't privy to. Lexi waited.

Minutes passed before he spoke again.

'What? You're leaving me so you can go be a porn star?'

'Of course not,' she said quickly.

Ethan raised his eyebrows.

'I quit already.'

Ethan scoffed.

'I quit when I realised I was in love with you. I was only doing it because I thought I was going to leave you anyway.'

This admission, which was meant to serve as an excuse, only managed to wound Ethan further. She hastened to go on. 'I was scared, okay? Everything with us happened so quickly, and it was too much. You and Lucas and this house and your family and living in Justine's shadow. And I couldn't find a job, and everything felt like… like it was happening to me. Like I didn't ask for any of it.'

Lexi, realising she was flapping her hands about wildly, tucked them back between her knees.

Ethan stared down at his lap, shaking his head as his mind laboured. 'Why would you even tell me this?' he finally asked.

As difficult as it had been to begin this conversation, Lexi knew it had been nothing compared to what was to follow. Resting her elbow on the back of the sofa, she covered her eyes with her hand. It was difficult to imagine a time when her body wouldn't pulse with shame. It was radiating from the depths of her bone marrow, buzzing throughout her like an electric current. She took a deep breath and dropped her hand from her face. 'Someone is blackmailing me.'

'Someone is blackmailing you,' Ethan repeated, the words sounding mechanical and devoid of meaning. 'Someone is blackmailing you,' he said again, willing his brain to make sense of it.

'They have photos. They're going to send them to you.'

Here Lexi paused, scrunching her eyes. 'And to Lucas' childcare,' she added.

'Fuck's sake,' said Ethan, resuming his forehead rubbing movements. 'Please tell me you've gone to the police about this.'

Lexi looked up at the ceiling for a moment. 'He is the police.'

'Is *he*?' said Ethan, putting extra emphasis on the pronoun.

'He works in cybercrime. He's covered his tracks.'

'How much is he asking for? I'll pay whatever it is. Lucas' childcare? I mean, fucking hell, Lexi. What have you gotten yourself into here?'

'He's not asking for money,' she said quietly.

'Not asking for money?'

Initial confusion faded from his features, giving way to pained comprehension. 'He wants…?'

Lexi nodded.

Ethan buried his face in his hands, his body static. He didn't even seem to be breathing.

Lexi looked on, resisting the urge to reach out and touch him, to rub his back and tell him that everything would be alright.

How many minutes passed like this, Lexi couldn't say. It was an eternity in the stark quiet of the house. It was as though all of Ethan's vitality had drained from him and Lexi had the disconcerting feeling that she was completely alone.

Lexi thought of what Linh had said earlier, about being able to work things out.

'I made some stupid decisions that led me to this point. I could have left without an explanation, but I wanted to tell you myself, before you get the pictures.' Lexi paused, waiting for a sign that he was listening but, receiving none, went on. 'If I could take it all back I would. The last thing I wanted to do was hurt you.'

Ethan remained hunched, his face still covered.

'I love you. I've never really loved anyone before, but I love you,' she added.

Ethan had been silent for so long that Lexi would have welcomed a tirade from him. Anything would be better than this excruciating nothingness.

She placed a tentative hand on his back. 'Please, I'll do anything,' she begged.

He said something, his voice so quiet and muffled that Lexi had to ask him to repeat it.

Lifting his head slightly and, without looking at her, he said, 'Go,' before dropping his head back down.

Lexi retracted her hand slowly, her traitorous contracting throat threatening to suffocate her. Smoothing her skirt, she rose and walked to the kitchen. The familiar room felt foreign now. Lucas' artwork crackled in her handbag as she removed her house keys and left them on the benchtop. She wheeled her suitcase towards the front door, hoping that the sound would rouse Ethan, that he might jump up and stop her. But as she walked past the living room, she saw that he still hadn't moved. Opening the front door, she kept her eyes on him, lingering with a fool's hope.

Out in the warm night air, Lexi strode towards her car, feeling the jarring vibration of her suitcase traversing every bump along the way.

FORTY-FIVE

'FUCKING fucker,' muttered Lexi, as she hauled her heavy suitcase up the dingy stairwell to Linh's apartment.

Should've left it in the goddamn car.

But Lexi would be staying at Linh's house tonight and she couldn't very well leave the conspicuous thing in the Mini overnight. She may as well leave it on the kerb with a sign saying, "Take me".

After walking out of Ethan's front door for the last time, Lexi had sat parked out the front, staring at the dimly lit windows as she dialled Linh's phone number. Through gulped sobs and a snot-clogged nose, Lexi had relayed the details of what had transpired in a haphazard and nonlinear stream of heart vomit. At this, Linh had insisted that she come over and stay the night, rather than continuing to a hotel at the airport.

Now, puffy and streak-faced, Lexi arrived at Linh's door and knocked. Almost instantly the door flung open, and Lexi was pulled down into a rough embrace by Vien. Linh, meanwhile, made swift work of the cumbersome suitcase, manoeuvring it over the threshold and into the small living room. Once within, Lexi fell onto the sofa gulping and sobbing again. Vien muttered something inaudible to Linh, who disappeared into the kitchen, before seating herself beside Lexi.

Vien clutched Lexi's heaving body to hers with an intensity that seemed at odds with her tiny stature and rubbed rhythmically between her shoulder blades. The initial vigour of the movement gradually petered out until Lexi's sobbing ceased and she was able to breath. Still holding her around the shoulders with one clamped arm, Vien produced a tissue from inside her blouse and wiped Lexi's streaming nose as if she were a child.

Lexi blinked rapidly, suddenly aware of the intimacy of their knot on the sofa. Lexi had never experienced anything like this and the newly acquired knowledge of what her own mother had been unable to provide, stung her anew.

Linh reappeared with a small cup of steaming tea and pressed it into Lexi's hands. She wrinkled her nose at the first bitter sip, but Vien nodded.

'*Trà đắng*, for your head,' she insisted.

Lexi complied.

Linh seated herself on the other side of Lexi and the three women sat in silence a moment before Vien slapped Lexi on the thigh and rose. 'I make dinner. I bet you didn't eat today. Only coffee all day long, right?' Vien asked.

Lexi nodded.

'You two, the same,' said Vien, shaking a hand between Lexi and her daughter before disappearing into the kitchen.

Lexi set down her empty cup and turned towards Linh, her eyes welling again.

'The worst is over now,' Linh said.

When Lexi nodded unconvincingly, Linh placed a hand on her knee and repeated more forcefully, 'The worst is over now.'

'What's wrong with me?' asked Lexi.

'You fucked up,' admitted Linh. 'But you're human, we all fuck up. That doesn't make you a fuckup. Everyday everyone has to wake up and decide what kind of person they want to be. So, tomorrow you'll do better.'

Lexi nodded, considering this.

'When did you become so sage?' asked Lexi, giving Linh a nudge.

'I woke up this morning and decided to be,' she said, pulling her body into a lotus pose.

Lexi couldn't help but laugh.

Linh rose and offered Lexi a hand up from the low sofa. 'You come eat now. You too skinny,' she said, poking Lexi in the ribs as she mimicked her mother's accent.

'I hear you!' yelled Vien, from the kitchen.

Lexi suppressed a giggle.

Later that night, in the quiet blackness of the apartment, Lexi lay on the sofa trying not to move. The plastic covering emitted squeals of protestation with every measured breath Lexi took, despite being heavily made up in Vien's best linens. At first Lexi had slept hard owing to the volume of cab sav she had consumed with Linh after Vien had retired to bed. But that respite from her own thoughts had been brief. Now she was awake, dry-mouthed and slightly queasy, both from the staleness of her inebriation and the freshness of her heartbreak.

She thought of the flight she would take in the morning, of staring down at the blue expanse of the Great Australian Bight for hours. Why had she drunk so much? She needed water and Panadol now. Flexing her abdominals with the intent of moving, the sofa squeaked. Lexi swore under her breath and changed tack, rolling off horizontally so she landed on the carpeted floor with a soft *thud*. She crawled over to a low table in the corner and switched on the lamp so that she might locate her handbag. In the small pool of light, Lexi's gaze locked on a silver-framed photo of the Pham family. In it, a preschool-aged Linh sat nestled between her parents, stern-faced under a home-cut fringe. Vien, young and grinning, appeared to have been captured at the precise moment she looked adoringly at her husband. Mr. Pham, an intense man with an impressive sweep of thick black eyebrows, remained oblivious to his wife's attention upon him as he focused on the camera. In her countless visits to Linh's home, Lexi had never noticed this photo amongst the collection on the side table. Lexi picked up the photo and shifted to a cross-legged position. Lexi knew that Linh's father's death in Vietnam had provided the catalyst for the family's migration to Australia. But Lexi had never stopped to consider the intense pain and insurmountable obstacles Vien must have overcome in order to create a new life for herself and her daughter in a foreign country. The floor creaked and Lexi turned to see a sleepy-faced Vien approaching.

'I'm sorry, I hope I didn't wake you,' whispered Lexi.

Vien dismissed her concern with a brief and rapid shake of her head.

She sat on the sofa, which accepted her noisily, and peered down at Lexi still holding the framed photo. 'Look at my hair!' she exclaimed, touching her fingers reflexively to her temple. 'Never get a perm. If you meant to have curly hair, you born with it,' she laughed.

Lexi smiled up at her.

'I don't think I've ever seen a photo of Mr. Pham before,' said Lexi.

'*Dep trai*. So handsome, eh?' said Vien, taking the photo.

Lexi nodded.

'Linh told me he was hit by a car, in Vietnam.'

Vien nodded, her eyes locked on the photograph.

'I wanted to move to be close to my brother. He was doing so well, even back then. Studying, working… but we had a textile shop in Da Nang. It was small but we did good business. Thào took it over when his father died. He felt pressure to hold onto his legacy, but I thought we could make a better life in Australia. More opportunities, you know?'

Lexi nodded.

'We fight all the time. And then one morning I told him he was being a coward. He looked so hurt, like I slap him with those words.'

'Oh, Vien,' said Lexi.

'He stormed out, but he didn't make it to open the shop that day.'

Vien polished the spotlessly clean photo frame with the belt of her bathrobe and replaced it on the table.

'I'm so sorry, I had no idea,' said Lexi.

'Sometimes we hurt who we love most,' said Vien with a resigned shrug. 'And forgiveness is the most hard when we have to give it to ourselves.'

Lexi looked down at her lap and nodded.

Vien smoothed Lexi's hair.

'Linh told me you lose your mother recently,' said Vien quietly.

'Oh, yeah. But we weren't close, so...' began Lexi, feeling embarrassed by the intensity of Vien's gaze.

'Well,' said Vien after a time, 'sometimes you find your real family later, right?' she said, pinching Lexi's cheek playfully.

Lexi grinned.

'Sometimes.'

FORTY-SIX

AFTER waking to the clatter of pots and the smell of frying, Lexi made her way to the kitchen where she was presented with a bowl of sticky rice, folded through with egg and topped with Chinese sausage. Despite her many protestations and a visceral aversion to eating while hungover, Lexi had eventually yielded to Vien's insistence. To Lexi's surprise and relief, the experience relieved her of any trace of the queasiness with which she'd woken.

Now, they walked through the airport in a tight knot with Linh and Vien flanking Lexi as if she were an international dignitary they were chaperoning. They arrived at the check-in counter and, seeing the line of people snaking around the stanchions, Lexi turned towards her friends. 'I guess this is it,' she said, forcing a smile.

'Text me when you arrive?' asked Linh.

'Sure.'

Vien, who had begun rummaging around in her giant handbag, pulled out a brown paper bag which she pressed into Lexi's hands.

'Mum!' groaned Linh. 'They have food on the plane!'

'You call that food?' shrieked Vien, indignant.

Thrusting a shoulder towards her daughter, she turned to address Lexi. 'Just a few things, sandwiches, cut fruit,' she said, patting the bag.

Lexi's eyes prickled and she hugged the bag to her chest. 'Thank you.'

She turned to Linh, willing the lump in her throat to cease its rapid expansion, and repeated, 'Thank you.'

Lexi knew that if she tried to elaborate, she would be overcome with emotion. Linh, sensing this, pulled her into a rough embrace that crushed the bag. 'I'll come visit soon. And we'll FaceTime heaps' she said into her ear.

Vien dropped her handbag to her feet and threw her short arms around them.

'Mum!' protested Linh as Vien let out a glorious sob and squeezed tighter. 'I'll visit too!'

'Mum!' Linh said again, wriggling free of the huddle.

Lexi, previously on the verge of tears, erupted into laughter. 'You better get to work,' she said, recovering herself.

Linh nodded.

~

At the boarding gate, Lexi plugged her headphones into her phone and slipped them on. She hit shuffle and her ears were flooded by a sorrowful yet pretty song lamenting the loss of love. She shook her head at the appropriateness of the random selection and, although it made her feel cliché, she didn't change it. The song was by a band that she and Linh had seen as a support act. The bandmembers, scruffy and young, looked as though they had been dropped off at the gig by their mothers. Their oversized jumpers and thrifted slacks made them look like children dressed up as old men. The lead-singer, a doe-eyed boy peeking out through a mop of shoulder-length, sandy hair stepped forward and sang. In a voice as clear and strong as bullet-proof glass, he conjured a sweeping image of first love and his own betrayal that ended it. The audience, previously bustling and oblivious, fell into a collective hypnosis. Heads turned towards the stage and mouths fell open upon witnessing the lucidity of the singer's pain and the orchestral melodies which accompanied it. Lexi could no longer recall the band who had headlined that night, but she could still remember how this song had brought her to tears in the crowded band room.

Now she turned up the volume and dipped her chin, creating a shield of hair to obscure the tears she knew were about to overcome her.

'Fuck!' exclaimed Lexi, jumping as her ears were assaulted with the sudden shrillness of her ringtone.

Nearby a mother drew her young daughter in nearer and scowled at Lexi, who scrambled to answer Jamie's call. 'Hello?' said Lexi, leaning over to gather up the contents of her handbag, which had been flung to the ground when she started.

'I've sorted it all out,' said Jamie, triumphantly.

Lexi sat up, still shoving things back in fistfuls. 'Sorted out what?' she asked, smiling sheepishly at the mother who was still glowering at her. She turned her body away, shutting out the woman's scorn.

'That arsehole Travis,' said Jamie.

Lexi bristled at the mention of his name.

'What do you mean you've "sorted it out"?' asked Lexi.

'I told Ali everything. All about me and you and Veronica and that stupid shit he's been trying to pull on you with those photos.'

Lexi scrunched her brow so tightly that her forehead throbbed under the strain of it. Jamie went on. 'Ali cracked it. She really doesn't like him very much. They barely even talk, normally. But he had that case he was working on, and Ali introduced him to Margot…' said Jamie, going off on a tangent.

Lexi shook her head as if trying to clear it. 'But what do you mean you've sorted it out? Sorted what out?'

'Oh, yeah,' said Jamie, focusing. 'I told Ali, and Ali told their Mum, and let's just say he's not going to be bothering anyone anymore.'

So many questions had formed in Lexi's mind that they seemed to have jammed in a bottleneck on their way out. She sat with her mouth open, oblivious that her fellow passengers were beginning to board.

'Apparently his dad is a retired cop,' Jamie snickered.

'His dad?'

Jamie was chuckling now. 'I don't really know the full story but apparently Travis has had a bunch of complaints filed against him at work. Ali reckons Travis' dad is going to make life pretty unpleasant for him after this. Especially for what he was trying to do to you. Apparently, the old man hit the roof when their mum told him. She was fuming too of course but I think the dad still has connections in the force, so…'

Lexi struggled to sift through Jamie's words.

'Anyway, I better go. I haven't slept yet; I've been on the phone all morning. So, I guess… you're welcome!' she said brightly.

'Wait!' said Lexi, rousing herself from her mind fog.

'Did he send the photos already? To Ethan? To Lucas' childcare?'

'No. I told you. It's all sorted. His old man cracked it. He's making him delete the photos and return the phone. Apparently, he lifted it out of the evidence room at work. The jerk.'

Lexi, who was focused on the floor, saw a pair of shoes come into her field of vision. She looked up to see the mother whom she'd offended.

'It's the last call,' said the woman, poking the air to indicate the curl of passengers disappearing through the gate.

'Oh, thanks,' replied Lexi.

'No worries, talk to you soon!' said Jamie, assuming Lexi was addressing her.

The line went dead.

FORTY-SEVEN

LEXI boarded the plane in a state of disarray with all eyes on her, the final passenger. Her head thumped with the knowledge that she had confessed everything to Ethan for nothing. Lexi hoped she'd be seated alone, affording her some privacy. Instead, she arrived at her row to find a middle-aged woman with short blonde hair typing feverishly on a laptop. Lexi tried in vain to jam her belongings into the overhead compartment until a terse flight attendant relieved her of the task and instructed her to sit. Lexi complied, buckled her seatbelt and snuck a look at the blonde woman who seemed oblivious to her presence. Covering her face with her hands, Lexi allowed herself to weep.

'Are you alright?'

Lexi opened her eyes to find the woman staring at her over heavy-framed spectacles, her fingers still resting on her keyboard.

'I'm sorry,' sniffed Lexi, smoothing away strands of hair which had stuck to her cheeks.

'I don't need an apology. I asked if you're alright,' said the woman, removing her glasses. She turned her body towards Lexi, as if she were her primary concern.

Lexi blinked and sniffed. She opened her mouth to spill everything, but an almighty rumble rose from the bowels of the aircraft, signifying their impending take off. By the time the thundering ceased, Lexi had thought better of it. When the woman prompted her, Lexi attempted to renege. 'I wouldn't know where to begin,' she said, shaking her head.

'Well, we have a four-hour flight ahead of us. And I usually find the beginning is the best place to start. I'm Asher,' she said, extending her hand.

Asher's bangles made a percussive sound as Lexi shook her hand. 'Lexi.'

Lexi wondered if she should censor parts of the story, but the effort of those omissions seemed overwhelming and anyway, she would never even see this woman again. Asher seemed nice enough and at the very least she would be furnished with a salacious tale to tell her fellow book club members or Pilates set.

And so, Lexi began at the beginning as instructed.

When Lexi had recounted this story just days ago to Linh, it had been a tale about a villain called Travis Nolan. Now, at its core, it became a tragic tale of ill-fated love.

When the cabin crew served lunch, Lexi reached the part where she had begun camming. When Lexi said the word "camming" she paused briefly allowing Asher to seek clarification as to what the term meant. When she didn't, Lexi elaborated.

'You know, with a webcam. Live streaming…'

Here Lexi faltered, finally settling on the cringe-worthy phrase, 'sexy things.'

Asher gave a nod and a long blink to indicate her comprehension, her index finger crooked over mouth.

'Something for lunch today, ladies?' asked the terse flight attendant, who was all smiles now.

Asher peeked at the passengers in front slurping flaccid noodles from polystyrene cups. She wrinkled her nose. 'Just a coffee for me.'

The flight attendant turned her face towards Lexi. 'And you?' she said, haughtily.

'I think I'll have a tea.'

'Hot beverages are coming,' she said, indicating another team member making his way down the aisle.

'We can land on the moon, but we still can't figure out how to serve edible food on domestic flights,' laughed Asher.

Lexi chuckled. 'Oh!' she exclaimed, remembering Vien's parting gift. 'My friends packed me lunch. Probably enough food for the whole plane,' she said, unbuckling her seatbelt and standing. She opened the compartment and pulled down the paper bag.

As predicted, the parcel was brimming with more food than Lexi could hope to finish in two days. Reaching in, she pulled out two baguettes tightly wrapped in wax paper and secured with kitchen twine. She handed one to Asher who took a moment to admire the obvious care with which it was prepared.

'There's some kind of rice crackers here too and fruit—mango I think?' said Lexi rummaging through the bag.

'This is fine, thank you,' said Asher, unwrapping the sandwich and biting into it. 'Wow!' she exclaimed. 'You started camming,' said Asher, between bites.

Lexi nodded with her mouth full, wondering at the nonchalance of this refined woman.

'And I'm guessing you didn't tell Ethan,' Asher added.

As the hours tallied and the snacks diminished Lexi came to the final instalment of her story thus far, the phone call with Jamie prior to boarding.

'So, it's all been for nothing,' concluded Lexi. 'I have nothing and no-one and it was all for naught.'

Asher remained silent, pausing to remove the cap from her water bottle and take a generous draft. 'You have yourself,' she said.

'Yeah, but—' Lexi began to protest.

'It seems to me, Lexi,' said Asher, interjecting, 'that all of this happened because you've been trying to conceal parts of yourself. You've been trying to run from yourself for years by the sounds of things. And I hate to tell you but, you are the one person you can't run from.'

Lexi, feeling the sting of Asher's observation, wished she hadn't shared everything with her. She had expected a little compassion, perhaps some acknowledgment of her bad luck. Lexi wasn't naive enough to think she was blameless but surely anyone could see how things had spiralled out of her control. How it wasn't really her fault.

Asher went on. 'And you know what?'

Lexi braced herself but tried to keep her face impassive.

'When you get off this plane in Perth. You'll be there too.'

Lexi opened her mouth to respond, but no words came.

'Any rubbish you want to be rid of, ladies?' asked the flight attendant, offering a latex-gloved hand.

Thankful for the interruption, Lexi shoved the spent wrappers back into the paper bag and handed it over before busying herself fastening her seatbelt for landing.

'Concealing parts of yourself the way you do…'

Lexi turned to look at Asher. Was this woman for real?

'…it speaks of an elemental issue. When you can't love yourself. When you can't be authentic. Happiness will elude you. Love starts and ends with you.'

Lexi turned away to stare at the seat in front of her. The seatbelt sign *dinged* and all around her passengers rustled into compliance. In her peripheral vision she saw Asher doing the same and was relieved for it.

As the captain announced their impending descent, the interior fixtures of the plane shuddered. Lexi felt as though the jarring motion was forcibly incorporating all the thoughts in her brain. The problem was her. In all her recent anguish she had been focused on Travis Nolan. She had cast him as the lynchpin of her misfortune. And while his behaviour had been abhorrent, it wasn't the reason she now found herself heartbroken and seeking a new start in Perth. Just like her suitcase, all of Lexi's problems would be waiting for her at the baggage claim. Dread engulfed her. She closed her eyes as they dropped from the sky.

Lexi's eyes remained closed as the plane thundered into contact with the tarmac. She gripped the armrests of her seat and fought her body's desire to lurch forward. Her eyes remained closed as the plane taxied to the gate. They remained closed as the fasten seatbelt sign was disengaged. She kept them closed even when she could hear her fellow passengers begin to stand. She kept them closed until she could keep them closed no more. Asher would be forced to clamber over her to disembark if she didn't move. Opening them, she unbuckled her seatbelt and stood in one swift movement. As she opened the overhead compartment, a sleek leather laptop case fell towards her. She caught it before it hit her in the face and offered it to Asher. 'Yours?' she asked.

'Mine,' Asher confirmed, taking it. She unzipped an outer pocket and extracted a square business card which she offered to Lexi.

Lexi took it and read.

Asher Solomon
Psychologist. Sexologist. Couples Therapist

'Ah, thanks,' said Lexi, sliding the card into her bag and turning away to take her place in the line of passengers. Her neck prickled as Asher rose and took a standing position behind her. The doors opened and the passengers in front began to shuffle out.

'I hope to see you again, Lexi,' Asher said, placing a hand on Lexi's shoulder.

Lexi nodded without turning.

FORTY-EIGHT

THE interior of the taxi was arctic but, although Lexi clutched at her bare arms to stave off shivering, she dared not speak to the driver. After the encounter with Asher, Lexi never wanted to strike up a conversation with a stranger ever again. The psychologist's words echoed in her head like a thumping beat. *Happiness will elude you. Happiness will elude you.* It was a shock to realise that future happiness was even something that her subconscious was hoping for. But the realisation had come at the precise moment it was swiped. Asher had been right about one thing, at least. Lexi couldn't escape herself. She was a mess in Melbourne and, as the taxi ferried her west towards the coast, she continued to be a mess in Perth. As Lexi's first cerulean glimpse of the Indian Ocean came into view, her phone rang. Absurdly, her first panicked thought was that it was Asher calling, although she hadn't given the woman her phone number. Looking at the caller ID her feelings turned to dread, and she considered letting it go to voicemail. *Run and hide, Lexi*, she mocked herself.

'Hi, Marija,' she said, answering the call.

'Was it all a lie? Were you using him?' Marija asked.

There was a steel to Marija's voice that Lexi was unaccustomed to, and it sent a chill through her.

'No,' said Lexi, simply.

She had no energy left to justify her love for Ethan.

'Okay,' said Marija, seemingly satisfied.

She fell silent again and Lexi waited, wondering if she was

expected to speak.

'Did you ever hear about the Yugoslav wars?' asked Marija, her voice losing its edge.

Lexi, taken aback by the question, faltered. 'I, ah, don't think…'

'It's okay, you were too young. It was in the nineties. 130,000 people died in the fighting.'

Astonished, Lexi opened her mouth to react, but Marija continued talking. 'It was a very dark time. My father was fighting, there was no work for my mother, no food for me and my siblings. Those with money, with food…' Marija trailed off before changing tack. 'There were bad people, smuggling arms, profiting from the bloodshed. My family was basically starving.'

Lexi, who was having trouble following the thread of Marija's story, attempted to clarify.

'What, did you become a spy or something?'

Marija laughed. 'No. But I was around it. I was running in some questionable circles, doing it all behind my mother's back. Every night I snuck out to parties. There was a feeling like we could all die tomorrow so instead of hiding, we partied. It was a way of dealing with the atrocity. We stared into the face of it and laughed.'

'Okay,' said Lexi, elongating the word.

'The people I was hanging out with. The company I was keeping. They had money. It allowed me to feed my family. We survived because of it.'

The taxi driver pulled up in front of Paige's apartment building and turned in his seat to gesture to Lexi. She held up a hand and concentrated on what Marija was saying.

'There were always rumours about me, but my mother turned a blind eye. When my father returned, he found out about it and threw me out. He called me every name under the sun, told me I had disgraced myself, his name, our family. He was furious with my mother.'

'Oh, Marija,' said Lexi.

'He told me I was nothing, would always be nothing. That the only respectable thing I could do was kill myself.'

Lexi's heart ached. 'But his family survived because of you.'

Marija scoffed. 'He was a man of superior principles. He would rather they had died honourably than survived with food in their bellies put there by a whore.'

A lump rose in Lexi's throat, preventing her from speaking. Instead, she nodded futilely as she tried to compose herself.

'The reason I called today. What I want you to know… is that no one can tell you what you are. Your story is yours to write. Your past actions do not dictate who you choose to be today.'

'But, Marija, what you did…' The words came out choked, in a voice Lexi didn't recognise as her own but she persisted. 'The reason for it. You were doing it for your family. I was… bored and stupid.'

'I was bored and stupid too,' Marija admitted. 'I wanted to feel alive when everything around me seemed to be dying. I wanted to be bold in a time when so many were frightened. My family survived, yes. But that was a by-product. A fortunate repercussion. I was seeking excitement and using my sexuality to find it, just like you.'

Lexi weighed this against the woman she had come to love. Marija was strong and intelligent with an easy manner and mischievous wit. She was a devoted wife to Ben and a loving mother to their four children. The idea that such a woman would share any semblance of Lexi's character mystified her.

'But you're so… you have so much integrity.'

Marija laughed and Lexi felt embarrassed by the formal choice of word. She scrunched her eyes tight, regretting it.

'Do you know what the secret to having integrity is?' asked Marija.

Lexi pondered this and, though she suspected the question was meant to be rhetorical, she had the distinct feeling that her future happiness hung on the answer. She struggled against the fog in her mind until the answer became clear.

'Transparency.'

Lexi heard the subtle sound of Marija's face opening into a smile 3,000 kilometres away.

'Well, I was going to say being able to own your truth,' she laughed. 'But yes, I suppose if you want to be succinct… transparency.'

Six months later...

EPILOGUE

'HOW'S the novel coming along, Lexi?'

Lexi looked into the jug of milk she was frothing and pondered the question. She poured the velvety liquid over two waiting espressos, creating identical filigree hearts, and slid the cups over the counter.

'At the moment it feels more like a process of extraction rather than a channelling of the divine,' she said, accepting payment.

'Maybe you need to base a character on me? The mysterious older gentleman. Spice things up a bit?'

'Why would anyone want to read about you, Alan?' the man's wife called from her position by the window. 'I married you and I can't even be bothered hearing about you!' she teased.

'Don't bother, Alan, I've been campaigning to be included for months,' said Paige, fanning out sliced strawberries on a row of take-away smoothie bowls from behind the counter. 'Apparently a middle-aged lesbian with a rescue cat doesn't make for compelling literature either.'

Alan laughed heartily and gathered up the coffees.

'Still more exciting than reading about how many Lipitor some old fart needs to take every morning,' yelled his wife.

Lexi laughed and watched as Alan walked over to place the coffees down in front of his wife. He kissed her and muttered, 'Cheeky sod,' before sitting beside her.

Lexi joined Paige at the food-prep counter, pressing lids atop the completed breakfast bowls.

'Pub trivia tonight. Wanna come?' asked Paige.

'I don't know. I've got a session with Asher this afternoon so I might need to go straight home and crawl under my doona afterwards,' said Lexi, grinning.

'Still dishing out the tough love, is she?'

'Something like that,' said Lexi. 'Plus, I want to get more pages to Clive…'

'Self-imposed deadline stressing you out again?' asked Paige, grinning at her sideways.

'Shut up,' said Lexi, bumping Paige with her shoulder.

'I don't know how you can keep in contact with that old guy. Isn't it creepy? I mean, he's seen you naked!'

'I know,' said Lexi shaking her head. 'It's not though. He was always just a lonely guy looking for connection. And he's amazing. I could never have gotten my writing to where it is without his guidance.'

'But does he ever, you know…? Ask for stuff?' said Paige, raising her eyebrows.

'Never,' said Lexi shaking her head. 'I guess our relationship evolved and, since his wife died…'

Paige nodded, familiar with the story of how, after a long battle with dementia, Clive's wife had finally succumbed to pneumonia.

'Anyway, I'm really close to finishing my first draft. Once I get it done, I'll go to all the pub trivia, okay?'

Lexi's phone vibrated in her back pocket, she pulled it out and gaped at the name on the screen: Ethan Thomas. She grabbed Paige hard.

'Argh,' Paige cried, reclaiming her arm and rubbing it. 'What?'

'It's Ethan,' said Lexi holding up the glowing screen but staying rooted to the spot.

'Answer it!' cried Paige.

'Right! Yes! Are you okay here?' she said, indicating a couple of customers making their way over.

'Go!' said Paige, giving Lexi a shove.

'Hello?' said Lexi, unable to cope with the intimacy of saying Ethan's name.

She strode out the door and followed the boardwalk to a bench seat, out of earshot of the customers seated outside. Although they were well into autumn, the Perth sun glittered onto the Indian Ocean with startling brilliance.

'Hi, Lexi.'

Lexi thought she could discern a wisp of nervousness in his tone.

'It's so nice to hear from you,' she said, wanting to put him at ease.

A light sea breeze whipped Lexi's hair about her face, and she smoothed it back, placing a hand against her ear so that she might hear better.

'Marija said you're in Perth now?'

After that initial phone call from Marija, Lexi had been surprised to hear from Ethan's sister-in-law again, a week later. Perplexed by the gesture, she enquired about it.

'I didn't break up with you,' said Marija, dryly.

After that they fell into a rhythm, speaking every few weeks, always at the initiation of Marija. Lexi came to look forward to those calls, enjoying the swell of pride as she summarised her life, only then realising her progress since the last call. She told Marija about her plan to turn her short stories into a novel, about how throwing herself into the gargantuan task had been the lifeline which prevented her from drowning in sorrow over losing Ethan. Marija shared the challenges of running her home-based web design business while raising four children. How precarious the balance was, how one runny nose or creeping deadline could throw the whole thing off-kilter. How everything she did felt spread thin and insufficient.

When Lexi spoke of her first therapy session with Asher after their chance encounter on the flight to Perth, Marija said, 'Good.' And that single word contained more weight, conveyed more meaning than anything anyone had ever said to Lexi.

Lexi returned to the present. 'Yeah, sea change and all that,' she said, immediately regretting the cliché. 'Actually, I came here to run away from myself. Turns out that's not possible so I'm working my shit out instead.'

The line remained silent a while and Lexi resisted the urge to fill it with small talk. She waited.

'I'm sorry I didn't call. I'm sorry I reacted, so—'

'You have nothing to be sorry about. I'm sorry I lied to you,' Lexi interjected.

Silence again.

Lexi knew from Marija that Ethan had made changes too, appointing another pharmacist to manage the business and cutting his hours back so he could spend more time with Lucas. He had even been attending a support group for widowed parents. Lexi had tortured herself for days, fantasising about Ethan meeting his soulmate there, until Asher told her to keep her stories for her writing.

Ethan spoke again as some nearby gulls rose, squawking their disapproval at a child thundering past on a scooter.

'I'm sorry, what was that?' asked Lexi, pressing her palm tighter against her free ear.

'I said, I'm coming to Perth next month.'

Lexi held her breath, not wanting to assume anything.

'Hello?' said Ethan.

'Yeah, I'm here. You're coming to Perth?'

'For a conference…'

Ethan waited for a response but receiving none, pressed on.

'Can I see you?'

ABOUT THE AUTHOR

Anne Freeman is a fiction writer, copywriter, social media content creator, health writer and publicist. From her little teak desk on Wurundjeri land in Melbourne, Anne writes contemporary fiction about women who are stuck in life and the extraordinary ways they shake themselves loose. They're always engaging and sometimes funny with reluctant adventures, sexy escapades and friendships that uplift.

Anne's novels and short stories have been recognised in many literary competitions including the prestigious Romance Writers of Australia Valerie Parv Award, the Grindstone Literary International Novel Prize and the Hawkeye Publishing Manuscript Development Prize.

Her hobbies include referring to herself in third person and making her family guffaw. Oh, and wine. She likes wine.

Me That You See is her second novel.

Acknowledgements

I live and work on the lands of the Wurundjeri people of the Kulin Nation, and *Me That You See* takes place here too. I acknowledge the Traditional Owners of this unceded land and pay my respects to Elders past, present and emerging.

There are so many generous people who helped bring this book to life but I must begin by thanking the friends who got sucked into the drafting process of a second novel before the first one was even published. I'm not sure how I got so lucky but I'm keeping my mouth shut and going with it.

To Marion Osmond whose late-night conversation is always so compelling that restaurants close around us every time we dine. May we never run out of things to say to one another. Thanks for your encouragement in the margins and in life. To Torie Miller who inspires me to be better, while making me feel as though I don't have to be. To Peter Gaitanis for generous words uttered at a campsite under the setting sun. To David Bowley for pointing out the 'cool lines' and always saying things like, 'I still don't really understand how you do it.' To Vicky Hanlon for unabashedly leaning into the spice and for her generosity with Post-it Notes. To Lisa Kelly for text messages, in real-time, chronicling her every reaction from the other side of the world. To Brooke Crawford for apologising for a lack of feedback because she 'just loved it.' To Nicole Butkiewicz for teary, late-night audio messages after she turned the final page.

To my soul sisters, Elysia Todd and Fin MacDonald, and my soul brother, Karl Phillips, for bringing light, humour and love. To my work family, colleagues and clients, thanks for the comradery and for helping fund my novel writing habit. To the countless friends who replenish my lifeforce, and by extension my creativity, with their love, tenacity and humour—it's a privilege to navigate life shoulder-to-shoulder with you.

To my dear writing pals, Camille Booker, Kelly Sgroi and Johanna Skinner for training their expert lenses on my story in the manner of *The Terminator*. Thanks for diagnosing weak areas and proposing myriad rehabilitation techniques. This novel is so much stronger because of your skill, support, guidance and encouragement. Thanks to two authors I admire greatly — Ali Lowe and Jo Dixon — for agreeing to provide me with generous endorsements to be printed for all to see on the cover of this book. Thank you for saying yes and then saying kind things. To Carolyn Martinez, my publisher and friend, for your limitless determination, humour and heart, and the Hawkeye Publishing family whose belief in great storytelling is soul-deep.

Mia Violet's memoir *Yes, You Are Trans Enough: My Transition from Self-Loathing to Self-Love* inspired me to create my transgender character, Jamie, while Mey Rude, writer, sensitivity reader and trans consultant, was my compass, steering me away from cliché and towards authenticity.

Thank you to Vân-Lam Trân, who meticulously sensitivity read my Vietnamese mother character, Vien, and provided wonderful insights to help bring her to life.

There are many real-life cam models who generously post blogs and vlogs online to help others break into the industry and learn the ropes. I found these resources to be invaluable whilst crafting my characters' perspectives. My forays into visiting *Chaturbate* allowed me to glimpse the user experience.

To the Bookstagrammers, reviewers, bloggers, podcasters, writers and general word nerds who give their precious time to enrich the Australian writing and reading community— I see you and I thank you. To readers who take chances on writers and bring our stories to life in their imaginations. Without you they are merely words on a page.

Finally, and most importantly, heartfelt thanks to my family, the centre of everything. To Paul Rabinovich, who has only read four books in the two decades I've loved him and two of them were mine. You may not be much of a reader but you are the best human I've ever met and I'm so glad we made babies together. To Davie and Edie, who are no longer babies and keep getting smarter, funnier and more delightful every day. Please never stop thinking I'm cool, or at least tolerable.

Book Club Questions

1. Prior to reading *Me That You See*, what was your knowledge of camming?

2. If you were stuck in Lexi's position—living a lacklustre life, desiring more but struggling to make ends meet—how would you shake yourself loose?

3. When do you think things began to go wrong for Lexi?

4. What was your initial impression of Travis Nolan and how did this change?

5. How did the sleazy real estate agents, and the slimy owner of Post Haste Espresso, frame Lexi's decision to become a cam model?

6. Lexi's relationship with Ethan cast her in a role of pseudo wife and mother. Do you think this contributed to her choice to become a cam model? If so, in what way?

7. Did Lexi's relationship with her mother contribute to her tendency to omit parts of herself or lie to those around her? If so, in what way?

8. What did you make of Ethan's relationship with his own sexuality?

9. Where do you think camming sits amongst sex work and pornography?

10. How do you think the rise of social media is influencing us to live our lives publicly, and sometimes performatively, online?

Book reviews can make or break a book. If you liked what you read
today, please do consider posting a review on Goodreads
or your favourite forum.

Me That You See is available at hawkeyebooks.com.au
and all good bookstores and libraries.

If you enjoyed *Me That You See*, you'll also enjoy

More Praise for *ME THAT YOU SEE*

'*Me That You See* is a fast-paced story and I read it in every spare moment! My growing interest in the world of camming has only been fuelled by Lexi's experience. It's so relatable, even in the scenarios that look nothing like my own life. I loved it!' *Melissa Kramer, Ljubljana, Slovenia*

'She's done it again! Anne Freeman has followed *Returning to Adelaide* with another hugely entertaining novel spiced up with just the right amount of raunch! *Me, That You See* will have you turning pages deep into the night as you follow Lexi and a great cast of supporting characters through this compelling story full of heart, romance, and self-discovery. Thanks for another great escape, Anne!' *Brooke Crawford, Altona North, Victoria*

'As Lexi finds, and loses, herself through camming, the lies she tells catch up with her. Perfect for those who like their books with a side of spice, *Me That You See* is a compelling glimpse into life on the other side of the lens.' *Devon May, Melbourne, Victoria*

'Freeman weaves a tapestry of vivid secrets, vulnerability and emotions that resonate with authenticity. The characters' inner conflicts are portrayed with depth and beauty. This book fearlessly addresses themes of sexuality and self-discovery and is a must-read for anyone seeking a heartfelt, thought-provoking and empowering read. Anne Freeman is quickly becoming my favourite author.' *Nicole Butkiewicz, Williamstown, Victoria*

'A powerful read written by a master storyteller. The deeper Lexi digs, the more she sinks into the quicksand of her messy life before she works out how to save herself. And I was there for all the drama and deliciously sexy details! This is a story with it all: relationships, financial pressure, self-love, shame and the power of finding yourself. Don't miss this one.' *Kelly Sgroi, Melbourne, Victoria*

'I was hooked from the start, and invested in the characters and a cheeky tone that was thrilling. I cannot wait to see what comes next.' *Carly Ruggeri, Geelong, Victoria*

'Such a thrilling read! A compelling and eye-opening story that breaks free from societal constraints, explores the alter ego within and challenges toxic behaviour with a sharp wit. You never quite know where this book is going to take you next. I was hooked!' *Lisa Kelly, London, UK*